*I*t Was the Goodness of the Place

$\mathscr{I}$t Was the Goodness of the Place

by

Lucinda Dixon Sullivan

For Martha, with warmest wishes to the sister of an artist,

Lucinda Dixon Sullivan

Fleur-de-Lis Press/Louisville, Kentucky

Printed in the United States of America

First Edition

Library of Congress Cataloging-in-Publication Data

Sullivan, Lucinda Dixon
It Was the Goodness of the Place
I. Title
Library of Congress Control Number: 2003103191

ISBN: 0-9652520-6-X
ISBN: 0-9652520-7-8 (pbk.)

Cover design by A. J. Reinhart. Printing by Thomson-Shore of Michigan.

Fleur-de-Lis Press of *The Louisville Review*
Spalding University
851 S. Fourth St.
Louisville, KY 40203
502.585.9911, ext. 2777
louisvillereview@spalding.edu   www.louisvillereview.org

Buffalo Bill's
defunct
  who used to
  ride a watersmooth-silver
      stallion
and break onetwothreefourfive pigeonsjustlikethat
           Jesus

he was a handsome man
      and what i want to know is
how do you like your blueeyed boy
Mister Death

      —E. E. Cummings

Contents

Chapter 1 . . . . Time Machine, 1934 1

Chapter 2 . . . . A Timeless Sweep 4

Chapter 3 . . . . Where the Money Grew 11

Chapter 4 . . . . In the Fullness of Time 18

Chapter 5 . . . . A Box of Noise 23

Chapter 6 . . . . The Edge of the Bluff 27

Chapter 7 . . . . Well Past Midnight 32

Chapter 8 . . . . To Make a Place 38

Chapter 9 . . . . Past the Time of Telling 42

Chapter 10 . . . . Sealed in a Bottle 49

Chapter 11 . . . . A Grip on Time 73

Chapter 12 . . . . . . A Place Imagined into Being 82

Chapter 13 . . . . In a Distant World 87

Chapter 14 . . . . . October 17, a Complicated Time 90

Chapter 15 . . . . A Leafy Nest, 1943 100

Chapter 16 . . . . Dead On 103

Chapter 17 . . . . In the Quiet 119

Chapter 18 . . . . A Rich Cup of Autumn 125

Chapter 19 . . . . . . Down a Dark Stream of Hours 139

Chapter 20 . . . . The Hard-Shelled Heart of Things 143

Chapter 21 . . . . The Mixing Zone 158

Chapter 22 . . . . Thanksgiving 167

Chapter 23 . . . . . . With Other Things than Time . . . . , 184

Chapter 24 . . . . Mercury Glass and June 195

Chapter 25 . . . . An Odd Kind of Space 208

Chapter 26 . . . . The Best Time in a Timeless Place 210

Chapter 27 . . . . . Inside a Tender Envelope of Skin 225

Chapter 28 . . . . Time as a Souvenir 237

Chapter 29 . . . . Sweet Time 248

Chapter 30 . . . . Absolute Summer 257

Chapter 31 . . . . In the Whirlwind 266

Chapter 32 . . . . The Goodness of the Place 271

Author's Note   285

Acknowledgments   285

For Dick, who didn't laugh

CHAPTER ONE

Time Machine, 1934

THE SKIRTED FENDERS and tank of Gabe Phillips' new Indian Chief motorcycle were red as apples and glowed like Chinese lacquer. On Gabe's instruction, Lucy Clement hiked her leg up behind the cycle's black leather seat that was big as a saddle and clambered over. Gabe pointed to the fold-out kick start pedal so she wouldn't scrape her leg. But who wouldn't risk it at the chance for a ride? The Indian Chief's suspension was so springy that when Lucy mounted, it bounced under her added weight. The thing not only felt alive, it was frisky as a summer pony.

Lucy wiggled herself into a comfortable position behind Gabe. Her arms slid forward naturally and latched around him at the waist. She seemed to fit precisely, like the shiny chrome cables and linkages that connected parts to the cycle's chassis.

It was a hot, dry, blue-white July day in 1934, and Lucy didn't care if she was wearing her best skirt. Sixteen-year-old Lucy would have this adventure no matter what her daddy said. Before she gave

Gabe the go-a-head, she pulled her skirt hem down until it all but covered the brown-and-white saddle oxfords which she had only recently scuffed to her satisfaction. The skirt was made of soft, fern green and gray plaid challis, and Lucy set almost as much store by it as Gabe did by his cycle. Besides, if Lucien Clement found out that she was racing around Milan County glued onto Gabe Phillips' back like "some tacky piece of Boxtown trash," what Lucy was wearing wouldn't make her father's wrath less thunderous or Gabe's company more suitable in her parents' eyes.

Gabe could hardly get started for bragging to Lucy about the Indian Chief's particulars. His cheeks were this minute as shiny-apple red as the motorcycle's paint while he showed off a "mounted shift lever." What Lucy loved was that Gabe loved it. He was eighteen years old and she, after years of studying Gabe, had never seen his face light up like this. For the first time ever, Gabe seemed simply to have no notion of the fact that his right leg was crippled.

They were at a pull-off way out at the end of Rose Hill where Milan started to thin out and blend into the countryside when fields expanded and stretched the houses farther and farther apart until turrets on the old, painted Victorian homes pulled away from their foundations and became silos on the horizon, near the enlarging barns.

Lucy's stomach hitched when all Gabe's noisy throttling and choking of the engine gave way to motion. But the very next minute they glided off the shoulder and headed down the road, then Lucy eased. Gabe would keep her safe. She could feel his back muscles flex against her chest. He leaned forward into the wind against them and she held tight, bending the reed of herself to the whistling reed of him.

They were headed toward the river gorge. The road was narrow but newly paved, one of the few county roads that wasn't a simple strip of oiled gravel. Lucy looked away to her right.

Already there was a backdrop of faraway palisades behind the unrolling fields. Gabe speeded up, gaining on the open country. The wind scrubbed against them hard but was no match for their red engine. It was exhilarating. Her red hair was liquid like the engine. Lucy laughed, head back, and caught cup after cup of warm summer in her mouth and swallowed, spitting out her curls. She and Gabe were flying. The trees were all one stripe of green against a wall of rock.

Without thinking more, Lucy brought an arm back and unbuttoned her blouse one-handed.

She untucked Gabe's shirt tail and raised his shirt as high as she was able. Lucy leaned forward and reclaimed her earlier hold, daringly atingle, skin to skin, brushing through the air. Gabe briefly pressed a hand on her re-locked fist, then they went faster still. Yes, oh yes oh yes. This was what she wanted. She and Gabe would fly and her life would be like this.

CHAPTER 2

A Timeless Sweep

SOME YEARS LATER a lone climber paused at the top of a ridge in the Hebron River Gorge. He shaded his eyes and looked off into the distance from under a brim of fingers. There was a profoundly timeless sweep to his view. The man then turned himself on brittle shale and gazed down at Milan, Kentucky, the town where Clara Phillips had been born and lived with her parents, Gabe and Lucy Clement Phillips.

From where the solitary figure stood, taking his pleasure slowly in the seamlessness of height and air and isolation, he could trace the Hebron's course, which looped around and all but severed Milan County from the rest of the state.

It was early December, 1948. Far beneath the man's feet, bare trees stubbled a wrinkled rug of tobacco fields and farms inside the river's ring. Dull as cornstalks today, only weeks ago the trees' leafy crowns had been as colorful as roostertails. While the climber watched, light spilled from behind a scooting cloud and splashed down onto a trail of sycamores. Branches gleamed out briefly, lacy white, like coral fans exposed by some receding sea.

When the man spied a vehicle inching away from Milan along a thread of blacktop, he smiled, faintly, at its whimsical appearance. The car, a maroon sedan, looked no bigger than a ladybug. He watched as the tiny, enameled shell beetled along, unimpeded, toward a toy-sized iron bridge.

Finally, the loner moved away and withdrew from the rocky lip of the overlook. The outline of his olive-drab jacket gently dissolved against the cedars on the ridge. Within seconds he melted into the brush and disappeared.

Lucy Phillips and her six-year-old daughter, Clara, could be seen inside the cab of the ladybug sedan. Lucy, absorbed, held a tight grip on the steering wheel. She nearly lifted the car off the road in her effort to hold the four-door vehicle and herself and Clara steady. Steadiness had become everything in the last few days.

Abruptly, Lucy flexed her right hand in front of the dashboard; then she lightly touched her left cheek where the skin was normally taut over prominent cheekbones. But this morning her face was puffy under a thick coat of pancake makeup and far too tender to press. Lucy didn't think any telltale bruises showed. At any rate, her daughter had not seemed to notice, disturbed as the child was by being suddenly uprooted.

After a glance at Clara, Lucy furtively, and for the thousandth time, checked her own appearance in the rearview mirror. Her willow-green eyes looked fevered. The narrow bridge of her nose had swelled. Because of the swollen tissue Lucy's eyelids appeared to have a Mongoloid fold. And her freckles, so like spatterpaint from the rust-red color of her hair, had disappeared under Covermark along with the ugly blue contusion. Lucy refocused straight ahead then squeezed the wheel again until her knuckles whitened.

Lucy had never been hit or slapped before. Stern as her father had been, he never once raised his hand to hurt her. That Gabe himself had hit her was not yet quite real. But the argument over his secretary, Joyce, and Lucy's suspicions was real enough. Gabe had struck her, though; it still took Lucy's breath to think it.

It wasn't even the intensity of Gabe's anger that was most shocking. She and Gabe were equally intense. That was part of what had paired them up as teens. Lucy had always seen Gabe's temper as the flip side of his passion, like hers. There was no gulf between them there. Lucy's own daddy had nicknamed her "little hothead" when she was a child. The name stuck and Lucy knew well enough that most of Milan had gleefully applied it. She supposed the fiery color of her hair had made the tag irresistible.

But the fight between her and Gabe had happened on a different plane. It was a confrontation that was as suddenly explosive as a war. When it was over, Lucy felt as though she was at the center of a vast landscape where Gabe seemed like a stranger.

Gabe had been standoffish as a youngster. As the result of a birth defect, a shortened Achilles tendon, he limped. But if he had felt humbled by his flaw, he never let it show. Two years her senior, Gabe's haughtiness had been enticing to thirteen-year-old Lucy. Shabby clothes and all, he seemed almost regal. He was a breed apart from the other boys at school whose goofy, crooked cowlicks matched their grins. From early days Gabe's posture of defiance plus his exclusion from any of Milan's clannish little groups had made Lucy more and more determined to disarm him. She had got her way.

When Lucy turned sixteen, Gabe had pressed her against a school locker and ardently kissed her out of childhood. This minute Lucy could still summon the press of cold metal against her back and the groin deep tug of sheer, unschooled desire within Gabe's enfolding heat. Lucy felt that she and Gabe had melted and fused. That feeling of oneness had been the bedrock of her life. But the fact was that Gabe hit her. He had struck her with his fist.

While her cheek was still against the rug that night a week ago, Lucy had opened her mouth where she fell and let a little rivulet of blood pool out between her parted lips. In spite of her fury, she had been conscious of the moldy taste on her tongue and the way the rug felt, nubbled up against her cheek. The light had reflected brightly off the tips of Gabe's specially made black shoes. She was too enraged to move when Gabe limped toward her, more careful of his bad leg, and the blood pooling on the rug, than he had been of her. Lucy had lain there noticing minutely, thinking this was fitting, that the end of love should be more bloodied than its sweet beginnings. She had now experienced both with Gabe.

Back with herself in the car, Lucy realized that she was driving too fast and breathing faster. The air in her lungs was icy. Clara had slowly rolled the passenger seat's window down halfway. Cold as the day was, Lucy didn't have the heart to make her daughter close it.

Clara climbed up onto her knees. She faced outward from the window and curled child's fingers, still dimpled, but slightly slimmed beyond babyhood, over the top of the cranked-down glass. Every now and then she lifted one arm and waved at the empty countryside. Lucy had watched Clara wave goodbye to Gabe, less than an hour ago, in the same deliberate manner.

Gabe had appeared pitiably astonished at their leave-taking. Lucy, too, had all but wept when they pulled away. But she had no intention of breaking down in front of Clara, then or now. Lucy could cry later. There was always a better time to cry, she thought, even if there would never be enough.

At the house, Gabe had stood off to one side, near the wooden porch swing. While Lucy started the ignition, he carefully laced his fingers through the big iron rings of the swing's ceiling chain. Gabe's ashen expression and the flaking gray paint of their home's façade had looked equally forlorn. Wordlessly, he kept the swing in motion, phantom of all the evenings they had rocked there, pleasantly hyphenated by their sleepy girl.

Lucy's announcement the morning after the fight had been terse. She told Gabe she meant to leave him. Most of the words had roared out of her in hoarse accusations the night before. That next day Lucy had asked her husband simply, "You know what that does?" without referring openly to their brutal confrontation. When Gabe didn't, or couldn't, speak, Lucy Clement Phillips bent near his ear, the silken ear her lips knew well, and answered for him. "Well," she said in a slow whisper which was as moist as if she had licked the lobe, "That does it." There were no truer words.

Afterward, she and Gabe agreed on how to handle things with Clara. They had never been at odds where their daughter was concerned. Lucy had taken a job in another town, they told the six year old. Times were hard. Like everybody else these days, they needed some cash money. If Gabe's new tobacco warehouse business got up and going, they hinted that they might reconsider. After all, just yesterday the world had been at war. Peacetime promise called for modern ways of life. In 1948 women everywhere were leaving home and seeking outside work. Gabe and Lucy spoke as one and gave their child these explanations. Fresh starts were ideal.

Thus the couple cooperated for their daughter's sake. No lies were told. Gabe and Lucy kept their answers to Clara's questions small, as Clara was herself. Every day, while Lucy exhausted herself with newspapers and a telephone, finding a rental house in Hickman, and while she arduously packed them up to leave, she kept up the ruse. She was so determined to convince and to hide her own heartbreak that she hardly noticed Clara. In those moments when she did notice, Lucy anguished. Her daughter also seemed distracted and far more than willing to let her grownups be.

This morning, Clara finally took a proper seat beside her mother in the car. There was an air of finality to the way Clara sat. Lucy waited for some stated indication of the girl's emotions. Clara was the kind of six year old who told you what she felt in a simple voice of bell-clear tones, like a hand chime. But today she merely twisted the window shut with a noted effort then held the knob awhile.

Now that they were sealed in, Lucy trusted her own voice.

"Can I tell you anything about Hickman?" Lucy asked. She tried to make the words firm in the air, polish them bright with her forced breath. "Or about the house?" Lucy had called a downstate newspaper to find a likely rental. Satisfied with a phoned description from the *Hickman City Press*, she immediately sent a check. Three months' rent depleted her small savings. Lucy hoped that Clara would finally show some sign of interest and gave the bait a tug. "There's an old lily pond in the yard," she said. "You and I can clean it out. You'll like water lilies. They look like fairy skirts." But her daughter wouldn't have it.

Almost slyly, Clara pressed the chrome lever on the vent just enough. She eyed her mother sidelong while Lucy's words sucked out and flew behind and trailed them like a pennant.

With the climber gone and the ladybug flown, the landscape encompassed by the Hebron was once again as tranquil as a painting, but only from afar. At ground level, in and around the town of Milan, the fact of Lucy's leaving was causing a considerable stir.

CHAPTER 3

Where the Money Grew

THE DAY LUCY Clement Phillips drove urgently from Milan also marked another milestone. It had been almost one year to the day since Gabe opened his new business, the carrot of solution he and Lucy had dangled for their daughter, Clara. For years Phillips had fed his family well enough; there wasn't a one in the entire county would grudge him that. But Gabe had earned his livelihood as a pinhooker. In the eyes of the town the very word pinhooker smacked of smalltime speculation and suggested a scrabbling life.

Through the years it became gradually, if grudgingly, accepted in Milan and beyond that Gabe had a knack that bordered on genius for sizing up a crop of Burley tobacco and buying it right. His reputation had grown like a good farmer's produce, bigger and healthier every year. It was told that Gabe Phillips could take fair-to-middling tobacco, including leaves not much better than the last rags of pea time, and sell it up. Even so, the townfolk all but gasped in unison when Gabe hit on his Big Idea. They put it about the county just that way: "Gabe's Big

Idea," snidely dismissive of its suspect nature. Next thing you knew he'd put on airs.

Gabe's plan was to open a local tobacco depot, make it imposing, and bring City buyers in for auctions. Based on such grandiosity, the town's thoroughgoing belief that Gabe Phillips had overstepped himself grew by leaps and bounds.

The fact that Gabe was known to be stiff-necked didn't help matters. One of the stories told about him concerned an instance right after he opened his doors for business. A tobacco buyer from the old pinhooking days had called him long distance. When Gabe answered at the warehouse, the man had greeted cheerily "Hello, Gabe, guess who this is." Gabe's response was immediate. "I haven't got time for guessing games," he retorted and smartly cradled the receiver. The buyer had told it himself when he started traveling into Milan for the auctions. He generally drew laughs with his little tale, but what the listeners wanted to know, they groused among themselves, was what Gabe Phillips thought he had to be so uppity about. There had never been a time they knew of when he'd been easygoing. It beat all, it really did, they just had to say. The part that rankled most was, Gabe didn't seem to notice their disdain.

Of course, a hint of jealousy or spite festering among the local population couldn't be ruled out. His sign, G. Phillips Central Burley Warehouse No. 1, was large enough to cast a shadow ten feet long over the far end of the Main Street sidewalk. This "big timin' it," a few sniffed privately, from a somewhat crippled, half orphan boy who had never known his place, was rash.

Outside town limits, however, in fields where the fertile and humus-rich soil ran soul deep, Gabe Phillips was in good standing with men who grew Burley hands on. Since high school the study of tobacco cultivation had increasingly taken Gabe's fancy. He would never have had the aptitude or patience for a farmer's life sentence of backbreaking toil, but he admired it fully. As a pinhooker, Gabe had worked the growers like they worked their acreage, in all weathers, with few words and from an equal measure of respect. From the lushest bellyband of bottom land near the Hebron to the scraggliest scrap of an allotment, the men who farmed it felt that Gabe would give them a fair shake. And Gabe somehow always managed to get the cured tobacco hauled to markets that were, for the most part, hundreds of crookedy mountain miles away.

What pinhooking came down to, after all, was merely buying here and selling there. But respect for a man's occupation rests on the base of his trademark style and drive. There had been plenty a one in the pinhooking line who took a crop and didn't pay as promised, or pinched way too big a chew for himself from in the middle. Not Gabe Phillips.

On the whole, tobacco farmers in Milan County were happy to see Gabe coming toward them through a field at any time. Characteristically he came head high, paying no attention whatever to his own shortcoming, his limp. Gabe was an otherwise well-made man, they thought, dark-eyed, considered to be good looking. And he was knowledgeable. With him, growers could discuss their hopes for alternating spells of wet and dry weather. He was as wary as they were if a drought set in or rain came on too long. Gabe knew every bit as well as they did what triggered the varying chemical processes within a leaf of Burley. Climate cycles brought out flavor. Without change, no taste developed.

If poor curing weather left Milan County farmers with a high-colored, yellow harvest, they held hopes Gabe would give them something for it. Usually that was true, even though company buyers didn't go for brightly colored leaf. On occasion Gabe's sellers confessed after a transaction that they feared he couldn't sell in turn what he'd just bought from them. Gabe was genial. "A deal's a deal," he'd laugh, "as long as it's a deal," in a lively voice.

Gabe had been pinhooking since high school. There was no way to exaggerate the smalltime nature of his beginnings. But thirteen years, a wife and one child later, Gabe Phillips had finally scraped up enough cash to fund the idea burning in his head. It had come to him that there was no reason to be carting mounds of tobacco all over kingdom come. Gabe's brilliant realization was that right here was where the money grew. In the midst of summer Milan was knee deep in money and didn't seem to know it. Long-leaved, spring-green, well-tended bills of Burley were multiplying at the very doorstep. Let the god damn cigarette makers seek their treasure here.

Gabe studied on his notion for quite a while, noodling out what he needed year by year. But when he had it figured how to proceed, he proceeded headlong. In 1947 the old Purina Feed Company building, two blocks west of the Milan County courthouse, went begging for a buyer. Within a month Gabe had wrangled himself a bank loan. Nobody would deny he had some manners on him when he wanted. Word went round that Gabe had somehow got a mortgage. Then there was joking that Gabe Phillips had put a shotgun in the chairman's chest at Farmer's Bank and asked him "Please." The night Gabe signed the note, neither he nor Lucy knew who had been the bigger fool, him or Sweazey at the bank.

Government rules that controlled tobacco farming had gone into effect in the late thirties. Gabe had immediately grasped how application

14

of the regulations transformed his business. He learned firsthand, but he didn't think it took a genius to understand the math. The surprise was that nobody else seemed to glean it. Allotments and subsidies, plus the boom in upgraded farm-to-market roads added onto the Burley farmers' gritty will to earn, and their flinty stoicism, could equal an influx of cash like this hick town had never seen. All Gabe had to do was put the first two and second two together in his very own clearinghouse. What he envisioned was a local auction setting where buyers and sellers could look each other in the eye. And the beauty part was, if he played the rules fairly and with imagination, he only needed to hold a hand out either side to collect his due. Everybody won.

On the Monday before Thanksgiving of '48, fifteen days before Lucy left him, Gabe's second year in business had gotten off to a bang-up start when the season's opening-day sale took place over to the Burley Warehouse No. 1. If the warehouse title seemed a little grand, nobody in Milan or thereabouts was inclined to say so these days. In fact, word on the recent event was good, the money even better. Each and every man involved could swear to that. Farmers paid Gabe's floor charges gladly from their surprising profits. The local gentry, the non-growers, were also singing a different tune. Lately those men of Milan who had smirked and doubted claimed, with knowing looks among themselves, that they had seen the promise in Gabe's venture all along.

Now this. In December Lucy Phillips had up and left her little house on Morgan Street right at lunchtime. The most influential gossips held she wasn't coming back. One neighbor lady swore that Lucy told her outright how she and Clara were after moving clear to Hickman, near the coalfields. The tale created a sensation that rippled its way around the town in record time.

By teatime, sides had been taken and defended in the matter. A majority of men and women thought it only fair to say that Lucy's leaving with his daughter was a crying shame for Phillips. These were kindly people, after all. That's how far their sentiments had swung toward Gabe within the circle of a single year. Nor did it make the citizens of Milan out as cynics if they quietly acknowledged something else: A goodly portion of the money in their pockets owed its presence there to Gabe.

Universally the townfolk shook their heads and muttered sorrowful asides about the Phillips family fortunes. What on earth had caused a thing like this to happen? An unnamed sage among them ventured that the trouble best be laid at Lucy's door. The woman truly was a Clement. Almost to a man, the town agreed. The feeling was, no Clement within living memory had ever been a piece of cake. This just went to prove it.

The story of the Phillipses ran along that way all afternoon and evening. To their credit, it was typical of Milan's population that the telling was straightforward in the main. But secret fears abounded nonetheless.

Most families prayed aloud about the situation over supper. They bowed their heads and clasped each other's hands and raised their sturdy arms in chains of flesh above their wide oak kitchen tables. "Keep Gabe Phillips here with us where he belongs," went the supplication, selfish though it seemed. In their hearts they couldn't bear to have him chasing after Lucy Clement in this rank removal from their midst. She'd come running back to Milan soon enough, they figured, if she had a lick of sense.

They had only just begun to take Gabe's measure. Milan's past, in town as well as county, had been full of want during the Depression then after that the War. This boy they'd paid no mind to until lately had somehow turned the local fortunes and got them facing forward. Phillips needed to stay put.

Under the cloak of that December's dusk when the farmers and the townsmen and their families finally fell to the business of eating glistening, purse-shaped rolls with steamy hash and latticed pies or custard, anxiety about the Phillipses died down.

CHAPTER 4

In the Fullness of Time

Between the end of 1948 and the summer of 1953, the roiling emotional seas around Lucy Phillips gradually calmed. Back in Milan during the same period, town and county came to accept their own growing prosperity with a somewhat complacent air.

Judge Matthew Stallard, Milan's model of rectitude and conservatism, unbent so far as to drive all the way to Louisville, Kentucky, in September, 1952, to buy a black metal Philco television set that came with a matching four-legged stand. The town was confounded when the delivery crew installed a contraption, mighty like a huge tinker toy it was said, on the roof of the Stallard's stately home. The ugly addition was soon determined to be an antenna; it sprouted from slate roof tiles like a stalk of geometric sumac. "Of all people, it wouldn't do for us to lag behind," the Judge told his wife, Belinda, when she looked bemused.

For her part, Lucy tried to grab as tight a hold on Hickman as she had on the steering wheel driving out of Milan. Through all her early weeks in the mining town, Lucy had felt flinty inside, sharp edged, ready to strike sparks if crossed. The severity of her determination served her well from the outset. She resurrected the initiative that had galvanized her youth. When a local bureau administered a Civil Service exam in Hickman's blocky, granite post office building, Lucy showed up first and scored high. Soon after, she was called to the Social Security Office and hired for a clerical position. The fact of Clara's existence, a child who might place inconvenient demands on an employee's availability, didn't suit the owl-faced manager at all. Lucy had brushed right past his puny objections with a hearty claim of self-reliance for her daughter.

The house Lucy had rented by telephone, sight unseen, pleased her well enough. It was dingier and smaller than touted but had possibilities. Day one, she stepped into the cottage's musty hallway and affectionately pulled Clara back against her so they could peer together into the large front room. Four big, old-fashioned-looking, triple-hung windows were set two and two on the front and outer side walls. "Look, honey," Lucy nudged, "when they're raised all the way next summer, it'll be as cool in here as it was on the porch at home." Clara slipped out from the mildly restraining band of her mother's crossed arms and went ahead into the dining room. Lucy's eyes followed. She missed the warmth of her daughter's encircled flesh, which had felt soft and yeasty. Her gaze returned to linger on the windows and the coal grate in the fireplace. In a few minutes, hungering, Lucy followed the slight sound of Clara's footfalls through the house until mother and daughter met in the back bedroom. "I'm sorry you're disappointed, Clara, but it will have to do." Though she felt a landslide of love for the child that minute, Lucy couldn't afford more democratic motherhood right then.

Clara seemed determined not to take to their changed circumstances. On the other hand, while Lucy fixedly pushed her way uphill in Hickman through the tunnel of an uncontested divorce and into a new life of advancement, towing a foot-dragging child every inch of the way, downtown Milan brightened. By the summer of 1953, the entire display of plate glass on Main Street appeared drenched in perpetual sparkle. The standards had been set by the couple who owned the Dixie Café. Before 6:30 every morning the Dixie's proprietors, Spiro and Sophie, were vigorously at their glass with wadded newspapers dipped in vinegar rinse. Fellow merchants followed suit as best they could.

Other manifestations of affluence were more significant. Milan's business district was mostly comprised of narrow, brick two-stories which ran deep to the alleys behind, connected each to each by thick-walled shoulders like a phalanx. The pre-Civil War era buildings, including the one that housed the Dixie, faced off down both sides of the street for at least two blocks. True to the period of their construction, the storefront façades were primly old-fashioned. Ornamented iron or wood-framed window expanses at street level modulated into a flourish of trims and lintels up above. They were presided over by a large, antebellum dowager of a courthouse at the head of Main Street.

Before the advent of Gabe Phillips Warehouse No. 1 many of Milan's structures had faded into a dotage of genteel poverty which seemed certain to claim them for salvage, the construction equivalent of death. Recently refurbished, adornments restored in green and black and cream enamels, in 1953 the stores proclaimed the town's self-satisfaction .

Eventually, a new car dealership opened up on the vacant lot one block over from Main, near the city park. Every day for a few weeks in the spring of '50, until he picked one, Gabe had walked over from the warehouse to sit in different vehicles on the lot. His routine seldom varied. Gabe left the driver's door open and rested his left foot on the asphalt while he leaned back, inhaled the smell of belting leather, checked the finger grips on the steering wheel for fit and tested the chrome radio knobs and dashboard lighter. He often put his hat on to see if there was headroom then tipped the brim and lit a cigarette. The salesman came to evaluate the level of Gabe's interest by way of smoke rings.

By then Gabe had bought a place of his own down at Tyrone. He had courted Lucy nearby, on the sloping banks of the Hebron.

Tyrone itself was a small settlement of summer homes and cabins on the Milan County bluffs at the tail end of the Hebron Gorge. The tumbledown house Gabe purchased near the Hebron river landing had appealed to him because it promised isolation.

For years the camp had disintegrated gently at the end of a narrow lane, forgotten on a shelf of land that hung out high above the water. The cottages up the road from Gabe's place were used only in June, July, and early August, mostly by weekenders from town and fishermen who kept to themselves. Before first frost, all but the harvest goblins chased back up to Milan for the cold months.

Gabe meticulously researched the title to the property and cleared it of several accumulated clouds before he closed the deal. He had in mind to winterize his place and make improvements because he planned to stay year round. The seven-mile trip from Tyrone to Gabe's warehouse in town was scenic. He could use the drive for thinking time. The main idea was to stop the gossips up in Milan from picking at the holes that Clara and her mother left, or prying at Gabe's shell of privacy.

Early on he had put a colored woman named Nonie on his personal payroll to cook and clean for him down at the river. She was also to mind Clara when the child came up for one of her painfully brief stays. Gabe and Nonie had more in common than they knew. Although Milan had tolerated Nonie Pulce for decades, it stuck in the town's craw that Nonie never curried favor. When his foreman stumbled so far over the line as to warn that Nonie Pulce was "no friendlier than she had to be," Gabe snapped, "That's just the point."

The vaguely unsettling constant in this otherwise even unfolding of days was Gabe's relationship with Joyce Oliver. In the fullness of time Gabe meant to break off with his secretary completely. The plan had been building in his mind from the minute Lucy left four and a half years ago. Gabe still had trouble believing he had dived in way over his head with Joyce before he knew it and lost his family. As full of regret as Gabe was, he was in deep as ever with an untamed girl who was driving him wild. There was groundwork to be laid, and he wasn't making much headway. He had reason to hope the increasingly successful Burley auctions would throw off enough money that he could afford to remodel and expand the Tyrone camp, reinvest heavily in his warehouse and still put aside an adequate amount to settle Joyce elsewhere. She was bustin' to be turned loose on some big town. That much was plain to see even if Joyce didn't see it.

Outside of Gabe's troubled and secret deliberations, the years rocked by in a pleasant lull in Milan as well as Hickman. Gabe nursed his warehouse enterprise along with care; the rest of it, his aching, bone-deep desire to win his wife and daughter back, he filed away for later.

CHAPTER 5

A Box of Noise

ON A LATE summer night in 1953, someone watching through Gabe's window might have thought that he and Joyce were dancing. They were moving their bodies in that kind of rhythmic pattern. Their hands stayed clasped while their arms snaked here and there.

Gabe was lover close to Joyce. When he turned, she turned. If she dipped back, he bent forward. They looked to be connected like Siamese twins, revolving on the axis of that point where they gripped the gun.

There was floorspace enough for dancing and the couple swung around with Latin-deep expressions, cellophane highlights on their hair.

But the sound was so important. In Gabe's front room the sound was different. His house, the simple river camp built up on blocks, had taut flooring which was suspended like a drumskin over air and dirt. As Gabe and Joyce thumped against it, deep-toned and threatening noises rumbled back. Gabe's footfall was uneven, always heavier on the one side, ta-*dah*, ta-*dah*, and Joyce's stockinged feet scuffled erratically a beat that didn't match his. Their breathing sawed into the din, harsh and loud.

Gabe couldn't believe Joyce's physical strength. This wasn't a woman with muscle. Her skin was a sweetmeat casing that allowed everything soft inside to shift as she tilted toward him or toward a desk. God damn her and that softness, he thought, spinning. Here was her hard center. This was pitiful, he told himself. Joyce was too sluggish and stupid to confront him. But with each turn of their struggle the peg of Gabe's anger twisted tighter.

Jesus. Jesus, he thought. Why didn't she give in? She wasn't too dumb to know he'd win. Threaten him? Gabe's face was so close to Joyce's that a fine mist of shared sweat flew between them and stung his eyes. Over thunder and pulse, he could hear a shrill sound that didn't seem to come from either of them. Her! It would be her. It was just like her! Now that she knew she was in too far, Joyce would whimper, back and scrape, say it was a joke. Gabe laughed a hateful laugh. She was craven as a coward. But she had not loosened her hold on the gun.

The pair worked their way over by the door where a table jutted from the wall, a step table with a lamp on the second tier. The lamp was Gabe's favorite piece, a bisque statuette of an old Chinese angler. Three tiny, hinged metal fish dangled at the end of a single thread that was tied like a fishing line into one faience arm. Gabe tried to avoid spinning into the lampshade but lost his balance when he pushed too hard off his bad leg. Momentum slammed him against the cabin wall, shoulder first.

In that split second Joyce was canny enough to exploit Gabe's stumble. She pulled away from him, suddenly. Slippery as a channel cat, she almost freed her gun hand.

Desperate, Gabe pushed at the table and clenched his left fist tighter around Joyce's right hand. He threw his free arm around her waist to steady himself before drawing her close again. When he did that, the lamp broke against the floor, and the couple twirled over the pieces in a Valentino-style embrace. They were oblivious to the minute ping of the Chinaman's fish amid the clatter of breaking pottery and thunder. Neither was aware that slivers of glazed enamel pricked Joyce's hose and needled into her bare, fleshy feet as easily as straightpins. With every pivot she sponged tiny whorls of blood on brass-colored heartwood planks.

In the diminished light, Joyce's sultry face could have been intent on any kind of passion, Gabe thought. And her throat must have been dry from breathing so hard, openmouthed. She licked her lips.

Oh, baby, Gabe whispered roughly, but he was unaware.

Their four hands were twisted together into two fists, one clamped at the small of Joyce's back, one knotted between them where they had caged the nickel plated .22, just under her breasts, waist high on Gabe.

Now, for both of them, the room was like a box of noise, an isolated cube in a still universe. The bullet, when it escaped on its precise, silvery path, was the only quiet thing; it pierced Joyce's skin below the sternum then, undeflected, sliced a hole cleanly through her heart before burrowing home in a spool-shaped chunk of bone.

Deadweight drops plumb. Joyce's body fell down to its knees straight and fast as a sandbag and hit the floor with a crack the same time as the gun. Gabe didn't move; he had opened his fists reflexively when she fell, but he didn't change their location, and now that he held her head between his hands, his palms felt rope burned.

Joyce was leaning into him. Somehow Gabe kept her from falling over while he knelt to her level. He wanted to lay his mistress over on her side, or back, but when he started some gentle rearrangement, she fell away from him completely, and her head struck the final note: a loud, unresonant, stockyard-singular clap.

Gabe knew that Joyce was dead although there was very little blood on her dress. What took his breath was the immediacy with which death overruled everything. Death was absolute—over Joyce's weight, over the collapsing way she fell—and his hands were as absolutely ineffective as feathers against her lifelessness. What terrified Gabe was that he could still hear a keening kind of cry, razor thin. Were her lungs deflating?

Slowly he stood and started to back away from the body. The noise didn't stop until Gabe folded his hands over his mouth, the way someone would soon settle Joyce's over her breast, like dovewings, crossed.

Gabe finally quit staring at Joyce. He went into his bedroom, lifted the bulky black telephone receiver off its base and waited for the operator. The time was ll:30. Almost midnight. Only one or two tired women would be working the night shift.

Gabe had not snapped the light switch just beside the doorframe. From the darkness, he looked back into the other room. He didn't want to go back in there, into its blazing light; he wanted to watch from where he stood and never enter the light again.

CHAPTER 6

The Edge of the Bluff

GABE, DISEMBODIED IN the darkness, was acutely aware of the operator's voice. The woman sounded aged and hollow and too far away. While he waited for her to ring the Sheriff, the pervasive mustiness in his bedroom, a river perfume mixed of mud and mildew and rot that came with living near the water and that no amount of spar varnish or cleaning could banish, seemed suffocating and more potent by the second, until its spell was broken when the call connected.

"This is Gabe Phillips down at Tyrone." His voice was terse. "Joyce Oliver is dead. You'd better come." Gabe hung up without waiting for a reaction. The hell with them. He would answer when they got here; his breath was gone anyway. After he fumbled the phone back onto its cradle, Gabe swayed against the headboard. The room squeezed him too tight; his face was cold but he was steeped in sweat.

His touch told him that the bedspread was so slick it would never hold him. If he sat, the mattress would certainly tip and the quilt's satiny surface would slide him away toward the corner where the room was narrowing. Gabe had to move, go outside, suck down real air.

Joyce was almost in the center of the living room floor. Gabe kept his eyes on the baseboard and like a blind man he rubbed his way along the wall to the front door. Her white shoes sat side by side on the hearth. The small, worn-looking pumps were as primly aligned as the halves of an open shell. They were powdery from being polished often and grayish where the coating hadn't taken. Gabe blinked them away.

Pea gravel lined the walkway out front. After a few lopsided strides, Gabe stepped off onto wet grass for silence. A cigarette would blunt the sharpness in his chest, but he didn't have a pack on him and he would never be able to go back, alone, inside the room where Joyce lay.

Gabe looked around the yard as the landscape started filling in gradually. That there was still a trellis in his yard amazed him. Its frame was so trivial, the scale so inappropriate. The hills were right sized, though, looming behind his slight house, blocking out whatever else there was, pushing Gabe up against the edge of the bluff, one hundred feet above the Hebron.

Sheriff Ben Gilliam would come through the notch high up on the left where the road from Milan cut the crest of a knob, two miles off. Gabe looked at the place in the ridge's silhouette and watched for headlights. He waited forever. When they appeared, the lamps were small and close set, like the eyes of a possum in highbeams. Gabe tried to track them through the series of switchbacks and hairpin curves that led first to Tyrone settlement, then here.

For a few minutes, he lost sight of the patrol car on the mountain-side. When it again crawled into view, Gabe could see that the lights were safely on a lower curve. Animal eyes coming closer, peering at him in and out of the dark, bigger each time.

About 12:15 A.M. Ben Gilliam and his deputy pulled halfway off the one lane road and parked on Gabe's grass. They got out of the car and walked toward him slowly. The way they moved looked almost leisurely. The short, younger man stayed close to his boss, but he studied the things in the yard, the trellis, the new terra cotta fountain which Gabe had just installed but had not connected to the water pump.

The moon was full, floating high, and, for August, the air was cool. The panorama had a silky look to it: Ben's rangy, easy lope, the deputy's head turning smoothly from side to side in a collar of fat, the soft mat of light in front of the open doorway.

The Sheriff nodded toward him and said his name.

"Sheriff." Gabe responded in kind.

The two men didn't shake hands.

"Jeff Bean, my deputy."

Gilliam didn't take his eyes from Gabe when he introduced the boy.

Gabe acknowledged Bean with a nod. Gabe hadn't moved since the black-and-white patrol car had pulled in; he was in the same spot on the lawn where he had stood to watch for them. It wasn't necessary to go toward what would happen, he thought. Things would follow their own lines to the center. Like spokes.

"I thought I better see how it was before I called anybody else in. You sure she's dead?" Gilliam sounded amiably cautious.

"She's dead." Gabe heard the dead tone in his own voice.

"What was it?"

"Gunshot."

"You hurt?" The compass of the Sheriff's questions didn't tip to

29

either side. So far there was no hint of blame, nor empathy.

"Not the way you mean."

"If she's in there," the uniformed man indicated with his head the lighted doorway, "you better show us. Come on, Jeff."

Gabe led the way. Ben Gilliam had reached out naturally and gripped Gabe's upper arm, holding Gabe slightly ahead of himself. The move and the clamped fingers startled Gabe. He wasn't used to being touched by men. Gilliam's hold was strong and intrusive, but Gabe controlled the impulse to shake it off.

Except for the overturned table and for the popcorn-sized pieces of pottery which were sprinkled near it, the long, sparsely furnished room into which they stepped was unnaturally tidy. Gabe, still in front, felt the other men's eyes ticking from spot to spot. He saw, as those two must, that nothing looked extraneous or casually placed. There were three books on the mantle stacked from large to small. Beside them a single candle in a brass holder knifed up sharply. About fifteen feet away from where they stood, Joyce Oliver was on her back, bent at the knees and almost doubled backward over her calves.

It hurt Gabe. It hurt to see her. Joyce's contortion was painful to imagine. Gabe was glad she couldn't feel or know how she looked. One of Joyce's arms was twisted under her body and the other one was at her side, palm up, fingers slightly curled.

Ben finally relaxed his hold a little on Gabe's arm. Together he and the Sheriff and the deputy approached Joyce's body. The short trip made Gabe feel exhausted.

Joyce's thighs were exposed. Her dress had caught when she slid to the floor and the material was wadded like a towel around her waist. The pink rayon slip she wore beneath had ridden up almost to her underpants. Skin showed at the top of Joyce's stockings, plumped out over garter bands, pasty white. Gabe jerked free quickly and reached forward. The Sheriff and his deputy both automatically barred him from pulling Joyce's skirt hem to cover her starkly exposed skin, to hide the hint of fernlike darkness above it.

"You can't change anything until the Coroner's gone," Deputy Bean cautioned flatly, as if he had newly memorized that rule. It was the first time Jeff Bean had spoken.

The Sheriff was now squatting beside the body, depressing each curled finger on Joyce's one exposed hand. Gabe wanted to restate Bean's rule just as cruelly to Gilliam. Instead, he stayed silent and looked on over the back of the Sheriff's head. The man touched Joyce's five fingertips gently, pushing them down like clarinet stops, until he seemed satisfied that they were still pliable. Gabe knew what Gilliam was thinking: that he probably hadn't waited long to call them.

"You shoot her, Gabe?" The question was soft. Surprisingly soft.

"She threatened to kill herself," Gabe said. No hesitation. "We fought. The gun went off."

"Your word against hers then, isn't it?"

Gabe didn't answer. Yes, that's what it came to. His word against hers. At this point Gabe knew he couldn't look away. He couldn't avoid seeing, and admitting what he saw. All Joyce's color had now settled at the back of her neck and limbs, where it showed through her skin, thick and purplish, as if she had absorbed her own shadow.

Gabe leaned forward and looked straight down into Joyce Oliver's eyes. Her pupils were fixed and staring, already hardened into a permanent view of him.

CHAPTER 7

Well Past Midnight

IRA TRUITT STAYED in the center of the Hebron, intent on robbery. He tried to pull up a trotline without disturbing the water's surface luster. It was late. So far, everything was right, Ira thought. River night was at the still point between the clicks and *brraacks* of tree frogs and cicadas and the first birdcalls of dawn. The air was just cool enough, not too far to either side of comfort, and the Hebron perfectly cupped moonlight deep between the trees. Good enough. He worked best, Truitt felt, atop the phosphorescent glow of a watertrapped moon. Ira's ghostly image, as pale as his own skin, stared back at him, floating in waves on the water's upward illumination. He was a rawboned man whose vanishing reflection was frightful.

What was that? Before Ira could continue his thievery, something over there on the Tyrone side of the river snagged his attention. A slight movement, perhaps. Ira wasn't sure. It had been way up high, something negligible, but disturbing. At that very next moment a sound, or a faint light, maybe even just a feeling, rolled off the limestone palisade, sped down the rocky hillside, and settled near Ira in the boat. Then nothing.

Unnerved, the old man shifted the weight of his big frame and steadied the quivering johnboat. He set one oar at a drag angle and went back to his skulduggery. First he braced the paddle with a knee that was thick as a club, then he dipped into the water up to his elbows and felt for the rig's central hook. The stageline had come up heavy from the bottom so Ira knew he would probably feel the rubbery *O* of a fish's mouth ringing the barb. A white bass maybe, or a fat, slick-skinned buffalo, even a sauger. If it was a catfish, he'd have to be quick as a wink and watch out for spines. Catfish spines were sharp as knife tips. Well, all cats got claws, he thought. He made sure his were sharper. Ira secured the paddle's angle, this time with both knees, and raised his palms before his face in the moonlight, fingers splayed. His long fingernails, packed with dirt, were filed to points that extended beyond his fingertips. Outlined against the sky, they looked like the business end of rail spikes.

Truitt stayed in that attitude for longer than he knew, rapt in studious admiration of the yellowish, cornshuck-textured pads that cushioned his broad, leathery hands. Ira's calluses were his pride. Before he was ten years old, their onion-colored thickness had replaced the pockets of tender, pink skin that popped and wept and bled until the youth was numbed and hardened out of them. It was then that Ira had been able, finally, to grab a splintery harrow or steer a plow under his father's stern eye without cringing. Ira would never forget. "God's gloves," he said aloud to the river in a solemn, benedictive voice and lowered his arms to their dark work.

The fish he was stealing reacted to Ira's pronouncement with a sloppy underwater smack against the bottom of the boat. Ira went back, unhurriedly, to the business of hauling it up. Yes, it was a catfish, the color and texture of mud. One that would go at least two or three pounds of good eating, Truitt assessed.

Suspended, the cat wriggled and glistened in the air like the very clay of Adam. Ira reared his head back to get a clear view of the long metal curl that protruded from the fish's cheek like an extra whisker. In spite of the fact that Ira's knuckles were stiff and as big as bulbs, he remained dexterous. When he did set to the task of freeing his catch, he slipped the hook with a thumbnail. The gill flap didn't rip.

Ira then grabbed the catfish midway between its flopping ends and pressed the fish firmly to the seat slat. Ira waited. The fish's mouth opened and closed rapidly, then the gulping motion slowed, gradually slower yet, as if to emphasize the message. When the catfish quit gasping and strained less against his hand, Ira mercilessly severed its head with his old hunting knife, cutting on the slant between the tip of the spike and the cat's backbone. He brought his blade out sharply just behind the bottom of the gill slit.

Chore completed, Ira stood upright in his boat and threw the fishhead off to one side, keeping his bulk and the boat's in perfect, practiced equilibrium when he swung. There was a soft plunk after the toss. A few reflected tree limbs rippled. Truitt's sense of power over the Hebron's surface pleased him. In the past he had been too much involved with land that didn't yield. He should have always farmed the Hebron.

Before Ira ran the rest of the hooks, he again felt the hairs prickle at the base of his neck.

Something was happening. Whatever it was, the sharpness of the

Well Past Midnight

sensation honed Ira's natural wariness. He bent at once until his bulky
torso was almost parallel with the johnboat's flat bottom and rowed,
pulling powerfully, over to his side of the river. It was a swift trip. The
oars bit deeply into the vein of the Hebron, and they hardly made a
splash.

Tucked away, back under the low branches of a sycamore, Ira
scanned the opposite bank then climbed his eyes upward to the land
shelf at the top of Tyrone's almost perpendicular fallaway. Unlit
campsites there were easily visible. From Ira's perspective, the cabins
looked like children's wooden blocks, clumped loosely together near
the righthand end of the bluff.

Nightly, before Ira paddled out on his midnight raids, he always
checked those sites for signs of life. He had done so this evening. Ira
Truitt wasn't in the business of overlooking details. There had not
been as much as a flicker of light the size of a match flare earlier, he
was sure.

At Ira's back, his own Moccasin County's immediate terrain
looked almost identical to the land opposite. The exceptions were that
Moccasin's banks didn't rise quite so grandly and there were no tidy
cottages crowning the bluffs. And in Ira's county the soil, like Ira
himself, was dirt poor, typified by scrub and rock.

Perhaps this apprehension he could feel was a warning, but from
whom? Whose trotline was it that he robbed? Ira had never seen it
tended. The line's tether had simply intruded itself on his side of the
Hebron one morning, like bait.

Ira put his hand up to a treelimb and anchored himself stealthily
in the shadows. A few bits of bark dropped like ashes onto his flap of
dingy hair. By now Truitt was pretty certain that whatever had caught

his attention wasn't at Tyrone settlement. Something though, Ira was sure.

But where? The old man squinted for sharper focus and tried to penetrate the darkened slopes above the Milan County bank. Nothing. Slowly, without turning his body, Ira scanned left from Tyrone. Hah! There. Starkly isolated, a towering chimney was backlit against an eerie, looping, bluish light. Ira had seen the stone stack before and assumed it stood in the ruins of a burned or abandoned structure. He saw now that the chimney served its own cabin. And, what's more, the cabin's roofline was intact.

Ira, always a man of minute attentions, peered as intently as he had ever done. He was determined to miss nothing, but the picture didn't alter for a long time. The beam scoured the dark sky repeatedly without illuminating anything. Truitt was certain there was a patrol car behind the cabin. But if there were policemen over there, why didn't they extinguish their useless light? Ira condemned such waste while the slack, blue lariat of light twirled around and around in the darkness.

The old man stayed at his vigil even when the mist at the waterline condensed into fog and obscured his view. His favorite time on the river was coming; the sky would soon lighten. The change would be all but imperceptible at first; then the vapor would rise from the surface of the water and hover there, just high enough off the Hebron for a craft to weave between cloud and liquid like a spindle.

Other such nights would have found Ira doing just that, once he had stolen the catch. He would lie stretched out, his shoulders fitted inside the raked bow of his boat, legs all the way to stern, and glide down the satin river staring upward, snug as Moses in a basket. Most of his imaginings while he drifted were sweet as the limestone-filtered river water, like his memories of dead Orena, and Ira was protective of their meaning. But lately some of his dreams had begun to be ominous and foretelling. Tonight Ira had turned stony from the last hour's tension. He would not leave his watchpoint for the water's solace.

At daybreak, Truitt finally got a payoff for his constricted sentry duty. A large, boxy vehicle pulled in and parked on the grass beside the distant chimney. It was a van with a bright bubble of red on its roof. Aided by the weak dawn, Ira could also make out the cabin clearly. It was a simple structure, much like other camps at Tyrone, except for an extension attached onto its back wall. The extension was supported by posts upended from the hillside, like pylons. Ira counted three sawhorses on the suspended flooring, or deck, before he pinned his eyes fast to the ambulance and waited, his barrel chest tight as a drum, to see if the vehicle pulled away fast or slow.

CHAPTER 8

To Make a Place

GABE STOOD OFF to one side of the long room and watched while Ben Gilliam and Jeff Bean and the ambulance crew and Dr. Halsey, the Coroner, dealt with the details of death. There was no conversation among the men, a few short questions that got shorter answers, but no talk. Nothing coarse, either. Gabe was alert for that; he half expected some smutty remark. But, as before, the sound was of knees and feet against the planks. This time slow. Methodical.

While Joyce's body was still on the floor, knees spread, one of the two ambulance attendants did what Gabe had tried to do earlier. The man reached over, after the Coroner nodded, and rearranged Joyce's skirt to cover her; then he smoothed the fabric with his knuckle, the way you'd touch a cheek. Dr. Halsey, squatting studiously beside the body, moved his arm purposefully and closed Joyce's eyes one-handed, his index and little fingers delicately extended. The deputy, Jeff Bean, straightened her legs.

It was a sad, quiet business on every man's part. At the end of it,

To Make a Place

Ed Halsey and the Sheriff and young Jeff exhaled in unison and stood aside, while the two attendants covered Joyce with a sheet, then lifted her onto the cot. Gabe took it all in without comment. He didn't protest when they strapped Joyce into place, but it was horrible to see her bound, tied to her stillness.

The men who belted Joyce in, the ones who had brought the ambulance, looked enough alike in their hospital whites to have been brothers. Bent over the tubular steel side rails of the cart, they secured her body and meticulously tucked the sheet tight.

The pair hovered above Joyce while they worked, moving up and down almost simultaneously, soundlessly, like pale wings attached to a ghostly shell. Their chin-length hair falling forward, the greased hanks that fell forward and hung over the white sheet, over Joyce, dirtied the job and made Gabe turn away, repulsed.

By 5:00 A.M. Gabe was alone. He brought a broom from the kitchen and swept pieces of the shattered lamp onto a metal scuttle. He salvaged the mess of delicately hand-wrought, miniature fish from a mound of porcelain dust and slipped them into his shirt pocket. Hardly anything else in the room was disturbed now that Joyce's body was gone. The Sheriff had retrieved her shoes from the hearth and taken them when he left. The sofa was askew. Gabe kneed the corner cushion back until he felt both ends of its frame bump against the wall.

Satisfied that he had done what he could to restore order, Gabe opened the double doors on the river side of his house and stepped cautiously onto the unfinished floor of the porch addition. In the warming air, he finally lit the cigarette he had craved for hours. Gabe pulled the cylinder away from his mouth and a tiny bit of cigarette paper stuck to his lips, paper and a few grains of tobacco, like coffee grounds.

The vapor had backed completely off the Hebron and left the water's surface burnished. Gabe saw that the river was gray-green and clear of debris. The leaves that would weep down on it in a month or two were lacily reflected but absolutely still. It was dead calm. There was no breeze at all, no current either. Locks No. 7 and No. 8 must have been closed for hours. Gabe exhaled through his nostrils. The smoke drifted into the risen fog and expanded, making Gabe feel as if it were all his breath that wound around the hills, that settled, downy and seductive, in a cleft or swirled around a tree. He raised his eyes. The early sky was slightly bluish, barely different from the river's green tint or the neutral mist. The sunrise should have been streaked and orange and mean, he thought, not velvety. But velvety it was, and Gabe would have reached to stroke the heavens if he could have. By ten o'clock in the morning, the August sun would burn the last wisps of mist clear.

Gabe knew that somehow he must step back into the ordinary of time. Gilliam had been plainspoken with him about what would happen next. Within two months the Grand Jury would meet. The Sheriff, forcefully and without apology for what was stern in his voice or manner, had told Gabe not to leave Milan County before the jury convened. Gabe clenched his jaw. It had been disgusting to be lectured and in such a tone.

All right then. By God. Gabe would stay at Tyrone. His tobacco warehouse up in town could bloody hell run itself. Just let them try to do it without him. Gabe would stay an exile in his newmade kingdom. Here in Tyrone, above the Hebron, he would breathe out smoke and inhale air, and he would burn clean, a crucible in the summer heat.

But whatever they thought now, those men in Milan could never lock him up. It wouldn't work. For all this time since his move to the river hadn't he, himself, tried to pen his seething anger at what life had dealt him? For Clara's sake, if not her mother's. Gabe had done nothing for the last four years but try by the hardest to break the concrete mold of himself. He had sacrificed, held Joyce at a mental arm's length, dwelled deep within himself to build and build, first the warehouse, now this house. His whole aim, except for the sordid detail of his mistress, had been to make a place in life that would lure his wife and daughter home.

And now his ferocious rage had slipped its tiny, iron cubicle and cornered him like this.

There was a claw hammer on the carpenter's bench within easy reach of Gabe's fist. He picked it up and tested its heft. Two thick, carbon-steel teeth bit against his palm.

When Gabe hurled the hammer, he yelled. The tool and his cry loop-loop-looped out over the edge of the bluff before they dropped: "Goddd damnnn yoouuu," he howled. The sound died quickly enough that Gabe heard the hammer thud softly, driving the words into the mudbank near his dock.

CHAPTER 9

Past the Time of Telling

NONIE PULCE'S HOUSE was little more than a shed. Long since abandoned, it had been an outbuilding on a sliver of property adjacent to Gabe Phillips' camp. Shortly after he closed on the first site, Gabe bought the extra land, bundled it onto his own plat, then set about making the shed habitable. Next, he hired Nonie to move down from Milan to do for him year round. Tenancy in the minuscule quarters was to be a good portion of Nonie's pay. In her view at the time, the promise of her own place had been all of the incentive.

The two domiciles, less than one hundred yards apart, were separated by something more than could be measured. Phillips' own house changed and elaborated as if elves were on the project nightly, Nonie thought, while hers weathered durably into the landscape. Today her tiny home seemed as grayish and permanent as some of the prehistoric boulders that were scattered, upright, near the lock.

Nonie's old feet had long since polished a narrow, crooked seam of earth between Mr. Gabe's camp and her own. But, slight and birdlike as she was, her route could hardly be called a path. Water maple roots knuckled up along the way, and in summertime broad clumps of long-bladed grass scalloped the edges of the cool, slick seam. The grass tickled Nonie's ankles as she passed.

That morning, before Nonie pulled open a wire gate at the back of what she called her yard, she saw Gabe Phillips coming toward her through the trees, staying exactly on the tiny trail which she herself had blazed. Nonie held on to her surprise from habit, but it was a fact that Phillips seldom came there. Fannie, Nonie's mother, had always told her that certain men possessed "poise." As a child Nonie had rolled the word around and around in her head, a silver ball, "poise." Click, click, click, it rolled over the hard first letter, sometimes too fast. Mr. Gabe was no more than halfway across when Nonie reminded herself that she didn't think often of things like that anymore. She was an old woman now, a woman aging past talk, well past the time of telling how her mother had given her words for toys. They'd had nothing else. But while she watched her employer make his halting way toward her in the pearly morning light, Nonie was sure that Gabe Phillips was the kind of man her mother meant with regard to poise, in spite of his being crippled.

Fannie Pulce would have had darker words for Gabe Phillips too, Nonie told herself; dark and secret words from the bitter, whispered store of mother talk that Nonie never touched.

Nonie grasped the top rectangle of her fencing and waited while Mr. Gabe neared. If he steadied himself by reaching for a tree trunk, she busied her attentions elsewhere. Usually, she mused, the only way to know that the man limped was to listen. Indoors he moved exactly like her silver ball, almost too smoothly. One shoe's heel clicked

43

against the floor with every other step. Out here on uneven ground, it was plain there was something wrong with Mr. Gabe's gait.

While Gabe kept his eyes hard on Nonie, in the way that he had about him, she met them in the face. By the time he was close enough to speak, they had said that kind of hello.

"Did you hear anything, Nonie?" As usual, Nonie observed, Mr. Gabe started talking right in the middle of wherever he was in his own mind.

Nonie quickly knelt down to pick some scorched leaves off a black-eyed Susan that was tangled in her fencing. "I heard you cuss, just then. And I don't know who didn't."

"Nothing else?" It wasn't like him to ask her the same thing twice, knowing as he did that her first answers, like his, were what the answers were.

"Mr. Gabe, I don't listen for much, unless Clara's here."

Nonie kept at her weeding business while Gabe stood gripping the top bar of the gate's frame. She stayed down, her hand now around a whole dandelion plant, working it gently from side to side, until she extracted it, root intact, like a tooth. Finally she looked up, shading her forehead with a wilted hat of greens. "What was it you were thinking I might hear?" Gabe didn't answer. Nonie didn't move.

And then he said it quietly. "The Sheriff was here in the night," he told her. "And some others. I thought you might have been bothered."

Well, no wonder he asked, Nonie told herself tersely. What would the man say next? Nonie gave a sharp little jerk of her head. "Not likely I'd be bothered by such as that after living in Boxtown. Ever hear of 'blue nights' Mr. Gabe? Up there 'blue nights' means law, not skies; it was their lights. And noise brought 'em, but it took a lot of it."

Nonie sighed. "You learned."

"Learned what?" His surprise sounded genuine.

"What to see, what to hear, and if and when to do 'em." Nonie told it with finality, the way she meant it.

Gabe's expression didn't change. Nonie wouldn't say the lines on his face were set angry, but they were set, for certain. Well, what did it matter, Nonie thought, concerning his expression. Nonie had decided long ago she wasn't going to toady to no Gabe Phillipses regardless of what they did to or for her. She wouldn't give them that power over her in her mind. Up in town, she never had done it once. There'd be no starting now.

However, this particular man and what he'd given had created a bad sense in Nonie of owing something with her soul. He'd got her down here to Tyrone, after all, and much as she had wanted to leave fear all boxed up in Milan, sometimes Nonie felt the fright almost open up within her when Mr. Gabe was near. Her feeling was just a glint off fear, something little, like the blade of a pocket knife that barely showed but caught the sun.

This shed was what Nonie feared for. It was what she had to lose and it was plenty. If Mr. Gabe fired her, though he'd never made to do it, Nonie had to go back to Milan. That would be some kind of painful journey. She hoped the Lord would let her die first. Nonie Pulce wanted to leave from right here where she was when it was time. At sixty-seven she was terrified she had more life than patience left, though these last years out on the bluff had helped her get real still inside.

She counted it a debt, that stillness, and Nonie guessed from eyeing Gabe Phillips where he loomed that her repayment started now.

45

The man she worked for had brought shadows with him from the trees. They hung around his deep-set eyes and wrapped his jaw.

Suddenly he confirmed it. "Nonie, I've got no time to say this right. Miss Joyce was fooling with my gun last night and she got killed. Clara and Lucy have got to know. I want you to tell them."

Whatever Nonie Pulce had expected, this was bigger. She gasped and said no, no, no, with her head. Slowly back and forth, no, no, no. She was still on the ground looking up, dangling the bird-sized dandelion weed over her eyes where it swayed gently, limp-necked, every time Nonie turned her silent no.

"You have to do this, Nonie," Gabe continued, pushing his rough voice toward her, demanding with his pressing stance. "Clara must not hear some other way and she'll be leaving soon for school. If we have trouble putting a call through . . . ."

"I'll do it; I never meant I wouldn't," Nonie said at last, her voice having strengthened first. "But it's her mother I'll tell. I'll say it to Miz Lucy. That's what's right. The child won't hear this on the phone. Not from Nonie Pulce. No sir."

Nonie stood then and tilted her head, a pecan shell, its graceful tip sculpted from her tightly gathered, tightly knotted hair. From that angle she took Gabe in full height, the tower over her, and brushed him toward the path with broomstraw fingers.

The oddly matched duo's parade back through the trees and thicket was quiet. A motorboat's buzz, the daytime river's hymn, rose and fell in the background.

They were at Gabe's door before Nonie asked solemnly, "What do I say?"

"I may be indicted," Gabe answered in the same tone. "There's some question of proving it was an accident. The story will all be in their paper tomorrow, I'm sure, and I can't stand to think they'll read it raw. But the main thing is about Thanksgiving. Clara should plan to come," Gabe said emphatically, at the last. "You'll be here like always, tell her, or Lucy if you mean to. But Clara can come. Even if there's to be a trial, Clara must come."

Nonie stepped up behind him from the stone paver that was so newly and neatly placed below Mr. Gabe's threshold. She balanced herself carefully before following the man into his shocking house.

At the funeral home up in Milan, Morton the undertaker smoothed the furry lining in one of his more expensive caskets, a steel-handled mahogany with fawn plush interior. This one should be perfect for Joyce Oliver since Gabe Phillips was paying. If there were to be a viewing, Joyce's cadaver would certainly appear rosier reflecting the pink tint of a copper clad. She looked so deadly pallid. But even Gabe's pocket might not be deep enough to buy a copper coffin. It was a shame. However, there was nothing wrong with hardwood. Not a thing. Hardwoods had been known to stay almost intact underground for years. Even without a vault.

While the embalmer considered the gleaming inventory of his casket room instead of the pitiably nude corpse in the cooler, Gabe was standing near Nonie down at Tyrone. As he stood, Gabe promised himself with a steely resolve that whatever he had to do, he would do. He would not let this anguish spread if he could stop it. That was the vow he would honor, no matter what oaths the powers-that-be made him swear in court.

Nonie settled sternly to her task at the telephone. She pictured Gabe's exwife. She saw Lucy Phillips' face coming up on the moment

47

when everything would change. Nonie's blue-ringed eyes had seen that change too often. And she knew Clara would be invisibly near while her mother got this news. Clara's telltale braids would dangle like ropes behind the hinged opening of the bedroom door. For at eleven years old the child had become a thin and guarded girl, always on the watch.

CHAPTER 10

Sealed in a Bottle

BEN GILLIAM, THE High Sheriff, unglued himself from his desk. Since coming up to town from Tyrone, he had sat filling out the required report on Joyce Oliver's death in a desultory fashion. It was almost time to meet the others for breakfast. If he went over early, maybe he could dig out of the bog that presently sucked him down. The air around him was dark as a dead zone while he gathered up to go.

At least the Dixie Café with its spotty morning chatter in the background would be a less lonely place for ruminations. Ben couldn't seem to quit running the rails of every casual brush he'd had with Joyce's living self or Gabe Phillips. It was his job to reflect on crimes, and this was a particularly shocking one which justified intensity. But Ben knew he should have been able to back out far enough from facts to get perspective. So far he hadn't. Details and their implications had clickety-clacked around and around in Ben's head for hours. If he shook his noggin, it would surely rattle.

$\mathcal{I}$t Was the Goodness of the Place

Out on Main Street, Ben paid no mind to the lingering pink tinge that rouged the storefronts he usually studied with affection. It was 6:20 A.M., a good forty minutes before even the Judge, punctual as a stopwatch, would show. Ben could ponder away until then and nobody would bedevil him. Good citizens of the early-riser ilk were likely to leave him be as long as steam could be seen curling above his cup. That part was easy. Spiro topped or hotted up the coffee until you never saw the bottom of a mug. Who knew what was down there.

Ben had been the High Sheriff for four years. He had been appointed to fill out a term before being rightfully elected in the spring of '47 and re-sworn. That autumn had also been Gabe's first season of running the warehouse. Before this morning the conjuncture of beginnings had been a great source of pride for Ben. The way he figured it, his life's course, the town's renewal and Gabe's prosperity had set off down the road together. He had thought they would continue, no more likely to cross than parallel lines, but headed in the same direction.

Gabe Phillips had ever been an outsized figure in Ben's mind. He had never known a man who had risen in life the way Gabe had. In Milan people were more or less born into what they would become. The security of such predetermination was comforting to Ben. Yet you had to stand in awe of any man who climbed an idea from the bottom rung of Milan's ladder to the top.

Ben was younger than Phillips and had had few dealings with him. None of those transactions had been significant. He sometimes called Gabe if one warehouse employee or another got himself hauled to the drunk tank, in that line. All the better to be awestruck, Ben guessed, no breeding of contempt where nothing was familiar.

Ben didn't have an ounce of jealousy. He sorted himself into an entirely different bin from a man like Gabe. In Ben's view society had rules. Ben knew his place. His own pride derived from having chosen a life of service. He was, after all, the *High* Sheriff. Until last night the role had fit Ben as easy as the uniform.

Across the street from his office, Ben stepped into the Dixie Café. In early morning the barnlike space was brownish, warmly dingy, and the whole place smelled like toast. The Sheriff took his regular chair at the back of the room and settled into a study that was as ripe and dark as his surroundings. For close to half an hour Ben wrestled to think things out. Strictly speaking, the precariousness of life was outside his job's concern but he couldn't let it go. That poor girl.

Last night, when Ben opened the door and climbed from his patrol car to cross Gabe's moonlit lawn, the most routine motions had seemed dreamlike, gradual, and hushed. Webs of that feeling still clung to his mood. There was no season, no year, no morning. There was no wet August heat waiting outside to be baked from the asphalt by noon. Ben's entirety was this: a dim room behind immaculately featureless glass, and timeless.

When Ed Halsey, sitting heavily, used Ben's shoulder as a handhold, he jolted Ben roughly into the present minute. Judge Matt Stallard, posture-perfect and hard-eyed as ever, followed closely behind the smaller man and also took his accustomed place.

"You look like a mouse in his hole, crouched back here," Halsey said. "You asleep?"

"I could use a nap, that's certain," Ben said. He started a tiny, counter-clockwise eddy in his coffee cup with a teaspoon.

The Judge was close to the wall on Ben's right, situated somewhat back from the circle of chairs, outside the circle of the table. Stallard placed himself apart then leaned in ever so slightly in a move that seemed calculated to make people edgy, as it currently did Ben. The tall, patrician-looking Judge customarily remained thoughtfully pendant above the group that way, putting in his oar seldom, if at all. From that oblique perch, as from the bench, the most ordinary of Matthew Stallard's words took on the quality of dicta.

First Stallard did exactly what Ben expected. The Judge angled smoothly forward and put a question ever so nicely to the Sheriff.

"There was too much paperwork, then? I thought you said you would find your way home immediately after our little phone conversation. I expected that to be so."

There was a pure line to the Judge's frame that focused him in the room's soft blur. Part of the older man's style was that he liked things simply done even in so small a matter as a social contract for rest. Ben knew his own failure here was minute, but of course he felt it keenly.

Ben answered Stallard about his tiredness, not about the implication of a promise broken. The Judge's dignity had a way of constraining argument, in court or out.

"Halsey's probably in worse shape than I am," Ben said, trying lightly to shift the Judge's focus onto the Coroner. "He had to go on to Morton's with her body. I've just been working on the file, sorting things out." He added, truthfully: "Once I got started thinking, it was harder to stop than to keep at it." The obscene picture of Joyce Oliver's pretzeled little body, previously the object of so much of the town's furtive and speculative desire, coldly exposed on Gabe Phillips' floor, screened across the back of Ben's mind while he spoke.

Because of that unsettling vision, Ben had longed to go home in the hours after he came up from Tyrone. He had yearned to be enveloped by that utter coziness with the familiar that was the slope of his wife's breast, which fell weighted into the deep bowl of his palm most nights when he curled to sleep against her back.

But Ben had doggedly stayed at his desk. His entire trip to the office before dawn, the ascending spiral from Tyrone to Milan, had been a rising, broadening lament, Ben finally realized, the worse for being silent. What had happened between Gabe Phillips and Joyce Oliver there in the house above the water? Ben Gilliam ached to know. What had really happened? And why did he personally feel the failure of it so?

The cubicle where Ben had spent the hours up until now was on the ground level of the Milan County courthouse. By 4:00 A.M., while Ben worried a minuscule train of paper clips around the clutter on his desktop blotter, the building's emptiness seemed as hollow and comfortless as a cave.

Ultimately, Ben had stayed because, thinking from the maze of those darkened corridors about Gabe Phillips and Joyce Oliver, and Gabe's young girl, Clara, braids flying like kite tails the last Ben saw of her, and Lucy, Gabe's forceful exwife, and on through the whole cast of this drama, he had felt threatened. Ben's own family had seemed fragile. Mollie and his boys were safe, the Sheriff had felt sure, only as long as he remained at work. Safety was innocence to Ben. He couldn't bear for his wife and children to wake to this rough new world of Milan where innocence was lost to evil and girls might die by violence in the night. It took Ben's staying in the half-lit room off the first floor hallway of the courthouse to preserve their egg-like slumbers.

Again, the Judge called him to his senses. "And have you done

53

that, Ben, sorted it out?" Stallard asked.

The question, uttered in the Judge's softly modulated drawl, was normal enough. But the voice and the query, no matter how gently put, was insistent. A satisfactory answer was demanded. Ben knew this was so because he had a life's experience with Stallard and his manner.

Was that, then, how Judge Matthew Stallard ruled them, Ben wondered, ruled him and Ed Halsey, and the entire town of Milan, and Milan County beyond, with what Ben could only think of as a sort of austere kindness? Or was there some benignity of grace that could be earned by having pleased the Judge? Ben had never pondered this before.

"Well, there's certainly no mystery to the what of the crime," Ben answered. "There were only two people there. One of them is dead. You tell me the why of it. If you're figuring a motive, it's a settled fact he didn't kill her for money. Or, I doubt, for love. So whatever is left."

Ben stayed busy with his hands during the short analysis. He thumbed a fold of the table's oilcloth into a sharp crease, then he reached for the milky, ceramic salt and pepper shakers and tapped them cautiously against a pressed-glass sugar bowl. Cautious because, since Gabe Phillips' midnight summons, Ben had been at odds with small items. He was vaguely wary of the sudden rebelliousness of inky carbons that floated from between tissuey office forms, of dry pens and misplaced cabinet keys and the razor-sharp edges of envelopes. They had all ensnared the Sheriff in nasty little traps of delay, delays that had kept Ben from doing what Judge Matthew Stallard wanted, from sifting through his sense of Gabe and Joyce and the things that men and women do, for the nugget of what happened.

Ben was not surprised that the judge had offered no preamble of sympathy for a young girl dead, before he focused on the cause. The man's concern revealed grief enough. But Ben couldn't remember a time when he had felt the importance of his own words to such an extent. If he just weren't so tired, so awfully tired. And being asked to make sense of a senseless thing.

A wedge of Halsey's grim face pried open the view to Ben's left. Those other people in the room, the same ones, mostly men, whom the sheriff saw daily, suddenly looked furtive in the sepia tint of morning light. They, too, wanted to know, Ben thought. They insisted with their silence. How did he, the Sheriff, see what had happened last night at Gabe Phillips' camp? No one looked at him directly, but Ben felt them waiting, knives and forks crossed above their plates. He sensed an edge of menace.

After his survey of the room, Ben's tongue felt as big as a sink stopper. He wished more than ever to speak plainly. But he had no idea what should be said. Something beyond words was happening inside Ben. In his simple way he had always done what he could to guard Milan. And he wasn't jealous of the Judge's status as a man of wisdom. Maybe Ben lacked something, though, that every single other person here possessed. Had they each inherited by birthright some ambivalence which held that all men born, conceived in sin as the preachers would rant, were therefore sinful? Perhaps that knowledge kept them from buying a man like Gabe Phillips whole, as Ben had done, or from assuming a common depth of goodness as Ben was wont to do with all. Was this withholding of whole-heartedness also Mollie's secret? Was it the part of his wife's unknowableness that Ben could never penetrate? Could he be alone, then, in not being able to fathom that the clinging horror of this death could entwine a man like

Gabe? And why delve into the mystery anyway? Particularly now, when he was exhausted.

While Ben watched his hands as if they were detached, the Sheriff's memory lit on a night shortly after the war ended. It was probably in the spring of 1945. Every boy in Milan County who was coming home from war had done so. Soon after their return, Gabe sent an invitation around by word of mouth. He was buying supper, treating veterans over to the steak house in Columbia, eleven miles from Milan. In spite of having earned a purple heart in France, Ben, at twenty-four, had been green as a twig in social matters. After considerable inner hemming and hawing, he went ahead and took the invite. If he could brave a bullet from the enemy, Ben had decided he could surely face the rigors of one man's hospitality by having dinner out with friends.

It turned out that Ben had enjoyed the evening as much or more than any soldier there. In 1945 Gabe had a few years to go before he would hit the jackpot with his Burley warehouse. Phillips was still struggling along during postwar as a pinhooker. There had been no doubt in Ben's mind but what the big-night spread of T-bone steaks and gravy set Phillips back substantially. To this day Ben wondered where Gabe and Lucy had scraped up the money to be so lavish by the standards of the times. Clara was just a mite. Ben had hardly dwelled on the evening's significance when it happened. As a returning G.I. he had been consumed with looking out for a handle of some kind on his own life. But Gabe's literal peace offering had been a goodwill gesture that lasted in Ben's mind. This morning wasn't the first daydream wherein Ben had relived the meal and comradery since becoming Sheriff.

At the dinner in '45, Phillips had sat off to one side of the restaurant's smoky room. The eatery was cheaply decorated. Crudely assembled tables rested on a floor made of pine planks so raw they smelled of resin. Ben didn't remember windows in the place. But the food was good as any. That evening it seemed appropriate to Ben that Gabe held himself apart. Phillips was six or seven years older than most of the boys he was hosting. And he hadn't been where they'd been.

At a certain point the party's boisterousness turned predictably maudlin. Ben had seen Gabe nod every time a waiter indicated that another whiskey bottle's seal needed to be cracked. Pretty soon Phillips' guests were universally red-eyed and lachrymose, as Ben remembered, calling out the names of boys who had gone over with them but would never be in their beloved Milan County again. Not above the sod at any rate. The shouts may have been drunken but they weren't emotionally false. God-almighty, Ben had reflected that night and did so again this minute, they had gone through something, that's for sure. And together.

It was right near the instant of that insight that Ben had sobered enough to feel with certainty how Gabe Phillips, a worldly seeming man by any count, was overawed by a group of graceless boys who were hanging on each other's shoulders over smeary plates. Ben, the veteran, guessed then that he had barely begun to glimmer what coming home from World War II victorious must have meant to someone crippled at the start.

Ben shook his head to clear the distant evening's clamor. He had always felt that life should be a clear, straight-flowing stream. His own life was, Ben thought. He was possessed of orderly desires, and he drew strength from an inner river of vastly wide and calm devotion that engulfed his friends and family. This morning his river had burst its banks. Other deaths had made him sadder, but none had shaken him quite like Joyce's at Tyrone.

A dim memory of the day Lucy Phillips had left Milan edged in on Ben. He pictured her muddy, mulberry-colored four-door going down Main Street, away from town. Clara, the girl, was up on her knees in the passenger seat watching Milan shrink and fade, her small face somber. Sad as it was, Ben had told himself then, it was no concern of his. Nothing on the books said you couldn't end a marriage. He'd been caught off guard, was all. But there had been something funereal about the pace of the car that lingered. Since that day, Ben had seen the child a number of times during her visits with Gabe. Clara was a quick-moving, dark-eyed girl who hovered at the edge of things even when she was on the street holding tight to her father's hand.

Once last summer Ben had watched Gabe's daughter from Tyrone bridge. Clara was out on the Hebron alone, diving off an anchored dinghy. From his distant vantage, she had sparkled silver wet in the sun, splashing seamlessly in and out of the water like a magic fish. This morning, Ben wondered, was she down in Hickman sleeping this very minute, damply nestled in the early heat? Was she dreaming of the river? Or had they told her.

Matthew Stallard interrupted Ben's reverie. "I hate to press, Ben, but how long might it be before you enlighten us with an observation? We do need an understanding here, if we are to right things." The Judge's speech was even, as always, no hint of impatience. His point was made.

Ben was well aware that most people in town had long since

practically deified Judge Stallard. The Sheriff's own wife, for instance, never failed to describe the Judge as "courtly." "A bit unreal," Mollie once observed, as if he were "trapped in the wrong era." Not at all the immutable power behind the county's life. No one ever said a word of that.

Ben's gaze settled on the Judge as lightly as a moth. If the town had secrets, Ben, too, knew what he knew. Every afternoon when the Judge passed their frame bungalow, going sedately toward his imposing Georgian brick residence at the end of the block on Oxford Street, Mollie watched for him. Stallard walked near the far edge of the sidewalk, his left thumb hooked into the pocket of a dove-gray waistcoat. The man was tall, and walking slowly, he raised himself off the surface of a small town afternoon by the glassy brilliance of his glittering black malacca cane.

In nice weather Ben knew that his wife tried to be on the porch drinking her afternoon iced tea when Stallard went by. Ben knew this was so, for more than once had he come home early, entering from the garage, and seen them through the front screen, seen his wife raise her tea glass slightly, seen the sheen of damp heat on her plump, pretty arm before she bowed her head in salute to the judge. Ben had watched, then, as Mollie lowered the glass, straightened her head and smiled, close-mouthed, over the sugary taste of something sweetly humorous she didn't aim to swallow just yet.

Judge Stallard, for his part, tended toward Mollie from his shoulders, without pausing, but he let her know that, oh, it was a pleasure just to see her there, and that his formal, gray-haired nod was an acknowledgment few in this town deserved. Ben's heart pounded. It was the absolute wonder of such gallant moments that he must protect. How was it that if Gabe Phillips fell, that kind of blame-lessness would disappear? Yet it would, Ben thought sadly, he was all but certain that it would. If nothing else, Ben had realized that Milan was a town as yet almost wholly unacquainted with its sins.

Ed Halsey and Judge Stallard had both pressed physically closer while Ben reflected. They waited, each man equally intent on Ben's silence. But what could he say? "You want to know," he finally asked, "if Joyce Oliver killed herself, or was it an accident, or did Gabe do it?"

Ben picked up a biscuit and tore it into parts, one for each possibility, then reached for the damson preserve bowl. He felt loosely collected. "I've got no idea," he said. "And, what's more, I'm not sure there's any way of knowing, even if we'd been there. But there's . . . something," Ben shrugged and bit the biscuit.

There was another interval of silence while the three men seated at the table handed around the sugar, cream, and butter, and performed smooth little rituals of politeness worn unnoticeable through the years, although, if analyzed, the careful order of offering and passing and refusing was subtly deferential to the Judge.

"If you're looking to me," Ben swallowed and continued, "it just seems like such a waste of something vital." His tone was mournful. "I'm not sure. But I don't think I know exactly what to solve. It's like something blinked. Everything I'm used to is askew."

"Well, then," Judge Stallard pronounced. He drew himself up with a swift breath. "Perhaps we should wait for Buell before we go on."

All right with Ben. Through the night, Ben's back muscles had gradually hardened into a thick plating. He would tortoise into that shell and wait right here at the Dixie Café for community order to reestablish itself. He could wait forever if he had to.

Ben swiveled to survey the room. Spiro owned the Dixie. But it was Spiro's wife Sophie who made the café what it was: a cozy chamber at the heart of Milan's three-block business district. She and the restaurant and the menu were an earthy stew of Southern mixed with Greek. Ben's favorite dish here was moussaka. Just thinking about the spicy, ground lamb, blanketed with an inch of fluffy custard, made his mouth water even this grim morning. It had taken her awhile but Sophie had even managed to educate Ben's simple palate. He was glad of it, too.

Last November, after Gabe's opening-day auction at the shiny new tobacco warehouse up the street, Ben had watched happily from this very table as, one after another, men crossed from the warehouse by noon for a satisfying detour through a plate of Sophie's Special. Regardless that the main dish had made their bellies bulge, most of the men promptly topped the meal off, groaning as they did so, with wide, sugar-crusted wedges of deep, transparent pie. One by one the farmers had then lumbered out to settle up their year-round accounts and buy what niceties they could for wives and children.

Ben wanted to think back on that this morning. Those were details, like the food here at the Dixie, that he understood. Not Joyce's ugly death.

While he and his companions waited for the Commonwealth's Attorney, Ben eased the thorn of death from his mind by picturing the farmers' wives at home when their men were up in town. He saw the women happily cool in big, square kitchens, with the roller blinds half down over the screens. In his vision, the wives rested their forearms against cold, granite tabletops and waited for the work to start up again, for the kids to run in hot and damp and grassy smelling; the women sat until they saw their men in place, back in the fields, perched high on machinery, mowing soundlessly or slicing into the turf with sharp blades, leaving a wake of almost black dirt fanned out behind.

In that serene world Ben never factored out the desperate joy of the Burley tobacco crop and its temple, G. Phillips Central Burley Warehouse No. 1, which held the entire county in thrall. His vision of farmers and women and the warehouse and the town and Sophie's dimpled presence was whole, spherelike, and perfected for a moment, just before Buell Smith walked over.

Ben sighed and let the present renew its sharp hold. He liked Buell, the Commonwealth's Attorney, but it was good that Smith was the last of the foursome to arrive. He hadn't needed to be here earlier. It was said that Buell was smart as a whip, but he didn't seem to have an inward knack. He was, however, right for expediting whatever it was the Judge was setting up. And Ben didn't doubt for an instant that a setup was in the works. Grateful to be off the hook, Ben eased back and cut himself some slack.

Buell jumped in directly, a habit honed by years of practice in crucial depositions. He sat at the noon point on the table, opposite Ben and next to the Judge. He first turned to Halsey: "I'm late because I've been by Morton's," he said, keeping confidences with his tone. "He called about an hour ago. Mr. Thoughtful said he didn't notify me earlier because he wanted to allow you and Ben time for some wee-hours rest before we met. Considerate as ever, he never mentioned having gone to sleep on the job himself."

Ben smiled at that description of Morton, the funeral director. No question that Milan's unctuous undertaker, with his swept-back fronds of silver hair, was slick as soap. Buell Smith, on the other hand, was all business. Smith moved on quickly from his Morton comment by inquiring about plans for Joyce's autopsy.

"Well, we can go ahead and get her in the ground," Dr. Halsey answered. His speech was gruff. It was well-known among the group that the doctor hated doing autopsies. His arts were for the living, not the dead. "I've explored the wound locally, probed it. Used letter opener hemostats, no additional incision." Head down, Halsey went on: "It was a sure bullet, straight to her heart. Minimal surrounding trauma and no exit wound. If she'd been twisted any other way . . ." His words trailed down. My. Every man at the table took a breath. If wishing could have done it, Joyce was snatched to safety in a flash. Reluctantly, the four exhaled and let time's slipstream take her.

The lawyer in Buell wanted a stated conclusion from the doctor. "You're saying no autopsy."

"What's the point?" Halsey asked instead of answering. "We've got the gun, Gabe's not going anywhere and she's got the bullet in her. There's no prize for ripping her up trying to prove something Ben says we can't know."

"The points being procedure and routine, if I have to cite chapter and verse."

"Come on, Buell. You'll be reelected regardless of whether parts of Joyce Oliver's heart get weighed in on a scale." The doctor's expression was as sour as his words.

Ben was surprised at the injection of sarcasm. In this group, that had never been their way. He couldn't remember a single instance when any man among them had been so much as curt to any one of the other three. Having witnessed it now, Ben knew he wasn't the only one who found himself off base this morning.

Judge Stallard interrupted the set to between coroner and attorney by passing the bread platter to Buell Smith. The Judge had been watching the other men sternly, but now his expression was invitingly benign. Stallard stretched his arms past Ben's chest, holding the stoneware plate as exactly level and carefully two handed as a communion tray. "Tell me this," he addressed the attorney with just the right ministerial hint, "Her people don't live around here, do they?"

This was more Ben's department than Buell's. Ben told what little he knew. "She didn't have kin in this county, not a solitary soul. Nor any friends that I know of," he said. "Other than if you count Gabe."

"Doesn't look like we can," Dr. Halsey contributed drily.

The last time Ben had seen Joyce alive was through the plate glass at Gabe Phillips' storefront up the street. Joyce had been perched on the narrow windowsill inside the warehouse office. Her face caught the sun fully. When she smiled up at Ben, she had a dab of almost purple lipstick on her eyetooth. She wore a tight, angora sweater that sported a garish rhinestone brooch near the bulging round of her breast. Ben remembered thinking that the fastener could have grazed Joyce's nipple if she were careless when she pinned it. The sweater's feathery wool was too white, next to Joyce's white skin. Her nails had been painted a child's pink and their tips gleamed with the hard enamel shine of little candies. She mouthed a hello at Ben through the expanse of the windowpane, then repeated it aloud when he cupped his ear. Her voice had sounded watery and indistinct.

Ben looked around and tried to read the face of each man at the table. What could any of them say for Joyce Oliver? She was a dumb girl, flirty, who hadn't begun to guess her impact, the explosiveness of brash and wistful with a beauty fuse.

Buell Smith gave his head one of his characteristically big loose shakes, like a horse adjusting its bridle, then paused and shook it again before he spoke. "I'll get on the line this morning. Try to find out if there is anyone to notify," Buell said. "Seems like if there were, we would have heard of them before now." Ben recognized that that was the deplorable conclusion each one of them had reached.

"Well, then . . ." said Judge Stallard as a prologue.

"My god," Halsey interrupted. The doctor muffled himself with his hand then somberly announced: "If there's no kin . . ." His voice, caught, squeezed out between his fingers. "She's like a rock down a well."

Pragmatic Buell said his part: "At least it's simpler. And Joyce Oliver doesn't care a bit. Not today." Polling their faces, he added flatly: "The inquest and Grand Jury will cost the county less. Few to summon," he went on, as if any one among them could have missed his point. He turned to Ben. "You did advise Gabe about the Grand Jury?"

The Judge again imposed himself between the men with his same commanding, leaning posture. "The Grand Jury convenes again in two months. Time enough."

Buell Smith removed his eyeglasses. On either side of the bridge of his nose, the only fleshy part of his face, there were deep dents which the attorney now tried to erase by massaging them while he talked. Barely eight o'clock in the morning and already he sounded tired and looked tired. In contradiction of his habitually brusque manner, there was an air of perpetual weariness about Buell that, for the first time since Ben had known him, fit the circumstances of the day. Spectacles back in place, the lawyer looked pointedly at the group and asked out loud the question Ben had silently asked himself in different words. "Well, do we hide in the blind by going for an accidental on the certificate and a No True Bill," Buell's eyebrows met and underlined the rest of his sentence, "or shoot ducks while they're flying? What's your call?"

"I don't see a need to be quite as specific or hasty as all that in our determinations." Judge Stallard spoke slowly while considering, mightily, the backs of his hands. "There's many a way to hunt. Some more sporting than others." With that he pressed his hands, palms flat, against the tablecloth: "We all have a stake in preservation, after all," he announced. "Let's make that clear among us. Certainly we can make it our mission to see that no one else suffers. In the meantime, to aim for equity, in the absence of absolutes, seems the honorable thing. And if Gabe Phillips is outside our laws, he's certainly not above them. There are always higher courts."

"And what do we say to Gabe Phillips while he waits for *that* hearing?" This from the Coroner.

Judge Stallard was his most precise: "Let's allow Mr. Gabe Phillips to stew in his own strong juices for the coming weeks. Such an experience can only edify the best of us."

From where they sat, Ben could see the broad front window that seemed to magnify the light that it admitted. Ben had the sleepy sensation that they were posed in a thick glass bottle. Puzzled as he was by what he could only call the ambiguity of the Judge's statement, it was increasingly difficult to stay awake. Ed Halsey was speaking, urging; he wanted Ben to think about Gabe, who would represent Gabe for the Grand Jury, but it didn't matter, did it? Weren't they

sealed here in their bottle? Ben wouldn't move. He would watch a fat
sleeve of light play on Mollie's arm when she lifted her glass to the
Judge. He would trace the icy sweat that dripped ever so slowly down
a cone-shaped, rippled, yellow tea glass before it wet her hand.

"Come on, Ben, get with it," Buell insisted. He thumped Ben's
chairleg impatiently with his foot. "Join us in this. We need you. Who
do you think Gabe will hire? You can see my problem. We're in
never-never land. There's nothing with which to convict but plenty of
evidence that can make up an indictment. I can direct the Grand Jury,
but I'll need help. Don't forget, a runaway panel isn't unheard of, God
forbid. Gabe's got to have a lawyer, regardless." Buell scanned around
the table, coming full circle to rest his eyes where they started, on Ben.

Ben groped his way back mentally. They had all gotten ahead of
him somehow. "Everybody has a stake in the outcome, you mean.
Except Joyce Oliver." His tone came out sharper than he intended.

"Harshly put, but a fair assessment." Judge Stallard's comment
was reticent. He had closed the book, Ben thought. Ben scratched the
stubble on his chin against his palm. Things were moving fast, gathering the same kind of speed Gabe Phillips had picked up with his talk
of going statewide with the warehouses. It suddenly was all a matter
of speed and power and forces outside the control of last night's pitiful
events. Better get this over with. Ben couldn't remember being on
display unshaven.

"All Gabe really needs is an attorney who hasn't purposely pissed
off, or on, somebody in the jury pool," Ben said. He watched for the
effect of his statement on the group. "Not the easiest thing to find,
even in this county."

Dr. Halsey concurred: "Especially in this county! We've been in this pond together for a long time."

It was almost half past eight, and all four men turned toward the storefront, where Sonny Nolan, having whooshed open the double doors, was shining in beatifically, brighter than the August sun.

Judge Stallard edged toward Ben and smiled his most patrician smile. "Well, gentlemen," he soothed. "If it isn't the rooster from the rooftop. I believe we are about to find out exactly which way the wind blows. Counselor Nolan may have just chased an ambulance until it caught him."

"Good God, Judge. You don't expect Gabe to hire that little prick, do you? I've seen him; he avoids Nolan like he's afraid of getting something on his shoe." Buell Smith radiated his disgust.

Stallard simultaneously sharpened the point on his goatee and his words. "Perhaps more should," he said. "Don't lose sight, Buell. What we need is an imprimatur."

On that note Robertson Nolan Esquire, known by request as "Sonny," arrived at the table. "Well, well. You gents looking for an Indian chief or will you settle for just another lawyer?"

Buell Smith hooked the fifth chair out with his overactive foot. "Awful humble of you this morning, Sonny. I've never known you to think of yourself as just another anything."

Nolan canvassed their faces but paused before sitting until Judge Stallard waved him into the chair with one of his spare gestures. When Sonny did sit, his tight, three-piece suit bloused his starched shirt breast dramatically. The lawyer's bright countenance now bulged like the bulb on a thermometer. Whenever the town gathered, picnic, dance, or death, Sonny Nolan showed up and cried or sang the loudest, danced the most and prayed the longest. He was patriotic, Ben thought, right down to his flushed skin tone. Mollie never referred to Nolan as anything but "the flag."

The first time Sonny stood and sang in Ben's presence was at the park fountain dedication. He had crooned the old mountain favorite "When the Roll Is Called Up Yonder" to a startled audience. On the least hint of an excuse since then, Nolan showed up and pitched into the hymn with gusto, to the point that Mollie allowed that she, for one, was willing to let Sonny go first when that particular call came.

Ben hadn't known whether to laugh or applaud after Sonny's park debut. The majority of the crowd had no doubt. They clapped and whooped and whistled around their little fingers. If Nolan had the stature of a leprechaun, he sounded like an Irish angel, should there be such a thing. His pure tenor voice had played on the air as clean as a high strung fiddle. One old woman nearby in the audience egged Nolan on. "Bless you. Bless you, Sonny," she called. "Your our'n." Tears made little rivulets down the dried clay runnels of her cheeks. Well, Sonny wept along and sang a little sweeter, but he never missed a note.

Like Joyce Oliver, Robertson "Sonny" Nolan had come to Milan alone and knowing no one, ready to take on the town. The difference had been that Sonny, the personification of shrewd ambition, seemed to have a future, not a past. Ben's dread was that Sonny's brand of artifice might *be* Milan's future at the rate he was going. The man was scary smart, more cunning than smart and more ambitious than either.

Judge Stallard brought matters to order with an exaggeratedly polite "Ahem." Then: "Since you presumably know of the deplorable event which transpired down at Mr. Gabe Phillips' Tyrone abode last evening, I wonder if you would share how and what you've heard, Mr. Nolan."

Sonny scooted up to the edge of his seat. Ben had seen Nolan try to impress the Judge before, by becoming foolishly formal. This morning Nolan merely flashed a sheepish smile for each man at the table before he spoke. It hardly hid the wolf.

What he did say was circumspect. "I don't need to tell you fellows that the party lines are humming. There's more than a little speculation going on. If you think my ear is closer to the ground than yours, your Honor," Sonny paused for effect, "I'm happy to be an intermediary."

The Judge indulged Sonny with his own brand of smile. He asked graciously if they might have the short version of when and what he'd heard.

"Word traveled pretty fast once you had the body up to Morton's." Sonny's response was also pretty rapid, and he allowed no time for interruptions before continuing: He aimed to hold the floor. "What I'm hearing is that people are more worried about what might happen to Gabe than what did happen to Joyce. Tragic though it was," he quickly amended.

Ben doubted that there was ever any "short of it" with Sonny Nolan. The lawyer made even this little speech with gestures of sincerity. Palm over the heart, hand on the brow. Who knew if they were false? And Nolan didn't stop there with the utmost "what" of what he'd heard: "Gabe Phillips has a host of people huddled under that big tobacco-leaf umbrella of his. They're right fearful of bad weather if it gets folded."

If three of the men at the table were aware of the Judge's impatience with Sonny's line, Nolan was oblivious. He summed up his importance to events by saying: "Some people look to me, you know." And he just had to add that, Ben was certain. A man like Sonny Nolan couldn't *not* say such a thing when he had the chance and Judge Matthew Stallard was so very, very near.

They all, in their official roles, meaning Judge Matthew Stallard; Halsey, the County Coroner; Buell Smith, the Commonwealth's Attorney; and Ben, the High Sheriff, hesitated in unison when the smaller man signaled by his silence that he had had his say.

Sonny, the blood pressure showing in his face, began nervously making coffee corkscrews from the ring under his cup, dipping his index finger in the mug to moisten it when the liquid dried. He did sit quiet though, painting bigger and bigger spirals while the men studiously considered him as if to do a drawing of his face. After a time Judge Stallard led. "Then, we may assume, may we, Sonny, that if Gabe Phillips wishes to retain you, you would be willing to have him as a client? In fact, by my lights, it wouldn't be unseemly if you were to volunteer."

Sonny grew a slow smile. "Now, tell me again, why would I want to do that? Sounds like a lot of potatoes for very little butter to me." His eyes gleamed. Sonny appended "Your Honor" to his question a touch too politely. Saint or sinner, Gabe Phillips would be no angel to work with and every man at the table knew it.

Judge Stallard answered, same smile, different eyes. "Why, prestige, Sonny. Presteeege."

Nolan nodded. "Ah, I see. And how do you cook that?" Then he stood. Before turning away, he feigned resignation and tossed out "But I'm proud to serve when called. Mighty proud," Sonny said again, as a goodbye, and left the way he came. At least they were spared the concert. Happily, Sonny missed the Judge's elegantly enunciated observation that in the practice of law Counselor Nolan no doubt ate only what he killed, and few potatoes.

Buell groaned in on the subject of Nolan's stated pride: "He already is too proud by half. And, shit. Now we'll have him with us every morning."

Judge Stallard unhooked his cane from the adjacent chair. The fateful coffee hour was over. Dr. Halsey stayed put. He looked permanent to Ben.

Ben rose to go, unfolding slowly, feeling the same resistance in unbending arms and legs he had felt in Joyce Oliver's.

CHAPTER 11

A Grip on Time

IRA STAYED HIDDEN through the night, riveted by the drama being played out on the bluff across the river. The scene intensified when the van with the red bubble arrived then inched away. He kept his eyes glued onto the vehicle until its light was no bigger than the head of a pin, redhot, then extinguished.

Just past dawn, Ira had been able to make out a figure that seemed to have materialized on the deck of the unfinished house. Yes, it was a man, Ira thought. Nothing spectral. Ira was waiting for the sun to show the man clearly when he heard a voice that could have only come from over there. The sound of the voice was immense, and it filled the river basin, repeating down the water's telescopic channel, modified by the high karst strata until the words thundered around Ira. They spread without limits: "God damn you."

Immediately, Ira Truitt was as wide awake as a clock. Damned? Oh, but he had to get out of the johnboat somehow, scramble up the bank, and scoot home without being seen. Hurry, hurry, hurry. Time had slipped his grip. Ira felt as hot and visible as the rising August sun.

He groped the seat slat for his stringer of stolen fish. Damned for fish? Ira's eyes were still fixed on the bluff. But you bet he wouldn't abandon the bloody metal wire that looped his catch, gill to gill. No sir. He might be damned—the voice said so—but Ira would have the fish. What he wrestled from the Hebron was Ira Truitt's to keep, no matter what had happened at the house on the bluff or what vile names had come ringing down at him from over there. These clammy, sluggish cats and drums and that one juicy bass were his by rights. Ira slipped the grisly bracelet of fish over his wrist and up his forearm, like a bangle dangling hideous charms, then he eased his smallish foot, considering the size of the rest of him, delicately over the boat's side into the shallows. Quickly and expertly, Ira anchored the lugs of his bootsole into the Hebron's mud. Then, in a single, powerful lunge, Ira freed the rest of himself without mishap and stood knee deep. "No baptism today," he growled. For a fraction of a second afterward Ira noted the river's eerie quiet, broken only when the johnboat's released hull bobbed up from his weight with the tiniest sucking sound.

Ira fought his way up onto the bank and climbed the steep slope from there to the shelf of Moccasin County's river frontage. "Hush now," Ira muttered harshly every time his boots slipped back and broke or dislodged a bit of flintrock. Usually he liked the rattling sound stones made when they cracked against each other. "By God, yes, you feel that weight of me," he had said aloud many times, year after year, but not this morning. No. No. This morning he had to hide under the trees, scramble to the top of the mud shelf and get home, creep from thicket to thicket, bent over in waist-high sumac, squinting to keep burrs and thorns from the soft bull's-eye of his pupils.

What had he seen? Ira wouldn't think about it, that's what. He wouldn't think until he reached full cover. Speed it up. Ira moved faster than an old man could. All this year, these last months, hadn't he known, hadn't he felt damnation coming on? And he had called it age, put it to the debt of time. He had gleaned the fearful coming of his own dark rest. Ahh, but now Ira was permanently startled, he was almost sure of that. He was fully conscious, he thought, maybe for the first time, mind jumping like a flame. Maybe it was the back part of Ira's life that had been the dreaming part, compared to now. He strained up and got a stranglehold on a sapling with his fist. Ira moved well for his size and age, and he would have snaked forward but he was creaky from his vigil, and terrified, too. No sound! Absolutely none. Mustn't even whisper again.

But contained within his scrambling body, Ira could safely allow his anger its full bloom. And he did so. His fury rippled open. It unfurled with a thrill that vibrated every nerve down Ira's back. Why should he be damned? He, Ira Truitt. Why had his life been damned? How wide awake he was! How full of mean wonder over what had happened!

Ira peered across the river a last time and lit out for home. Below, the mist that had hidden Ira was burning off fast. Even though he was moving well now and panting deeply, Ira's legs still cramped from waiting and watching out the night hunched over in his boat.

Damnation! It was that message which had ignited Ira as if he were dry tinder and sent him flaming up the bank. Tiring and frenzied, Ira heard the magnificently devastating curse in his head again and again and began to stumble. He tripped more than once over abrupt ruts and sharp-edged rocks. But if Ira had been called out for a bout with destiny, he would not rest. Grim-faced, he clamped his forearm and the stringer of fish to his chest ever more tightly until the coiled white hairs beneath his shirt were matted and slick with blood. Ira pushed and pushed through several cornfields. He brushed in terror against loud husks. Ira staggered on through a few tattered strips of tobacco until he reached the haven of his own ragged farm, his very own land, until he made it to the spot where the voice's damnation would die away. Safe. He had made it. Here the skinless pain from the burning of the words would surely be extinguished.

Ira had homed on an area right in the middle of his eighty-five acres where there had been a scraggly, tear-shaped swale of earth with a sinkhole at its center, like an open throat. Years ago, when he moved into the ham house next to the sink, Ira had planted the depression with water maples as a windbreak and tediously groomed the undergrowth from between them. After all these seasons of rapid growth, today the saplings' trunks were thick. They formed an almost impenetrable barrier of stakes, some as big around as telephone poles, supporting a nearly circular dome of entangled, deeply lobed foliage that shimmered whitish underneath and broke the light like bits of leaded glass. The ring of trees started and ended at the side walls of Ira's shed so that only the back side of the shed was visible from without.

In summer the cool vaulted hollow, dimly lit, which the trees protected, was Ira's sanctuary. It was a dank, tenebrous place of endless possibility. This morning, when he reached the windbreak at last, when he finally made his rough way there, Ira sidled in through a V-shaped cleft between two handsome, silver-skinned beech trunks, volunteers among the maples. Here he was sheltered. Within his asylum Ira straightened and took possession of himself.

Ira gave himself only a moment to savor the victory of having reached home. Then he worked his way slowly through the trees like a shuttle, weaving an invisible trail around the refuge and almost out the other side. Still concealed, he spied on the front wall of his cabin.

Even though the shed's face was completely within the windbreak and protected, Ira's trick was to leave his door hasp propped at a certain angle. If any intruder so much as touched the hammered iron, the outrage was detectable in a trice. With his free hand, Ira fumbled his glasses on and scrutinized the crudely fashioned door made of corrugated tin. The latch was undisturbed.

But before Ira edged the last few feet around the sinkhole and up onto his doorstep, he completed what had become a morning ritual. He peered through a slit of sunlight at the corner of the shed before looking up the hill at the shell of his old house to reconfirm that it was so: charred, roofless, and bristling cedars out the doors and windows, like the tufts of hair that sprouted from his ears.

If the swale and thicket were the rooms of Ira's asylum, the ruined farmhouse on the hill was his high holy of holies. Tendrils of grape and heart-leaf vines were creeping up what was left of wooden walls. They climbed and claimed the blackened, blistered boards until the place was shingled with leaves and laced with woody stems, a green dwelling shaped more in the imagination than real. It was under Ira's close watch that the burned-out, frame two story had got to this verdant state. There had been no marked change from one day to the next, after the fire. This had been first his father's house, Ira's birthplace, then the home where Ira had lived with his own wife, Orena, before she and the structure burned.

The morning was already hot, near eighty degrees one hour past sunrise, Ira figured, and windless. There was no motion on the hill to suggest the young Orena as she had been: as lacy and finely scented on the breeze as a spray of pink astilbe. No breath from any puff-cheeked cloud rippled the weeds and let Ira imagine his wife walking down slowly, slowly stirring the air with a soft wave in his direction. Ira finally pulled his eyes away. When he at last crossed to the shed, it was with the jumpy stealth of a ferret.

Inside his one-room dwelling, Ira slid the metal bracelet of fish down his arm and over the outsized knob of his wrist, ignoring a smeared crust of ooze where they had pressed his skin. The fish were alike now in being dead, the freshwater drum and the catfish and the buffalo and the bass. Their eye buttons, except for the headless catfish he had strung through its tail, were dull. Ira was too upset to clean them immediately so he pumped water into the granite dishpan under the faucet and left the catch submerged. In the gloom, the tinge of blood that marbled slowly through the liquid was unnoticeable.

Now Ira needed light. And absolute privacy. There was an old blanket folded and tacked above the filthy, four-paned window between the sink and cot. Ira pulled the blanket's hem down and pressed until every inch of glass was completely covered. He switched on a bleak, overhanging bulb and sat, ponderously, at the fair-sized table so he could work this out.

Dead. That's what the slow-moving ambulance meant. If there had been the least bit of life left over, the vehicle would have boxed it up and raced away, wailing. The way it had with Orena the day of the blaze.

It didn't always work, though, did it? The wailing or the speed. Neither one had saved Orena. Over twenty years ago. Could that be? At least that many. Hadn't he cut each and every one of those eternal nights into the plaster? Ira raised his eyes heavily without lifting his head and scanned the rows upon rows of crookedly slashed indentations that further marred the walls. Don't get lost in those bottomless lines, he warned himself. Concentrate on now.

Who was it then? Who was it who was dead? Ira was parched with curiosity. There was the man's voice left behind. The profane man who'd damned him, Ira. The man who had found Ira out on the Hebron and raped the silence of the river with his big voice to call damnation on Ira there. A man like that would do anything. But the ambulance had left from that man's house. The yell had burst the structure's walls. But it wasn't that man who was dead. He was there and loud and profane. Oh, whose life was lost? The middle of the night, who was there with that other man, and now dead?

"Some humans are no better than the beasts of the fields." His father's remembered tone, sonorous with disgust, was almost audible. Ira pulled his hands apart and flexed his fingers with difficulty. The lamp's warmth eased them. He reached outside the light for a pencil stub and a pad of paper scraps that he had laboriously torn and then stapled together. The biggest piece was the size of a postcard, which Ira tore off.

The flood of Ira's loneliness, unabated for decades, ebbed. His starvation for connection was so overpowering that the curse was like a morsel. The voice had addressed him! He had been called. He mustn't miss this chance. Under the light, Ira struggled to express himself on the card, printing deliberately something only vaguely remembered from the Bible: Watch as a watcher in the night. Then he put his own biblical cast on the next phrase: Find the one who calleth.

For who was it who called out damnation for him, Ira, with a voice as big as God's or his father's, but himself was not damned? Yes. Yes. Ira had heard that in the voice, too. A vitality, a defiance that would not be crushed.

Ira bit the inside of his jaw and pressed harder on each succeeding word. His saliva was richly metallic from the taste of blood as he kept at the even-sized letters, squared off at the top and in a perfect row, like baby teeth. After the first two lines, he exhaled harshly. Shortly, Ira leaned forward again and scratched much faster. His printing went a little crooked then bucked toward the end: I will watch over them for evil not for good. That one Ira could have written out chapter and verse. He had heard Jeremiah ranted often enough. His father had hit him with the citation like a belt when he was a child.

There. Still gripped by the intensity of his effort, Ira scanned the list. He spoke the phrases aloud and liked the preacher-like sound of his voice in the overstuffed room. Satisfied, Ira stood and extinguished the bulb. He had left it burning so long that there was a strong smell like hot tin on the air. In almost total darkness Ira at last pulled his knife and turned to gut the fish, sure-handed. He amended the words he had written and repeated them aloud, dramatically: "Watch over *him* for evil, not for good."

Ira was grim with exhilaration over the things he wanted to know. About the curse, about the ambulance, about the voice. Ira had never asked what caused his own life, the whys of Orena's death, or what left him alone here. Infinitely alone. He had been all but comatose in his isolation. The awakening heat of his questions seared his spirit and burned a desert in his mind.

God damn you. It should be him, Ira, who shouted down the night, whose voice filled the long pit of his life. Not that man whose rage could not equal Ira's rage, Ira's losses.

Ira slipped the tip of his curved, eight-inch fillet blade maliciously into the silky skin of a drumfish right at the top of its backbone. His split along the lateral line to the tailfin was immaculate. He put the knife aside on the drainboard and eased the halves apart about half an inch, exposing a delicate, calcium frame. Then, with no more than a third of the knifeblade protruding from between his right thumb and forefinger, Ira expertly freed the meat from each side and lifted out the drum's skeleton, intact. It looked like an ivory feather. A quill of bone.

CHAPTER 12

A Place Imagined into Being

THE WEEKS OF late August and early September were quiet at G. Phillips Central Burley Warehouse No. 1. There was little to do before the tobacco baskets started coming in for November's opening day auction. At Gabe's command, Gilmer Crow, his man of all work, did what simple daily chores Gabe set him onto. Gilmer could oil and prime equipment with the best of them, though he was creaky enough to have used a drop or two of oil himself. For his part during that period, Gabe went up to his office at sunrise daily. He spent a few stringent hours in his place of business then left around noon with nothing to consider until the next morning except his clouded future.

On sunny days, after he left the warehouse, Gabe often drove his car down the twisty little lanes that tangled up the Milan County map like knotty fishing line. He sat up high in his open-topped convertible and steered it easily, one-handed. Powered by the Buick's huge, straight-8 engine, the car slid around the backroads smooth as any cruiser on the river.

A Place Imagined into Being

When the chance presented, Gabe aimed his surging Roadmaster over to a grassy shoulder and left it parked at an angle to the roadbed. From there, he gazed out at whichever field of tobacco had caught his eye. He liked the viewing all the better if the strip was being worked.

He was gratified that the Milan County tobacco farmers had been lucky in their weather lately. A sweetly aloof late summer sun had dried the fields. And there had been no night fog to speak of. Most of the Burley plants that Gabe sighted on his forays appeared to be robust. Often, tissues of circulating air delicately lifted and fluffed the gray-green layers of leaves while he watched.

Gabe didn't spot even a hint of blue mold anywhere during his impromptu inspections. If frost held off until November, this year's yield would likely be the biggest yet. Tonnage might even rise high enough to boost Milan's crop allotment for next season. Gabe stopped short of wondering if he be would be a free man around to see the day.

Sometimes, when Gabe parked to look or watch, he got out of his car and clambered across the strip of ground between the chrome front fender and a rail fence. When he did so, he planted his good left leg with care and smoothly swung the crippled right one forward like a scythe even when he negotiated tricky gullies.

Before Gabe ever unlatched his car's heavily enameled door, he invariably pushed his hat brim straight up, allowing the sun use of his fine forehead for a mirror. "Halloo," he might call, distantly, if there was a crew in the field, before he crossed his arms and propped himself against a post to watch. Always, the scent of ripening crop was thick as musk on the air around him.

If the farmers Gabe hailed had not recognized him by his limp, the tip of his hat would have done it. That and the short-sleeved shirt, spanking white, which was Gabe's summer uniform. All that autumn, from forehead to shirt to vehicle, Gabe Phillips sort of blazed out at them from the roadway in a light more concentrated than the diffuse brightness which lit their hard, hot chores.

Since it was a handmade crop, the draining lifeblood of tobacco was labor. In any given field this time of year there would likely be a melt of families, friends, and neighbors, all ages stirred together, who had pitched in to help.

During the time of Gabe's daily forays, the workers had set themselves at breaking out the individual pink blossoms that topped each Burley plant like a crowning star. From his sideline, Gabe sometimes heard the flowerstems when they snapped with the sound of bird bones breaking. He heard it as a necessary cruelty, for it was only after topping that the plants began to bush and ripen; it was then that leaves grew long and became as wooly-soft and dense as mules' ears.

On some acreage, where early set plants had already been topped, the Burley needed suckering, a poisonously juicy chore. Gabe had hated it himself when he was young, but he had done it many a day in a claylike, clammy sweat and had forearms to prove it. Lucy had despised it too, when he came home in coveralls so soaked in dark tobacco juice that they were slick as spit. But, if left untended, suckers dried up green and ruined the other foliage.

Under Gabe's eye, now, mothers and children mingled companionably in the field with men. Some women moved capably from plant to plant, shaded by old-styled poke bonnets. The colorful cotton hats that were sprinkled so quaintly among the chartreuse rows looked like oversized taffy wrappers. All around the women, plants trembled as youngsters ran beneath the tents of leaves and tagged each other in between squeezing puffs of Paris Green on foliage. Worms could appear at any time and it was up to small fry to see that each worm's meal was his last supper.

Gabe felt stabs of envy while he watched. The unyielding memory in his muscles was of the laborers' sweat and a shared portion of dignified pain, like within a family. At times he edged up on the daring required to take the fence and fall to work among them. But he held back. As always.

By mid-September, beneath the lowering pendant of his life, Gabe regularly cruised near rectangular fields of tobacco that yellowed evenly across the view. Alternating next to acres of ripening corn, the maturing Burley created a fanciful yellow-green checkerboard of countryside that made the landscape look imagined into being.

From the first, whenever he stopped, farmers acknowledged Gabe but let him be, as he would have had it. After a week or two Gabe thought his appearance was expected. Word had gone round, he guessed. He took some solace for his sense of loss from that.

Gabe never once turned on the car radio while he drove from site to site. Gravel flew up behind him, rattling like a beaded curtain as he went. While on the move, he attuned solely to the ravenous roar of his powerful engine, which swallowed up the road and devoured the days until October 17, when he would appear before the Grand Jury.

If a sour taste singed Gabe's tongue during his side trips, it was the thought of lawyer Sonny Nolan or the man's advice, or his own dreadful need of either. But Gabe swallowed his distaste, burning, down down down, and rinsed it with a sip of even hotter whiskey from a long-necked bottle that he carried in the car where once a gun had ridden. After every gulp, the fields sped up, and the landscape became as sharp-edged in its detail as his memories and concentration. The emptying fifth of Ancient Age, gently cradled on the leather seat beside him, rocked a tide of tiny amber waves within.

CHAPTER 13

In a Distant World

THE SHADOWS IN the barn were as deep and cool as pond water. Ira Truitt submerged himself up to his chin in the farthest corner, behind a stack of posts and tobacco stakes that had been piled up aslant at the same angle as the late afternoon sun. The barn's open door showed the bright technicolor outdoors as vividly as if it were focused on the wide new screen up at the Milan movie house.

A red tractor splatted with mud pulled a flatbed wagon slowly toward him through the barnyard. The wagon was piled high with long yellow tobacco leaves, chopped and staked and hung, like clothespins, over wooden sticks. Some farmer had left his cutting late. Any night now it would come a ruinous frost. Since early September, every vent barn Ira had seen, until today, had been full. The narrow doors, which ribbed those barns' sides from the ground to the rafters, were propped open. Ira liked the sight of a black barn fat with tobacco, breathing, showing toast colored Burley through its gills.

Since that August night on the river, each sneaky thing Ira had set his eye or hand to seemed to have come to profit, even unto today, October 3. He could hardly believe his own good fortune. Not once had Ira been caught slipping up the hill, creeping around, spying on the house with the tall chimney, the one at Tyrone. He had peered unnoticed into its rooms, had even seen the man, limping through the hollow space. A crippled man, "broken-footed," like the one described in Leviticus, chapter twenty-one who must "profane not my sanctuaries," said the Lord. That same man whose name was on the mailbox, GABE PHILLIPS, and who had nailed a miniature frame, shaped like a tiny house, to his front doorjamb. The toy house had its own, four-inch door and a stubbed pencil for a chimney. Something that would please a child. Puzzled, one black night Ira had furtively prized the little house open and found a tablet for messages inside. It was all he had been able to do to refrain from leaving a small note of his own. For he felt less lonely spying on Phillips. In spite of the curse that started it, Ira had grown dependent on the task.

So Ira had grown bolder. He wasn't only unseen. It seemed he was unseeable. He would stay where he was in the tobacco barn for a few moments more, steeping in its watery shadows. Because he had spotted, way up by the road, nothing less than Mr. Gabe Phillips' own car. Ira's eyes glittered like spangled lures while he looked into the picture, over a wagon, over the farmers and the golden leaf, and strained to see his broken-footed man somewhere in the distant autumn world of jewel-colored trees and rusty silos.

Ira's nerves tingled with the danger of the wagon coming closer, ever closer. But if he could stay and hear the man's voice. If he could hide long enough to find out what Mr. Gabe Phillips' business was down here with these tobacco growers, down here in this bottom land by the Hebron, where the rich earth ran deep beyond digging, but only on this side of the river, not Ira's.

His sense of safety snapped when the tractor came to a full halt. Ira pulled back and squeezed reluctantly between boards he had tediously prized loose earlier. It hurt him to leave without hearing Phillips' voice. Hurt him bad. But that must be slated for another time. Ira had come this far, after all. It seemed miraculous to Ira that he had chanced upon the sight of Gabe's showy car. Today it would lead to nought, as Ira had no car of his own with which to follow. But there might come a time, there might come a time when the two would meet on equal ground. Ira would not despair.

Ira backed soundlessly until he bumped the tines of an old hay rake then he turned and crept into the whispering brush behind the barn. He let the picture show dissolve behind him and aimed for the Hebron. No more visible than a furrow of breeze in the head-tall weeds, Ira made his getaway unnoticed.

CHAPTER 14

October 17, a Complicated Time

CLARA, JUST IN from school, couldn't settle. Somehow, in spite of her fidgets at the slowness of its passing, time had elapsed, and the calendar had finally landed on the seventeenth of October. Up in Milan today, Daddy was on his way to the Grand Jury. Clara thought maybe he was there exactly now, at 3:15. This very minute, which ticked away while she watched the sweep hand on the white moon of a wall clock in the kitchen, he might be standing, he would be the only one standing, in the windowless room Clara pictured, in front of blank-faced people. Daddy appeared suddenly in her mind, standing there before the jurors with his smile tilted at the same angle as his hat, wearing a sky-blue suit. And the jury panel, the featureless men and women, looked at Gabe, thinking, Clara was sure, of windows, gazing right through his sky-blue suit all the way to the river.

By four o'clock Clara, fearing to study any longer the image of her vulnerable father outnumbered, had searched for her worn leather, child-sized pilot's jacket, had scrambled through the cottage until she fished it from the jumble of clothes on the floor of her closet. Then she stood still for a moment, only a second or two, with the soft pouch of a coat hugged close, and listened to the Hickman house. Now that the noise of her search was stilled, the rooms, where she slowly began to tiptoe, were frighteningly quiet and had grown impossibly tall. The tongues of glass transoms hung open hollow-mouthed above her.

She sniffed the leather jacket she yet cuddled, for after three years it still gave off, although muted, a wildish smell of tannins that thrilled her. After struggling a bit with the zipper—its teeth wanted to catch and bite—she donned the coat and determinedly snapped two large snaps that closed the jacket's overlapping waistband. The sound reverberated loud as pistol caps throughout the silent house.

With the vision of Gabe before her, Clara opened the front door. The cottage's entry door was little more than a large, framed pane of glass, and Clara slammed it behind her in the very way Lucy constantly admonished that she mustn't do. Clara hesitated. She was nervous, until the pane of glass stopped shivering, that she had in fact "done it this time."

Three oblong panels of cracked concrete walkway bisected the small yard and connected their property to State Street's sidewalk. On their portion, Clara had laboriously chalked a hopscotch grid over the rough surface. From the porch she squinted marksman's eyes at the game's awkward outline and briefly felt in her jeans pocket for her throwing stone. But, as she had known inside the house, it was not possible to dally in mere play while Daddy and all else hung in the balance. It was only possible to move. Clara jumped flat-footed from her perch and landed jarringly hard on two chalky squares. She tipped up her face and sniffed, soft-nosed as a rabbit, and tried to catch a whiff of burning leaves. Nowhere could she locate anything as mysterious as leaf smoke in Hickman's ugly autumn.

This time of year in Milan there would be bushels and bushels of gathered leaves. Clara was sure that houses there were now adrift in dunes of papery, rusty-colored foliage raked from under pin oaks and whitebud and redbud and maples of all kinds, or fallen, each leaf like a breath, from the spreading crowns of towering ash and hickory trees. When the leaves were set ablaze by the grownups of the family, exotic, butter-yellow gingko fans sputtered in the smoke while children watched. After the flames subsided, a curl of bluish haze usually lazed from street to street for days. In fact, Daddy might smell its comforting smoky odor in the courthouse this very afternoon if the haze rose, as well it might, and nuzzled mossily against the clock face on the building's third-floor gable. And in a cozy town like Milan, with such attributes as perfumed pyres of leaves and gabled buildings, how could people think that her daddy had hurt Joyce? Clara could not stop asking herself that question even as she tried to concentrate on other things.

What grass Clara could see, down the block, was dormant and colorless. A line of umbrella trees on the other side of State Street had dropped a few of their big, ungainly leaves. A slight wind rattled the leaves and scuttled them noisily against the base of the trees' warty bark. Disgusted, Clara bent over and retied her oxfords.

Cool air had pinked her hands, so she snugged each of them into a hip pocket, flapped her elbows back winglike a time or two, and waited for a notion that would fly her forward until Lucy came home from work.

Then they could get the news from Milan. Then Clara would find out the exact quotient of hope divided into fear. Because as she understood it from Lucy, if this Grand Jury did not "indict," that strange word with its silent *C,* if they did not indict her daddy, then every step of Clara's secret plan might yet be doable. But if they did, Gabe faced trial. And Mother said trials were things where anything might happen. Clara could believe her, terrifying as that was. Clearly, it already had.

One thing was certain. It was no help to just stand here in chilly air until her skin turned completely blue. Clara's ears were so cold already that she wondered if you could get frostbite of the head. Slowly, and without inspiration, Clara started toward the end of the block. Slender as a sprig, she almost rattled inside her bulky denim and leather clothes. Shoulders sloped, she plodded on. State Street's sooty sidewalk curved away before her until it disappeared over a slight rise that led to the noisy bypass where Lucy bought groceries at the A&P. The whole town really was worn and dirty, Clara thought, like the faces of its miners.

For if there was an aspect of Hickman that Clara studied tirelessly, it was the plight of the men who dug coal and their families. And not just because Mother's job was to help the government help them. No. They held their own fascinations for Clara. When she saw miners in stores, what she noticed most was their hands. Miners were men of hands, men who pointed first, on meeting, then punched each other's shoulders lightly, or rubbed their own faces or pulled their earlobes. She could tell that they were used to tools, not words. Their creosote stained fingers—nails and knuckles outlined in black—took on a silvery sheen and worked thin air like metal while they talked.

Clara stopped walking and fished her throwing rock for hopscotch

93

out of a pocket. She had pulled the stone with her toes from the mud-squishy bottom of the Hebron. The hardened brown sediment was about the size and shape of a marine snail. Porous, it was perfectly weighted for a controlled toss. A petrified twirl of whitish material, which Lucy said was a mineralized shell from the geologic past, wheeled out of the rock's side. There they were right there, Clara thought, time and secrets fused.

Clara pressed her thumb on the fossilized stone and glared at the stunted, ugly trees and yuccas that flanked her path. Yuks, she called the smaller plants. Clara had never come any closer to using a curse word. But Gabe used curse words all the time. Daddy's words were "damn," even "god damn." And worse. Clara tried one out loud: "Damn ugly trees," she said tentatively and looked around in spite of herself. Then, louder: "Damn chopped back stunted yuks and trees in your ugly hard mud yards." She stomped the words against the sidewalk. Jarred, she realized she had shocked herself. The words didn't come out the way they did from Gabe. Clara fell quiet and resumed her normal gait.

Well, if she wasn't one to stamp her feet or curse, what was she? Maybe she was a whisperer, Clara thought. Nonie and Mother were. They had whispered the day Nonie phoned about Joyce's death. At least Lucy had. Clara could only guess about Nonie. But at its loudest Nonie's voice was soft, coming out at odds with her steely little frame. When the long-distance call came that morning last August, something in Mother's manner had been secretive. Lucy had answered then nestled the phone like a baby's head between her hair and lifted shoulder. The moments went off like flash bulbs in Clara's mind. She recalled each specific move. Lucy had bussed her lips against the cradled mouthpiece. Immediately, Clara had slipped into the front bedroom and hidden behind the tall white door that stood ajar. There she had stayed, watching through the narrow slit of space between hinges, while her mother stood deathly still and heard and whispered secrets on the phone with Nonie.

Secrets had been a loaded word for Clara since she was a tiny girl. Her face went warm on thinking of it now. In the bathroom in Milan Mother had called her own bosoms "secrets." Lucy had been soaking in the tall bathtub, languid, resting, leaning back. Clara must have been only three or four years old, she thought, when she raised a chubby arm from the cold, rolled ceramic tub rim, where she hung on tiptoe, and pointed at her mother's heavy breasts that fell apart easily, rubbery and pink-looking below the steaming water, absolutely white above, except around the nipples. "What are those?" Clara had asked, in love with anything so ample. Mother had pulled her arm across her chest and rested the ivory bar of her hand against her left side. "Secrets," Lucy said to Clara's question, but Lucy's mysterious smile had asked more than it answered. So "secrets" was the word they still used and smiled about when they must speak of such as breasts, but Clara had all but forgotten the sly power in her mother's voice in that memory from Milan, that hot room memory of Milan that was fading with the others, clearing from her child's mirror of the past, like bathroom steam.

Holding onto and sorting memories had become as complicated as the problems of clinging to or hurrying time. If Clara thought about scenes from their old house in Milan, the one where Gabe and Lucy and she had lived together, or if she worried over Daddy and then the Grand Jury, she had next to think about Joyce. There was no way around her. Clara bit her lip hard enough to stop tears. Poor, pretty Joyce was where the problem of time became so difficult. The amount of time Joyce got for herself just seemed pitiful to Clara. And Clara had her own regrets with regard to Joyce and time. How could Clara possibly have known that you couldn't put off acting nice to a person?

Nonie was known to harp on Clara's need to be considerate. Clara always did aim to try. But in Joyce's case it had been hard. Preceding loyalties paralyzed Clara. She had ignored Daddy's girlfriend when she could. There had even been times when Clara had been so hardhearted that she looked right through Joyce. Clara's behavior had sprung from the same deep-seated fear that kept her from stepping on sidewalk cracks, an almost trembling apprehension that somehow Lucy would be hurt in either case. In her uttermost thoughts, Clara had certainly planned to be pleasant to Joyce eventually. Just not anytime soon. Now it would be never, ever, and Clara's burdened heart simply broke to think it. Never was horrible. Maybe it was even the devil. Hell certainly.

Clara blushed to recall that in spite of her own behavior, Joyce had given her things. The last gift was a simulated-leather book satchel. It was an enviable possession with heavy straps and gleaming potmetal buckles. Clara kept it safely stowed under the farthest corner of her bed. Whenever she could, out of Lucy's sight, she wiped the satchel clean and carefully re-hid it.

But Joyce had scared Clara a little too. The way she might suddenly make handles of Clara's narrow hands and waltz away with her into Daddy's kitchen or clear through the double doors where the new porch floor was being installed. Clara remembered Joyce's laughing too loud and the cistern pumps of their arms, while they danced through the house, with Clara stumbling clumsily to keep up. Or when Joyce sang at the top of her lungs while she cooked, shoeless. "Today I passed you on the street . . ." she crooned, and exaggerated "my hort fell at your feet," when she came to it, winking broadly on the word "hort" to allow to Clara that she well knew it wasn't pronounced right. What was scary was that you never knew which Joyce you might get, the shy one timidly holding out that good satchel, a huge tacky bow streaming from its handle, or the dancer full of silliness, or somebody else entirely who appeared when you weren't looking.

One late night, Joyce had stared directly at Daddy and drunk straight from a gin bottle, then set it on the kitchen table with a defiant smack. Clara herself had seen that happen. The bottle was square and flat bottomed and Clara registered that the little bit of clear-as-water liquid left inside it splashed high as a fountain when Joyce slammed it down. Clara was supposed to have been in bed. Gabe had tucked her in tight, but when she heard something like a cry, she freed herself. She had padded silently in her gown all the way across the living room to the kitchen doorway. Clara pictured again the cold-eyed light in the kitchen and the white stove's glare and Gabe's eyes and Joyce's, full of meanness, that had justified Clara's every fear and worry.

"Little pitchers," Nonie teased Clara whenever she noticed the girl listening in on grownup talk, "I see you listening. Don't think I don't!" "Snoopers going to be finding out something they don't want to know," she admonished.

Nonie generally didn't shame Clara though. Soon as she caught Clara with an ear out where it shouldn't be, she shooed her away towards some other activity, most often a trip to the river. And that suited Clara fine, because as a rule Nonie went with her. Sometimes, they waded in with their skirts tied up between their legs like oldtime bloomers and dug mussels. Gabe liked to bait his trotline with mussel meat, so their forays were useful. It was quite a chore to wag the catch up the hillside in muddy pails to be left in the porch sink overnight, but well worth the effort for the next morning's surprise. By breakfast time the elongated, dirty mussel shells would have popped their lids to reveal unlikely, satiny, rainbow-tinted linings, and each mollusk would be trying to leave its carriage shell, daintily stretched forward like a foot. One time Clara had actually spied a seed pearl that looked like a large, lustrously fat grain of rice, embedded in the revealed flesh. Daddy had skillfully dug the pearl from the mantle and dropped it onto her palm, a treasure.

If Gabe didn't need all the shells they had dragged to the house, Clara and Nonie hurriedly toted the leftovers down the hillside and tumped them back into the Hebron before it was too late.

If only Clara could bring Joyce back that way this minute, splash her right into life and let her float down and settle onto a smooth, safe, river bottom of time. The floating would be dreamy and the settling, oh, so deep.

But this was Hickman, Clara reminded herself. She brought her eyes down from watching a red-tailed hawk spiral purposefully and saw what he saw from his tightening gyre. This was not Milan or Tyrone. There was no sweet Hebron flowing here among the rocks. Here in Hickman she stood exposed, small prey among huge surface scars and flattened, raw, red knobs where strip mining had disfigured the countryside's face. What was beautiful, the shining, blue-black coal, the treasure of the place, was hidden underground.

And all of Clara's grownups seemed hidden also. Or they were caught up in mystery and unsafe. Even, like Joyce, beyond saving. As much as she had heard, as hard as she had watched, Clara understood adults less now than she ever had, and only from the outside.

At State and Fifteenth, Clara turned to go back home. But Daddy did not hurt Joyce, she told herself. He never. On that point Clara's mind was as silver clear as a mussel shell's nacreous lining.

CHAPTER 15

A Leafy Nest, 1943

WHILE GABE APPEARED before the Grand Jury, Lucy tried to busy herself at work. She didn't dare believe that it was October, 1953, and that Gabe, heart of her hidden heart, father of her child, was on the brink of being in jeopardy of his life. Lucy stared fixedly at a stack of files. In her head it was ten years ago. Lucy's younger voice was as clear as if she stood behind herself and spoke. But she had been in the second-floor hallway of a Milan house when the conversation took place.

"That water is so hot you'll melt and stop the drain," Lucy said, but Gabe didn't open his eyes.

"You think I'm like the Wicked Witch of the West?" he teased.

"More like yourself," Lucy answered.

Gabe slid farther down against the back of the tub. The bathroom in their upstairs apartment, converted to rental from the top of a big frame house on Newberry Street, was narrow as a closet and was this minute boxed full to bursting with steam.

A Leafy Nest, 1943

It was tobacco cutting time, September, 1943. Every hand available had been pressed to service. Gabe had come in spent from the
fields, laboriously peeled his way out of his work clothes and mud-
caked boots, then dropped them right next to the bathtub. He was no
butterfly, Lucy thought, but it was almost as amazing that a fine animal
like Gabe could emerge from such a casing. His coveralls oozed
tobacco juice, which had also soaked his sweat-stained shirt.

All of the "able-bodied" young men were gone off to war that
autumn. Lucy, silently appraising the lissome, tan, and naked man in
the tub, thought her husband looked pretty able-bodied himself. She
couldn't say it, though. It was nothing short of tragic to Gabe that he'd
been passed over for service because of his bad leg. Nobody in these
parts would ever mistake his limp for a war wound. And a bitter birth
defect was certainly no badge of honor in Gabe's eyes.

Lucy gathered up his slimy clothes and left Gabe soaking the
nicotine out of his pores into the bathwater. She went to the kitchen,
which must have been the sleeping porch before the owners decided to
let. Big squares of screen mesh had been filled in with glass. The room
made a pleasant enough place, early mornings especially. The yard
outside was studded with trees. Not elms or oaks, mostly locusts and
walnuts and maples, but still they had age on them and were big-limbed
and leafy. Lucy felt like she was living in a nest when she came in of a
sunrise to boil coffee, listening to the tobacco report on the radio while
she fried up bars of honey-colored mush and warmed some syrup.

There was a wringer washer in the kitchen corner, up on legs.
Lucy rolled it near the sink and hooked its hose to the faucet. So far,
year-old baby Clara had slept through all the machine's sloshes and
gurgles these last nights. Lucy stuffed Gabe's filthy clothes down into

the Speed Queen's barrel stomach and poured in a liberal measure of Fels Naptha. While the agitator chugged its rhythmic half swirls against the soggy dirt, the water darkened. Soon it would be as umber-colored as the water in Gabe's tub.

Now that she had a few minutes, Lucy tiptoed into the front bedroom. She soundlessly pulled open the bottom bureau drawer, but she couldn't shush the whisper of the tissue packet she withdrew. Clara, in a corner crib, didn't stir.

Lucy tipped back down the hall, past the bathroom door, which was still closed, and into the pantry alcove off the one solid kitchen wall. In half light, she opened the tissue and unfolded its prize. She had, by the hardest, saved enough money from skimping on groceries to buy a pure silk nightgown. In the end it cost her more than the gabardine dress she wore when she and Gabe went to the Justice of the Peace to marry. Lucy skinnied out of her chenille housecoat and stood exposed for a second, savoring the chill of the silk fabric against her even colder, bare skin. Gabe would love this. He would be thoroughly warm and still slightly damp when she pressed up against him and opened her own silk-tissue wrapper with a whisper in the dark.

Suddenly, Lucy felt something wriggle right between her breasts, something slimy and slithery and small. She yelped aloud and dropped the gown. Without a stitch on she made a little leap into the full light of the open kitchen. There, suckered complacently onto Lucy's chest, was a squishy, fat, maggot-colored tobacco worm almost two inches long. Lucy plucked it with all her might and hurled it across the room. But she didn't squeal. When she quit gasping, Lucy decided there was no need to tell.

From the future, Lucy's mind swam into the depths of that night.

CHAPTER 16

Dead On

Over time, the haughty, beaux arts exterior of the Milan
County Courthouse had softened into something benevolent. There
was about it, in the minds of the people it served, an air of dignified
neglect that only magnified its charm. But the Grand Jury room tucked
away inside the structure, where Gabe Phillips would appear that
afternoon, had no shred of faded grandeur. That venue was oak-floor
plain.

Gabe took the courthouse steps slowly. He silently rehearsed his
practiced, "Up with the good, down with the bad," as he stepped up
each time, left-footed. Gabe never touched the bannister. He would be
god damned, he thought, if he let the sons of bitches see him clumping
up to the second floor in an awkward rush to his own judgment.

When Gabe topped the last riser, he saw Ben Gilliam and the
Coroner off to one side of the hallway. They spoke to him amiably
enough. Gabe glanced at his watch. He was, as he had planned to be,
on time but not abruptly so. Still he felt winded after the one flight

climb. He took a deep breath and entered the door that was indicated by a posted bulletin: SEATED GRAND JURY. 3 P.M. 10/17/53.

Gabe opened and closed the doors firmly. Inside, the Commonwealth's Attorney Buell Smith turned and acknowledged Gabe, briefly. The other people present, presumably the jury members, tended to their own arrangements regarding chairs and coats. They ignored Gabe for the moment.

So this is where it would happen, Gabe thought. He hated that the drama of his terrors would play out here, within the confines of such a woefully ordinary space.

Centered in the bare courtroom under a four-bar flourescent fixture was an old, library-style table, exactly the size of a surgical bed. Gabe sat heavily there where Buell Smith pointed, onto a swivelback chair at the table's narrow end. One of the overhead light's mercury vapor tubes flickered intermittently. The effect of the lighting was dismal and cheapening. Under it, Gabe took hold of the table's corner with his right hand and pulled himself around. From that ground would he hold himself in place and face his questioners dead on.

As Sonny Nolan had described, there seemed to be no rigorous courtroom order to the setup. Opposite Gabe, the jurors, now seated, had organized themselves into an informal assembly. They talked quietly to each other, scattered in groups of two or three.

When he could, Gabe caught and held the gaze of whichever panel member briefly looked his way. He kept his expression neutral. But inside his head, Gabe's hearing was almost completely muffled by the swish, swish of arteries pulsing in his neck. The danger in such deafness made him feel icy. For whatever advantage he could have, Gabe knew that all his senses must be keen. If, this instant, he told himself, he were to slap the table with his hand, flat out and hard, the rush of sounds that filled his ears would cease. Gabe immediately relaxed his frozen grip, wiped his coldly melting palm on his knee, then frigidly renewed his hold on the corner of the table.

According to Sonny Nolan, Buell Smith, as the Commonwealth's Attorney, would be the only officer of the court present at the hearing. Gabe took a deep breath and watched as Smith stood, now, from among the veniremen and walked to a point two or three yards away from Gabe's chair. The attorney's posture as he approached, his head hung heavily forward from his lanky frame like the blade of an upended garden hoe, suggested defeat. Gabe knew better. He didn't doubt for a single minute that Buell's demeanor caught people off guard. Or the fatal effect of their dismay when the slouching man pounced and sunk his sharp legal teeth into the nakedly juicy belly of some wrongdoing. But Gabe was not unwary, nor was this a mismatch.

Smith stopped and slowly turned. Gabe scanned the faces of the people who were still seated in casual clusters behind the attorney. He counted seventeen who would decide. In one of Gabe's many tiresome wranglings with Sonny over how to prepare for this hearing, Nolan had cautioned him to "hope for a woman's panel." As if hope figured in, Gabe thought disgustedly. But in that and all else, Sonny was never wrong and never in doubt of his own notions. Nolan's idea was that women would be more alienated by or suspicious of such a one as Joyce. Well, Gabe would find out soon enough. He had decidedly not got a women's panel. Fourteen men and three women. Grand Juries were described as "hand picked." Ah, but by whose hand? And with what aim in mind?

Gabe recognized several men who regularly brought their Burley in for sale. How vengeful might they be, he wondered, these plain-spoken, stalwart men of Milan, at being shaken from a wispy dream, some dark, tumescent dream of Joyce Oliver that they scarcely knew they'd had? How bitter? And what made Sonny Nolan think that women had not seen in Joyce's face, though beautiful, a kind of lostness, and blame Gabe for the wordless sin of taking what they themselves had never, ever had?

As Gabe looked across, one of the three women, seated just behind and to the left of Buell Smith, returned his scrutiny. She was narrow lipped and her large, round face was pale. Under her eyes there were blue-gray depressions that looked hauntingly like lunar seas on a distant moonscape. Gabe and the woman studied each other frankly. Her arms were crossed and each of her forearms supported and protected a little sack of bosom like a treasure. Only the marine depth around her eyes muted the force of her expression. Gabe, his forehead damp, looked down. He concentrated on the area beneath his chair where the varnish had worn away and the grainy oak floor, preserved and glossy in other places, was dull. Thus he sat encircled in a kind of reverse spotlight.

Finally, upon Buell Smith's direction, Gabe rose briefly within his circle and took the oath that the Commonwealth required. He rested his strong hand on a red, clothbound Bible that the bailiff held on fingertips. Gabe straightened and swore to tell the truth, the whole truth, and nothing but the truth. "So help me God," he announced evenly to his audience in the plaster-walled, white-box theater of a room. For what was that oath to him?

Holding himself in check, Gabe could almost feel Sonny Nolan's impatience outside the chamber, worrying his own unimportance to

106

proceedings into a knot in his handkerchief, stewing that Gabe would "hang himself on a rope of words," as he had constantly urged that Gabe not do. For weeks Sonny, in his insistent, banty rooster way, had pressed his advice on Gabe. The one relief to Gabe this afternoon was that lawyers, other than the Commonwealth's Attorney, weren't allowed inside the hearing. A good rule, Gabe thought, which bore expansion. And if it had surprised him to learn that Sonny could not enter the jury room, it surprised Gabe more that he was himself allowed to leave during questioning. He could actually go into the corridor and consult with Sonny if he felt the need to. Of course, Gabe would not do so. The very idea of dependence on Sonny Nolan chafed. But if he did leave, Gabe mused, just how far beyond the courthouse corridor did that freedom stretch? At what point could the bailiff stop him if he did not stop himself? The same was true of judging. Gabe's eyes ran the faces from Buell Smith to the last juror. As if they had the right to judge him. They only had the power.

After the swearing Gabe reseated himself. For an instant he felt that time might conquer him. Gabe felt as still as he had ever been until the moment passed.

Gabe's shoulders briefly slumped. He had been immaculately faithful, nearly, to his own vision. Had been that close to its perfection. Business at the tobacco warehouse boomed. He had almost completely remodeled the camp at Tyrone. It was now a place of substance, good as any up in town; a lasting place that weathered and fronted on the bluffs, with the look of their same permanence. He had made a home for Clara and Lucy they could not have resisted. The life Gabe wanted had been within an inch of his grasp. Except for Joyce. Except for Joyce. If today this small group of farmers and shopkeepers and teachers and wives handed down a True Bill, it meant he would stand trial. Whether true or not, a 'True Bill' in his case would declare to one and all that there was reason to believe a crime had been committed and probable cause to suspect Gabe as the culprit. If this panel did that, if today he were indicted, Gabe knew that the sins of one kind would be punished for another.

All right then. Gabe took a deep breath and held a globe of air between his fingertips and the heels of his hands. Then Buell Smith moved from where he stood. He came and sat on the far end of Gabe's table. With one crackly snap of a manila folder, Smith began.

It would happen now.

Shortly, Smith read from a typed sheet: "The jury is instructed as follows." After describing that each juror must fill out and sign the provided Verdict Form, he emphasized that the verdict need not be unanimous. Dissenting jurors were advised to so indicate after signing. Then the meat of his instructions thickened. "Under the evidence presented to you in this case, you may find as follows: That Joyce Oliver met her death on August 19, 1953, and it was the result of (1) Natural Causes, (2) Accident, (3) Homicide." Gabe winced inwardly at the deep slice of that last word.

But the Commonwealth's Attorney had not said his worst. He further instructed: "If the death is determined to be a result of homicide, list the party or parties responsible in the appropriate space on the form. The following definitions are applicable: 'Natural Causes' is defined as an event conforming to the usual and ordinary course of human existence. 'Accident' is defined as an event happening without any human agency, or, if happening wholly or partly through human agency, an unusual or unexpected result attending the operation or performance of a usual or necessary act or event."

Buell Smith finally read his final, chilling paragraph. His enunciation was sharp as he did so: "'Homicide' is defined as the killing of one human being by the act, procurement, or omission of another. A person is guilty of homicide if he purposely, knowingly, recklessly, or negligently causes the death of another human being."

Chilled to the soul by Buell Smith's emotionless recital, Gabe tried to *not be* until the words were over. At last the attorney put his document down and passed duplicate pages of what he had just read to the empaneled men and women. Smith sat again, handed Gabe a set of the same papers he had given to the panel, and faced him.

"State your name," Smith directed.

"Gabe Phillips." No sir. Not Gabriel today.

The lawyer then leaned aside and spoke informally to Gabe. "Since I am the representative for the Commonwealth and to an extent this jury, Gabe, I'll start the questioning. Jurors can break in at any time." Buell Smith paused before tuning up the volume of his more official voice.

"Mr. Phillips, are you familiar with a Miss Joyce Oliver?"

"I am."

"And what was the nature of your relationship?"

"She was the secretary at my tobacco warehouse."

"Merely your secretary?" Smith's tone implied nothing.

Gabe answered in kind: "We also saw each other."

Smith looked briefly at the jurors. They seemed satisfied with that description of relations as applied to Joyce and Gabe.

Back to Gabe, he asked "How long did this 'seeing' of each other go on?"

"Five years. Give or take a month or so."

Smith looked at the jury but addressed Gabe. "Were you with Joyce Oliver the night she died?" In spite of its simplicity and the fact that all assembled knew the answer, the question quietly exploded in Gabe's mind.

"Yes." No more. No way to alter now the fate of "yes."

The attorney changed course. He deliberately placed a small pistol on the table. The jurors' eyes flew to the gun and lit there.

"Is this your gun, Mr. Phillips?"

Gabe hardly glanced. "My gun," he said. His tone and manner were firm, recovered from the "Yes."

"All right, Gabe. Regarding Joyce Oliver's death, would you tell the people here, in your own words, what happened?"

Gabe was ready. His voice would not shake even as the terrifying night threatened to rise again around him. "It was fairly late of an evening, in August," he said, barely keeping his head above the black memory. "After eleven." The bailiff had set a glass of water nearby. Gabe sipped. "Joyce had threatened to kill herself in an argument. She had tried to scare me before, by saying that she would, you know, do something dire. When she showed me the gun, of course I tried to take it. We struggled." One more word and Gabe's voice would be tremulous. He fell silent. Neither wide nor deep, that story of the night was all he meant to tell and must suffice.

Smith shuffled until he found a certain paper. "When Ben Gilliam got there at midnight, you told him or his deputy that you kept this gun hidden and kept its hiding place secret from Miss Oliver. Is that right?"

"That's right. I told him that. It's also true." But the gun wasn't hidden, was it? It was never hidden. Gabe had kept it in an unlocked strongbox or near it, even recklessly loose on the seat of his car, when he took cash home overnight for safekeeping until a morning deposit. Joyce had always known where the gun was. He had taught her to shoot it, how to let her hand rise with the kick of the shot. She had loved the wildness of the thing. They kept the .22 in plain sight, often between them, on a table perhaps, as it was now, temptingly small and potent—a little, palm-sized beauty that drew them both. Like Joyce's eyes, the pistol's nickel plating watered sapphire blue in certain light.

Gabe looked at the attorney, then the jury. He did not look at the gun. One juror, a man with thick brows, had cocked his head, waiting for more. Gabe coughed before he spoke and said, hesitantly, as if this next would be something he was loath to reveal: "But . . . you have to understand, Joyce was suspicious. She was always nosing around, trying to find out if I was hiding something, covering up. I don't know why but Joyce seemed to think that life was out to trick her. She meant to catch it in the act."

After a pause Gabe continued: "I could tell when she had been through my pockets, bureau drawers too. Nothing ever went missing except . . . obviously she found the gun."

When he stopped there, some men had altered their expressions. Directly inside himself, Gabe was startled to hear the whispering rush in his ears sort itself out as Joyce's voice. The familiar sound of her was softly distant but her words were distinct, although mysterious. "I'm thinking of the time . . . ," she whispered.

In front of Gabe, Buell Smith bent and picked a piece of fluff from his trousers then studied it, as if a particle of lint were the one illuminating clue: "And do you know, Gabe, why a twenty-six-year-

111

old woman, this twenty-six-year-old woman, would want that? I mean, to kill herself?"

"No I don't. I don't know. She'd been sad. . . ." (One of Sonny Nolan's commandments had been: Don't be afraid of I Don't Know). "I can't say. Joyce wasn't a talker. She was a moody girl. . . ." All seventeen across the room were with Gabe as they seemed to fill the blank. Yes, we understand, they all but said aloud. Girls like that. They sadly shook their heads.

("I'm thinking of the time you promised . . . ," Joyce soothed again. Gabe shook his head to banish her words. She surely hadn't thought he'd marry her. He had been so blunt about his plans, for the house, for Clara. Had even told Joyce his scheme of someday wooing Lucy back, the mother of his child. Or had meant to. Maybe, drinking one night, or in bed, he'd forgotten himself and said something loose about marriage. But Joyce should have known the truth of his affections. At any rate, men said things. Gabe wasn't the only one; these men here in this very room shared that with him at least. And they meant them more than life, the wooing words they pledged, for a little while. Gabe squeezed his eyes shut for a second to stop Joyce from picturing some sugared scene, some foolish, heart-shaped cutout of a time he had never really promised.)

"I believe you told the Sheriff you were fighting?" Buell was undeflected from the march of his questions.

"Struggling is the word I used. We were struggling for the gun. I meant to take it from her." Gabe bowed his head. "She won." A darkeyed, female juror shifted her face toward the wall and exposed the sallow indentation just beneath her earlobe. Gabe touched there lightly with his eyes. The woman must know he had to save his life, for Clara and for Lucy. Or else the niches he'd left open just for them, the only spaces which remained in the re-creation of his life, would allow the wind to enter and the world he'd made, the one that was a hair's width from perfection, would shatter from the power of the storm within. This was Joyce's fault. Gabe knew it plain as day. She must stop whispering; he could barely hear above the sound.

Smith took his time with the next question. He made it conversational. Gabe's tension tightened up a notch. He'd be damned if he would drop his guard.

"The main thing, Gabe," Smith nearly drawled, "what the state can't understand is, is why would a girl bent on shooting herself try to kill herself in front of you? You're a big man, Mr. Phillips, powerfully built."

That wasn't a direct question. Gabe waited.

"What I mean is," Smith continued, sounding curious as if he were thinking of this conundrum just now himself, "she's bound to have thought you could stop her." The attorney suddenly stared intently at Gabe and said, somewhat more harshly, "She's bound to have thought you *would* stop her."

Members of the panel and the state they stood for looked at Gabe in multiples of disbelieving eyes. Put that way, so reasonably stated by so reasonable a man as Buell Smith, the statement had the ring of an unavoidable truth. Gabe's fear stabbed its deepest. He had no answer now or then for Joyce's thoughts. He had paid them little heed, if they existed.

Gabe went spinning back to the instructions. Silent, sweating, he replayed the last: ". . . Purposely, knowingly , recklessly, or negligently . . ." So that's how they aimed to get him.

"Negligently." The word itself was damning.

"I don't believe that's right," Gabe answered, defensively. He caught himself. "But I don't know what Joyce was thinking, do I?" He mastered his voice. (Don't be afraid of I don't know.) "I know what she was doing." Joyce was going to best him for once. And she had, hadn't she? That's exactly what she'd done. Little Joyce Oliver had almost beaten Gabe forever. Unless he won today.

The minute hand on the clock above the jurors ticked forward once; a heavyset juror twisted his watchstem. Gabe went on, allowing a slight plaint to raise his tone: "Here was a girl who was never the same two days running." Gabe spoke slowly and almost to himself. "Who knows what her plan was?" Then he paused, unclenched his hands. "She was secretive. I tried . . ." This time he waited so long, Buell Smith had opened his mouth when Gabe continued. He said it to his tensed chest: "I always tried. After a while, you just wear out." Yes, beg. If there were a time to do so, it was now. Some good might come. At last, looking up, Gabe concluded: "Then, I guess, I really didn't think she meant to do it." He had felt it, though. God damn Gabe had felt it, as their rage united that sweaty August night. Joyce had been determined to defy him, for Gabe to know, for once, at last, the truth of her, Joyce Oliver, in the ringing, bent steel tangle of their arms.

Not hearing what Gabe thought, the State and its Grand Jurors were moved by what he said. The poor man, after all. Gabe felt tension in the room subside as he fell silent. He might yet pull it off. This would be the end. Joyce kissed his eardrum. "You'll see," she said huskily, like whiskey talk, over and over through a pulse that was now as emphatic as his limp: "You'll see, you'll see, you'll see . . ."

114

The Commonwealth's Attorney came and weighted down Gabe's shoulder with his hand. "All right, Gabe." Smith pointed at the grainy double doors on their right. "When we've heard the Coroner's report and Sheriff's, we'll meet you on the first floor. Judge Stallard's courtroom off the rotunda."

Gabe collected himself before he screened the panel one last time. The woman whose eyes made him so picture the moon, looked pensive. Her expression had shaded, darkening toward the night of a frown. Gabe stood to leave. He balanced himself carefully before setting off, shrinking from the inescapably heavy thump of his next footfall. His desperation brimmed within but did not spill.

Downstairs in the main courtroom, Judge Stallard sat black-robed and immaculately silver-haired behind his high, mahogany desk. He was its perfect finial. From Gabe's vantage in the back of the court-room, he watched the Judge straighten papers, smooth his goatee, and lean forward, barely, when a diminutive clerk hooked tobacco- stained fingers over the tall desktop and craned upward on tiptoe for a conference. Propped up that way above them, Stallard was the essence of austerity and power. After a long study, it seemed to Gabe that Stallard's authority was visibly widening and spreading as his robe spilled wide and wider from his shoulders, until, in Gabe's eyes, it finally encompassed the dark wood of his high bench and overflowed the room.

Stallard looked at Gabe directly only once, but then it was with such force that the jury foreman stopped in his tracks between them and moved to one side. The foreman had just come into court with Buell Smith, Sheriff Gilliam, and Ed Halsey, the Coroner. All three passed Gabe by without a nod. In their wake, the entire panel of jurors filed in and formed a semicircle in front of Judge Stallard, who arranged his countenance for their benefit.

"First thing he'll do, he'll ask the foreman if they've done their duty." Sonny Nolan said this. He had pinned Gabe by the elbow and, though the pewlike bench they occupied was empty except for the two of them, he had wedged Gabe tightly against the end of the bench that abutted the courtroom's center aisle. Even though the wood was slick as glass with accretions of varnish, Sonny was unscootable. Gabe had tried and failed several times to shoulder the man away.

Nolan, undeterred, kept up his raspy line of commentary. "They'll read the names from all the cases they've heard this week. You were the last. Then they'll post the lists. True Bills first." Sonny pointed frontward, as if Gabe's attention needed direction.

Within twenty minutes of Gabe's arrival, Judge Stallard gavelled the small assembly into silence with one sharp rap of the mallet. He then consulted the foreman, who answered "Yes," they had done their duty.

Buell Smith, for again it was the Commonwealth Attorney's place to do so in this ceremony, stepped forward. He held up a single sheet of paper. Gabe was supercharged with concentration. He felt his spine lengthen where he sat. The True Bill list, those people who would be tried for their misdeeds, was fairly lengthy. Two of the names Smith called were Gabe's ex-employees. He had never liked either man. They were both cheap men, Gabe thought, repeatedly accused of piddling crimes such as hog stealing and petty assaults at a bar out on Granny White Pike. Gabe could not bear to stand among them.

Each time Buell called out, Gabe's sensitivity was more pronounced. He counted on his fingers nine separate swells of terror in his sea of

Dead On

fear. Even Sonny Nolan didn't move a muscle during Buell's catalogue. When the rangy Commonwealth's Attorney fell silent and turned away, Gabe Phillips' name had not been read. Nor was it, evidently, on the list.

At first, Gabe didn't dare breathe. Utter quiet was imperative to preserve and clarify what had just happened. If that nattering Sonny Nolan so much as said a word . . . Gabe looked at the jury foreman, who studiously scanned a second sheet of paper before he handed it off to Buell Smith. Buell eyed then dangled the solitary page at his side and announced, "No True Bill." From the graven slate of his memory Smith read one name, and one name only. His pronunciation was emphatic: "Gabe Phillips."

For the eternity of seconds during which Gabe had known it was coming, he rose. Upon standing, Gabe gripped with all his might the seatback in front of himself to keep from toppling to the floor.

No True Bill. He had gone free.

The air around Gabe quieted, infused with freshness. The courtroom, Judge Matthew Stallard presiding, became edged, more distinct. It was as hushed and pristine as the first sight of a landscape after snowfall. Not one print or track was visible. Gabe stood in this miraculous clearing with these other men, blinded to their presence by the light of his own exhilaration.

After Buell Smith's pronouncement, and after Sonny gaped and Gabe breathed in the deepest breath of all his life, Judge Matthew Stallard asked grandly of the Grand Jury Foreman: "So say you all?"

"So say we all!" the man resounded.

This time Stallard banged the gavel twice. The sound was smart but there was no report. Gabe turned and looked at Sonny Nolan, who

117

stood foolishly frozen, openmouthed, apparently unable to gulp down the fact of this success. Gabe extricated himself almost gently from the tight corner where Sonny had him wedged. Everything must be touched with such care. Gabe then concentrated his dignity and limped into the aisle. While he hesitated, the only thing he wanted, the one thing left to wish for, was that his hand could have fallen easily to cup the crown of Clara's head, there where her watersmooth hair swept exactly from a center part to either side.

The court clerk nodded at Stallard then started toward Gabe. Gabe stayed where he was lightly, almost weightlessly suspended, arms easy at his sides, one hand slightly curled. He felt, then, that Joyce might have faintly brushed his cheekbone from inside, tenderly, the way she had sometimes touched his face in life. "See the pyramids along the Nile . . . ," she sang to him in her throaty voice. Gabe could barely hear her, but the murmur was sibilant and haunting.

CHAPTER 17

In the Quiet

AT SUPPERTIME THAT same day, Nonie sat out on Mr. Gabe's new screened porch in Tyrone and watched the Hebron change colors. She rocked ever so slightly in one of four tall Gatlinburg chairs which were lined up, two and two, on either side of the french doors. "I declare," she said aloud, then declared silently in spite of it. The spoken words hollowed out around her where she sat, alone.

Below Nonie, the river's surface reflected available light as bright as a sheet of button pearl. She followed the shapeshifting colors with her eyes. Silver and violet curled liquidly, back and forth, from the riverbend on her left to the gap between palisades on the far right side.

Nonie rocked and rubbed cold from her hands and made absolutely no move to go inside. Soon the whole stretch of water before her would catch as full of sun as a God-sized orange in a teacup. The sunset would then make a last, desperate flash of protest before the channel gulped it down and began its glow of satisfaction. When those splendors faded into the blue hour, Nonie would step inside and warm herself in the kitchen. Until then, this was a better place than most for her deep study.

The meal was cooked. All Nonie had to do was hold it warming on the gas ring. She had lowered the flame before coming outside until the fire was a mere feathery rim of cobalt blue, same as the outline she could now see behind the piney, knobbed hills across the Hebron.

She had also laid a place for Mr. Gabe at his kitchen table using the good dishes. A grayish, gold-rimmed dinner plate of antique Haviland china, with soup bowl to match, from the full set he bid and won at Miss Blanche Sumpter's estate auction, gleamed proudly from a solitary white mat that was as pristine as a maiden lady's collar. With regard to the placemat, Nonie thought it fitting that she had broken open the cellophane wrap on his new set of linens, even if they were bought specially for Thanksgiving. In her book *this* was the day of days. Mr. Gabe could fuss if he had a mind to.

The dish Nonie would serve Gabe Phillips had been cooking down all afternoon. She had poached harvest vegetables on the stove and roasted a pan of beef shanks and onions in the oven under a coarse sprinkle of pepper and rock salt, which she'd cracked with a ball-peen hammer. When the bones were glazed and the onions crusted, Nonie had carried the heavy pan to the sink and filled it to brimming with limestone springwater fresh from the tap. Heavy as they were, the long beefbones lifted slightly in the liquid, and swayed. "And the bones shall dance," said Nonie, when they moved. The faucet's force against the bottom of the deepwell deglazed a thick sediment of marrow and juices. Their fine, caramelized threads beckoned toward Nonie in the rising water like strands of mermaid hair. She simmered the broth for hours, skimming, sipping a taste now and then from the side of an old, hand-carved wooden spoon, frowning every time. Around four-thirty the stock concentrated to her satisfaction. It was dark, rich, and almost thick as aspic. Nonie approved with a politely wet smack of her lips and turned away.

Supper was what solace Nonie felt she could offer. No matter how late, when Mr. Gabe arrived from his singular day she would allow him to seat himself and slowly gather up the afternoon inside until he could distill for her the clear truth of what would be. Then would Nonie gently, gently ladle out the healing soup. As soon as Nonie had served the meal, she would slip away and disappear into the dark. Until she climbed her own rough steps and touched the door hasp with unaccustomed tenderness, Nonie would keep her feelings to herself about their conjoined fate, whatever it might be.

Out on the porch, Nonie replaced her missing collar button with her finger and gripped her coat together tightly underneath her chin. She shifted her hips in the rocker. The kitchen would feel good; heated gas was like a pillow against her skinny limbs.

Whatever happened, whether they were to try Mr. Gabe or not, the blond sheriff and the town would release their hold on him tonight. Gabe Phillips would be here this evening, regardless. The last few days Nonie had heard her employer arranging bond in case he needed it, promising up his money to stay free. Not a thing in what he'd said surprised her. It was the same she'd always heard with white men, just bigger sized. They almost always found a way. After such an accusation as Mr. Gabe was under, a negro might have never seen the jail. The reasons would have had nothing to do with bail; there would have been darker-hearted grounds.

Even in the half-light of sundown, Nonie could make out a clump of gnarled riverbank grape dangling a few withered pieces of blackish fruit just outside the screendoor. Nonie knew that acid taste. She had been hungry enough to try to eat some once when she was seven or eight years old. She nodded. Seemed like everything was turning acid now, and all the fruit was dark.

Nonie moved forward and sat tautly away from the woven rush chairback. A fat, spot-legged wolf spider, big as Mr. Gabe's hand, ooched itself through the space between the screendoor and the door's uncured frame. At first she glanced for the broom then merely watched the spider insinuate himself where he didn't belong. She settled back, lips pursed, eyes narrowed. Yes sir. Mr. Gabe had brought something bad down here with him to Tyrone, all right. It must have been just enlarging somewhere, hidden, blending darkly in the shadows like that water spider, waiting to crawl out.

Nonie shook her head. These white people held too tight. She must ease away from Phillipses, even Clara. Except for her mother, Fannie Pulce, Nonie had done that with her own people, too. The gingerbread man had forever danced in Nonie's head. All her life it seemed she had ridden lightfooted on the fox's back, ready to run, run, run as fast as she could if he turned on her, fanged, snarling, before they reached the bank. Even if she had somehow landed on safety in Tyrone, one of these days Nonie planned on heading directly into that dazzling sunset in front of her. Until then, she must stay free of anything that would haul her back from glory.

Now the riverscene demanded her full attention. Nonie swivelled, faced squarely west and let all sights turn red from the sun's full force burning on her watchful eyes. The porch struts and the hillside and her coat and even her skin, her creased brown skin, were shiny red for an instant. And if Clara or Joyce were here their skin would be red too, and the emerald river would have the sheen of melted rubies, in that brilliant last flare before the sun exploded and was gone and all their differences returned tenfold in sooty shadows.

After the brightest burst died away, Nonie stood up and listened hard. The blue hour deepened around her; small sounds intensified. But Mr. Gabe's powerful Buick was not what she had heard. What Nonie heard came from the river. The insistent purr of a small outboard motor was briefly loud when it passed Mr. Gabe's float then trailed mournfully after the skiff. Who could it be on the river this late of a cold evening? Nonie shrugged. It wasn't up to her to question souls who sought out landings in the dark.

Mr. Gabe should have been home by now. Nonie filled her lungs; for a few seconds she kept them inflated. Yes. She could detect the first melancholy smell of winter on the faintly smoky air. Nonie sympathized with what must be the airlessness of Clara's waiting down in Hickman, and with Lucy. The very atmosphere this evening seemed taut from a kind of aged tension that had to do with waiting. Would those blunt Milan farmers step outside tonight and feel that too? She wondered, and, lacking air, would the people up in town, the coloreds in Boxtown and the white folks in their solid brick houses, would they take themselves outdoors and gape at the thin sky stretched above them, stars pulled tight, and long to draw at least one sweetly deep and unsuspicious breath of the ether that all beings breathed the same?

In the quiet, in the dark, Nonie exhaled and summoned Clara before her from shapes on the wide plank flooring. There she and the child appeared, suddenly, in a remembered morning of her mind's delight. A slight black woman and a slip of a white girl weaving up a world of real and fancy by the riverside, like the glistening, lime-green garter snakes that wove ribbons in the silky hillside grass.

Dusk changed to complete darkness almost in a moment. With the change, Nonie's cold discomfort was sudden and forceful. Her old coat wasn't lined. There was finally nothing for the chill but to go inside and wait for what would come.

CHAPTER 18

A Rich Cup of Autumn

IF SEMI-DARK WERE portable, Ira would have moved around encased, protected by it, looking out. But this afternoon, tucked into a hidey-hole between the Dixie Café's façade and an entrance to a flight of stairs, he was more and more agitated. Two hours ago he had seen Phillips flow up from the steep left side of Main Street, as if risen, and enter the courthouse. Gabe's head had been high and he had come on in that artful stride of his that made him less a cripple. Oh, the man was prideful.

By now, the long October shadow of the courthouse leaned heavily onto the squat bank building and Ira had all but given up, convinced his fish had slipped its hook. Then Gabe appeared in Ira's line of sight. Phillips stepped carefully out onto the broad limestone stylobate that supported the courthouse pillars and, briefly framed under the arched and columned entry as if fitted there, surveyed the block and started toward the crosswalk.

With that, Ira eased out of hiding and across the street, up the courthouse steps, and into the building's cavernous first-floor vault. There was a diagram on a sign near one of twin stairways, which curved upward on opposite sides of the circular room like a pair of raised arms. Ira paused long enough to study the building's layout. Pale, mote-filled rays of sunlight splayed out around him from the dome's skylight but Ira found a dark eye at their center.

There it was! *X* marked it. Ira located a judge's courtroom indicated on the drawing. He headed off to his left and burrowed under one stairway and emerged from there into a wide corridor. Gravelly panes of glass in some closed doorways lit the hallway dimly, shrinking as they receded. On the second door to his left, Ira found what he had come to find.

Clipped to the door of Matthew Stallard's courtroom was a single sheet of paper. It was all but impossible to read in the subterranean gloom. Ira leaned in as close as he could, tilted his thick bifocals, and with the fingertips of his other hand, rubbed the page where hard strikes on old keys had quilted the vellum. He squinted and peered. At first, the few marks he was able to make out doubled mischievously; they jiggled upward toward his face and hovered over themselves before Ira forced some of the letters back into place with his forefinger. He then fiddled his eyeglasses until he managed to cant the lenses at a proper angle. At last the script defined. On the page, under the heading "No True Bill," one name was distinctly embedded: GABE PHILLIPS.

In a shadowy way Ira was aware that there were other people in the hallway with him. Faint and weblike creatures brushed near, out beyond the edges of the all-important white notice.

Ira deciphered the message a second time. He slowly mouthed the words as he read. With the last syllable of PHILLIPS on his lips, Ira turned heavily away and knocked clumsily into a grayish shape. "Shit!" the shape hissed after him, like some animal startled into noise in its lair. Undeterred, Ira went back to the rotunda. He stayed over to one side and moved slowly, not an arm's length from the wall. The people on his path glided soundlessly by.

Ira circled around under the steps until he heard a typewriter. Inside the office where he ran the sound to ground, he found himself awash in a heatless, bluish glow from the startlingly flourescent tubes stretched overhead. The planes they lit were bare except for a hanging clock as big as a platter. Thin, cheap-looking paint gave the walls the fragile look of bisque. They were tan and dirtyish, the color of egg-shells. Ira furtively scratched his fingernail against a spot of plaster near his hand. Cold and thick as rock.

Against such walls and in that light, the clerk, a petite woman in an orange dress, looked pert as a bird. She was almost as delicately sized as his wife had been, but Ira could tell by the sharp way this one moved that she was free of the filmy veil behind which Orena had seemed to dream her life.

Furtively, Ira shut the door then waited while the clerk stepped briskly from one small task to another involving pens or folders. Although the service counter divided them, Ira was close enough to study particulars and did so. The backs of the woman's hands were triangular and thin. With each gesture she made, their tiny bones splayed out and closed inside her faintly speckled skin like the slats of a fan. He was starved for that kind of womanly detail and could hardly pull his eyes away from their feast.

"I'm Ira Truitt," he said at last when the woman paused behind the counter barrier. She was unruffled but alert.

"Yes?" Small green eyes checked Ira, ticked off wire baskets on the shelf behind him, then came back to his face.

"Ira Truitt." He tapped his chest. "From across the river."

When she didn't question him, Ira said, "There's a notice down there. Outside the courtroom, on the door."

"This is the Tax Assessor's Office," she emphasized.

"I've come to find out about the list that's taped up. Under the Judge's name. What it means. I need to know." Ira couldn't help his insistence.

"Oh. That. It's a report on the Grand Jury proceedings. But this is the Tax Assessor's, and we don't do Moccasin County. The place for that is at the county seat over there."

"I'm not here about property. It's about the page that says 'No True Bill.'"

Even if the woman wasn't being helpful, Ira liked being alone with her in an isolated room, cut off from rude interference, he thought, by the dusky aisle outside her office. "I need to know what comes from that," he finished up his request. His voice, at the last, rose up, strengthened by his need of her and his sense of what was due him.

"Oh. If that's the question. Yes. About Gabe Phillips. Everybody up here knows. There won't be a trial. They've gone and cut him loose." The woman clicked a sliver of metal, a paper clip, with her thumbnail before she turned away.

"You're saying he's got off scot free? This Bill means nothing else happens?"

"Yes, sir. That's right. Free as a bird. And flying high right this minute, I expect. Yes."

Her chirp of yesses pleased Ira, and he wanted them to continue, but the other things she said were disturbing. His sense of disappointment was almost overwhelming. Ira had counted on watching the trial. He would have come into town every day, the way he had when Orena lingered before dying, curtained off in an otherwise empty ward at the hospital. And this time, too, Ira would have been desperate to prolong the connection. This clerk didn't even seem to feel regretful. Now Ira was free of duties. Free among the dead, he thought, as the Bible stated. Free among the dead. He decided not to quote that to the clerk. A matter of fact was all this business was to her. Just some girl dead, another man set free. What difference to this sparrow? What did she know about life lived in isolation?

The woman efficiently collected several loose form sheets, clattered them against the table until she was evidently satisfied with the packet's neatness. She busied with a comb in her hair then looked around pointedly at the clock where it hung on the back wall near the ceiling. The hour and minute hands were ornately black, like ivied iron, and there was no mistaking them, or that they pointed out the lateness of the day. Six minutes after 4:00 P.M. Ira's eyes and the clerk's eyes synchronized, they moved from the clock face to each other's simultaneously. She wanted to flee, did she? Well, he would salt her feathers.

For Ira had more questions, and it was the clerk's job to tolerate them. He meant no harm, but if he had to catch and hold her in his grip until she answered, her little heart aflutter against his palm, he would have to do so. He had a citizen's right; she was a public servant. Ira's forearms weighted the counter. He wouldn't quite believe that it was over now with him and Gabe. And that's what this woman was really saying. Ira refused to take that in as fact. Gabe separate from Ira? How could it be?

Over the last weeks while he spied on Phillips, the man had assumed utmost importance. Ira was entitled to his fascination, he thought. He and Gabe were almost blood kin through the fate of their women, after all. And this secret following of Gabe Phillips had the urgent power of a mission. The task filled the empty surfaces of Ira's life.

Finally, when Ira had stood there so long that even he could feel the passage of time, he asked: "Who come out for the girl?" Ira knew her name, the dead girl's. The fresh wound in the cemetery's soil and its temporary metal marker had told the tale. Ira wouldn't show it, though. What he found out, like all the rest he had discovered, was strictly for the swale or mulling in the shed. He would chest his cards. Did they think that he was stupid?

"Joyce Oliver? Is Joyce who you mean?" the clerk asked. She continued without his answer. "It's not like that up there, at the Grand Jury. It's all secret up there, but they say it doesn't go like that. Nobody appears for the dead ones unless there's a trial."

"I heard he had a gun." Ira took a guess.

"Yes, well, there's cause and there's coincidence. You don't go to jail for standing real close to a dead person, even with a gun in your hand. Not in this state you don't. Who knows? Word is, there wasn't any proof. They didn't think they could convict. Gabe Phillips has a lot of friends these days, at least there's plenty are beholden. That right there sounds like a lack of evidence to me." The clerk sighed sharply then lowered her voice. "Joyce, the dead girl, she's not from around here."

The whole time the bird woman spoke and fluttered with some bit of work and spoke again, Ira tried to quell his own rising sense of urgency about getting out of the courthouse before the front entry was slammed and bolted for the night. Phillips would still be near enough; it hadn't been half an hour since the sign went up on the courtroom door. Deliberately, Ira slid his belly to the left against the counter and stopped where the laminate was hinged, presumably the gate by which the clerk would leave. He held the woman's gaze until she looked unsettled, then Ira turned away. With the same awkward grace he possessed from being a big man who had learned to balance his bulk above delicate feet, Ira left and pulled the door behind him in one smooth swing, closing it swiftly, on a pad of air.

Ira knew most of Gabe Phillips' routine by heart. Lately he had tracked Gabe to the Dixie, the restaurant across the street, around this time almost every day. There was no need for Ira to consult his ragged little sheaf of notes to picture Phillips where he sat alone at a corner table. Or to imagine that unyielding nod of Gabe's when people looked in his direction, the hint of distant mischief in the smile. Gabe never stood or offered a chair, but neither did he back away. Something invisible about the man kept him apart but drew attention like a lodestone. How would today's act differ? Or would it? Same or not, Ira mustn't miss details. He slipped effortlessly back into the gloomy corridor and retraced his steps.

Even in sunlight, the late October afternoon was cold as cider. Ira, keeping his momentum, steamed right into this rich cup of Milan's autumn, powered by deep breathing. He was blinkered to the red-tinged, golden oaks that licked up like flames.

Ira started down, taking by twos the courthouse steps where Gabe had halted earlier. Haste was imperative, even if it meant Ira ran the risk of being noticed. Well, let them look, Ira thought. He had more than one little secret. Gabe wasn't the only man with a certain way about himself, was he? And Ira's special quality was the opposite of Phillips'. Because no matter who saw him, Ira wouldn't be remembered. Had he ever been? Not once.

Besides, Ira had found a hidey-hole attached to Spiro's building where he could disappear completely. Almost as good as his own swale, right here in town. His find was a stairwell next to the Dixie's plate glass front, a nook that ran as dark as river water even when there was full daylight outside. While hidden there, Ira had roughly brushed his coveralls on more than one occasion to make sure he wasn't somehow disembodied in the shadows.

The place was created by the angle of Spiro's window wall. It indented away from the street on one end and a leg of building stuck forward. In the ell was an arched doorway and behind that, stairs to second floor storage.

Wedged into the alcove, Ira had watched from the stairwell for hours, hours and hours, over the last days. He was always fearful of being seen. What if Spiro himself came out to roust him? Ira had stayed, sometimes electrified by fear, but nothing drove him away. For no force had proved as powerful as his desire to know what Gabe was up to. Even when Ira's bladder was full to bursting and he had to wet himself, he had to, or when he was desperate to start his long hike down toward Tyrone so he could be back on the Hebron by midnight, he stayed. Ira was as determined of late as he had been when he was a boy. He would show his daddy yet. This was real work. This was a Man's job.

Ira ignored his own hunger while the people he watched, huge babies wearing napkins tucked like bibs, bit into greasy corn muffins, or cut fried steaks and dribbled gravy on themselves. Ira's good fortune was that no one ever did come and find him out. Not a single, solitary soul. Fate was with him. Ira was its instrument. He felt it more and more.

So Ira had stayed in the hidey-hole, in the murk, at least until Gabe left the Dixie, every afternoon for weeks, glued to the silent show behind the plate glass window.

And Ira used his time well. He didn't miss a lick. Oh, just look at the way eyes moved and danced in pairs like matched sets of small, exotic fish seen through the wavy wall of an enormous fishbowl. And Phillips, it was always Gabe Phillips the eyes loved, on whom they caught and held then swam away and darted back all through Gabe's time at supper. Though Phillips hardly ate the food before him.

Gabe never got himself involved in conversations, but the others in there did. Their mouths moved almost as often as their eyes and just as fluidly. Words slipped between their lips as easily as pits from plums. They amazed him. Ira never had been one for talk, except inside himself.

Ira was now crossing Main Street, but he kept going back and back in time. He had been too quiet with Orena. From his first day, first seconds, with her, words had been too heavy in his mouth. What was there to say? Ira was stunned that his daddy had wanted a woman on the place or any kind of good for Ira. "Better to marry than burn," his father said, or Saint Paul, Ira had the two mixed at times, he knew. But Orena had burned anyway. At the thought of Orena's burning, Ira almost groaned aloud in the middle of the crosswalk, but he mustn't, he must not break his silence, not now, now of all times.

Ira plodded ahead, heedless of a truck that slowed inches from his left side. In his mind, he was looking at Orena. He had seen her waiting for his sentiments, had seen it, the waiting, and known it for what it was. Those long looks of hers at the end of his few daily remarks about chores or weather. He'd just never got used to her enough. To having such a treasure in his care. Ira counted one thing to his credit. He had done his best to preserve her. If clumsily. His only guide was what he knew from farming, crude facts to know and worse to act on with a woman.

Ira felt some relief when the farm and farmhouse came down to them on his daddy's death. He didn't doubt for a single minute that the old man would have given his bequest elsewhere if he had seen his judgment coming. (The Moccasin Baptist Church, Ira guessed.) Well, Mr. Death had showed old Truitt who was boss. Death had snatched his daddy's breath right there from between those sheets where he'd begot Ira and marked his corpse with the same hateful grimace the man had probably worn when he did the first.

Ira looked up, momentarily into the present, and guided himself to the stairwell; then he sailed immediately back to the past. The morning Ira found his father dead, twenty years ago, was plainer in detail than this very moment. Ira had turned his back on his father's body. He had sat, heavily, on the mattress beside the cadaver. He remained almost as motionless as his morbid father, there in the back bedroom upstairs, staring out an open, unscreened window for the longest time. It was early May; at 6:00 A.M. the room was still cold. Even so, a fecal smell rose from the corpse.

Slumped there, breathing the ugly odor, Ira had smiled calmly, while he traveled over ridge after rippling ridge of cedar trees with his eyes. Finally, he spread his gaze and let it rest where the evergreens grew indistinct and blended themselves into velvet gray-green folds that blanketed the horizon. Plain curtains made from "cottons," lengths of white tobacco canvas, hung on either side of the window. Stirred by a soft breeze, the gauzy panels swayed occasionally, like animated shrouds. They were comforting companions.

After that day, Orena seemed to take real pleasure in the farmhouse's spartan rooms. Ira believed that, for a while, she saw him as a man of promise and was heedless of his poverty in words.

There were even a few pure months between the two of them before Ira's fear of his father had started up again. That period had been an airy time that seemed to soothe them both. The reawakened dread had come on Ira small. At first it seemed little more than simple wondering at how his father would make the thing turn on them, how he would control the couple from the grave. Ira later thought he could hear the man's dark march outside their room at night. When alive, his daddy had paced there, on the landing, for hours, and his footfall stopped every furtive touch of Ira's hands on Orena, stamping him with guilt. Ira remembered the centuries of heat while he had lain there with his hand suspended over the curly nest of hair between Orena's thighs, the millennium of waiting for the flat clomp of his father's next, ponderous step.

But Ira never guessed that the house itself would do them in. It was his house, though, his father's house, that had been so dry of all emotion that it went up like tinder when the spark, a forgotten, melting candle, was lit.

At some point between his father's dying and Orena's suffocation as a result of her burns, Ira had gone silent like his mother had been.

Even so, Orena never hardened toward him. For the two years she had lived between his daddy's death and her own, her face stayed soft, as soft in his direction as her body in the night.

Ira, back with himself in Milan, secreted now behind the grimy doorway, stopped himself right there. He would not think of nighttime with Orena; that was for the shed. If he couldn't twist away and escape and had to plunge those memories deep in his belly until he almost exploded from the pain of them, he would do it in real dark, not gloom but the inky midnight black of years of lightless nights and secret, dirty beds.

Ira suddenly realized that he had been looking at the past so hard and clear that his eyelids were squeezed shut. He opened them just as Gabe left Spiro's. Ira sucked back into his dank alcove. Phillips seemed to be following a tall man of distinguished appearance who was several yards ahead of him down Main Street. Ira craned to watch Gabe trail the other man. Each of the pair was intent on the sidewalk as he walked and, seen from the back, with their necks bent that way, they looked prayerful. It suited Ira to think so.

For the millionth time, Ira noted Gabe's crippled stride. Yes. The Broken-Footed Man. It awed him to consider how exactly Leviticus described this very one to Ira, the man with a blemish. Profane. A lame man who must be barred from places that were sanctified, kept from the altar.

Ira sidled out cautiously, looked around, and when he had the chance, moved onto Main Street. He had decided that he wouldn't stand out because there were several farmers dressed as he was, in coveralls and boots, who already headed down the sidewalk in the same direction as Gabe Phillips and the man Phillips had followed. Ira stepped in among the farmers and went along, different by the color of his skin. On every side of him the faces were pinked or reddened from wind exposure and the sun. Ira, himself, hid so religiously from the sun that his creased features had no more color than a wad of dirty dough tossed amid a crate of apples, but he had to chance it.

This was new and ominous, this going off of Gabe's in pursuit of a companion. Ira briefly touched his pocket-sized pad of notes where they bulged just over his heart and rubbed his fingertip along the pencil stub beside them. There was nothing there to account for it. Gabe was usually as singular as he was.

While there were men nearby, Ira listened in. The words and their fragments hummed close. Voices were muted. One or two farmers pointed down the block. "The Judge," he heard. Or "there goes Phillips," over and over again.

Up ahead, Ira saw where Gabe turned off onto a side street leading from Main. The other man stepped up beside Gabe when he turned, as if he had waited by appointment. Late, low sun made elongated scarecrows of the duo on the sidewalk behind them.

Ira followed them into the subsiding flow of heat and light as the afternoon ended, picking his way cautiously down a dark and unfamiliar block in pursuit of shadows.

One by one, porch lights came on. Their yellow bulbs lit up almost sequentially. The ones at the end of the street, nearest Gabe and his cohort, looked as small as lightning bugs trapped in dwindling, identical globes that were as glittery as bubbles.

None of the apple faces had turned when he did, so Ira was following alone. He plodded deeper into the thickening dusk, fists balled at his sides, eyes accustomed. He wasn't seen, and Ira never lost sight of Gabe or the older man with the walking stick. Ira could hear the cane. A block away its tap-tap-tap was faint but steady against concrete, a metronome set to the rhythm of Gabe's limp. The whole hollow avenue was otherwise hushed. Just that eerie, far-off sound tinkled in Ira's old, cold ears.

CHAPTER 19

Down a Dark Stream of Hours

In Hickman around ten o'clock that night, Lucy Phillips watched from her pillow as a sheen of violet, cobalt, and lavender traveled a silver picture frame, disappeared, then started up again every time a vehicle sped down State Street. The lines of light went black in a muffled whoosh when each car passed, as if that were the sound of their extinction. Lucy was in the front bedroom of her small house.

Nonie should have notified them well before now what the Grand Jury had decided, whether Gabe was to be bound over for trial. Even the term, "bound over," was stunning to contemplate as applied to Gabe. Lucy adjusted the afghan around her legs in the dark and waited for the blinds to leak another headlamp onto the frame, opposite on the wall. She hoped, but doubted, that Clara, in the next room, was asleep.

Lucy had made her way on rubbery legs to the bedroom and stretched herself across the double bed. Mashed flat, she was afraid, by the power of the past. If she remained here and held herself completely still, Lucy hoped the rouged bits of crisp, tart apple she had tried to eat for supper might also stay in place below her throat.

The middle ridge of the mattress, which had risen over the years of her marriage like a bulging fault line between her weight and Gabe's, urged itself against the flesh of Lucy's back. But she didn't move to either side. Instead, she gave herself up entirely to the boat of a bed and hoped it would float her safely down the dark stream of hours until Nonie called.

In spite of the mounting tension of the last few weeks, it was those damn songs, Lucy thought, that had left her here on her back, helpless of rising—those syrupy radio songs, sung by lonesome men and strong-voiced women who, with their mouths inches from the microphone, smeared the air with emotions thicker than their lipstick.

Early in the evening, Clara had knelt in front of the Philco and twirled a dial until suddenly a warm tone had expanded into the room, a pure tone, beamed through the night, magically invisible and inaudible until its sharp ray penetrated their modest Hickman living room, from however far away, and speared Clara and Lucy with the utter plaintiveness of its sound. Clara had immediately raised the volume. The radio's Bakelite plastic case rattled, faintly, against the spindly wooden table where it sat. A male duo wailed out "When I Stop Dreaming" through the metal woofer's mesh veil. "Joyce's music," Clara had then said, guilelessly. No mistake. Clara had spoken clearly, had bowled each word out slowly: "Joyce's music." Weighted, rolling, each syllable found its mark.

Well, who was this Joyce, anyway, to own a thing like music? On the bed, Lucy covered her eyes with her forearm and let the weight of it press in. She didn't want to start crying now for Joyce; she didn't want to feel anything for that girl. Lucy had forcibly ignored the fact of Joyce Oliver since the night her own marriage ended, one week before Lucy left it. Gabe had yelled that night that Joyce didn't matter, shouldn't matter. His and Lucy's bond was elemental, braided together, he said. They had entwined as saplings and grown that thick and strong. There could be no separation.

But oh, how blind in his passionate rage; how Gabe had misjudged Lucy! Those first tendril's of Joyce's presence, vining up between them, had clutched greenly at Lucy's solid, mountainous heart and choked it dead.

Lucy was amazed by this much pain. It was as if the plant renewed its squeeze inside her chest. Five years since she had taken an axe to their marriage and divorced Gabe Phillips. But he had been right. She had not severed their connection. Now, under the passive heaviness of her arm, she felt again the urgency of Gabe's arms, the dark nighttime thrill of the man, the warmth and weight and moaning breath of his that sucked her world inside and pulled it deep away. Only with Gabe, in that way, had Lucy ever penetrated anything in life that was as easily serene as breathing.

It was the same feeling, amplified, that she knew when Gabe was adrift inside her after making love, when he lay spent and lulled and seemingly dreamless, held tightly yet within the slickly salty sea of her. At those times Lucy had often asked him in a dark whisper to stay, stay, please stay inside. The two of them had even wakened hours later, connected only there, between their legs, cemented with sweet, soft glue.

What pain it was to have been pulled apart. Lucy lay there

knowing she had been fragile in the weeks since Joyce died. But never more than now. She must move little, and that, right carefully. More might break. If, this far from Milan, Gabe could yet smash the center, what was safe?

Her bedroom was thoroughly chilled, but a trip down steep basement steps to fill the stoker was more than Lucy could manage. She well knew Clara wasn't cold under the tattered but heavy comforter the child dragged out every winter. Lucy, though, was half dressed in a slip and skirt, on top of the bedspread, with only a bit of loopy wool for loose warmth. If the phone rang, she must somehow dredge the energy for a walk to the hall.

So Lucy waited, motionless on the bed. The very next second the void of silence could end. She felt her mind tick forward. There, again. She glanced at the silver frame for a glint of distraction. Few cars went down State Street after ten o'clock.

Lucy did not wish to live isolated like this in heatless, too-thin air. What she most wanted was to live her own new life ardently and to forgive, to let go even of Gabe's trespass against her that mean, long-ago, night. Lucy yearned to embrace and embody an artless kind of sympathy that would enfold them all. Dead Joyce, as well. Perhaps its purity would even soothe and smother Gabe's lifelong howl of fury that he wasn't perfect, a noise she had only this moment identified, but it had whistled in the background from their childhood. The overloud, long-distance ring, when it finally trilled from the front hall, hardly muffled that sound.

CHAPTER 20

The Hard-Shelled Heart of Things

G ABE WAS TOO elated to concentrate. He strained slightly to stay abreast of the Judge, even though his thoughts had raced away, leaving both him and Stallard far behind on Montgomery Avenue's narrow, concrete sidewalk. It took effort merely to regulate his own breathing. "OllieOllieOllieInFree!" Gabe wanted to crow to the heavens, at the top of his lungs. And damn all below who heard him, if they thought his behavior was unseemly. Damn Matt Stallard, too, for commanding this little powwow—tonight of all nights, though Gabe's euphoria was hardly tempered by the prospect. There would be no changing of the facts. Gabe had been victorious, for Lucy and for Clara. His bath of sweat in the Grand Jury hearing had washed away their shame.

Most men hitched their stride a step or two when they fell in beside Gabe. Judge Matthew Stallard decidedly did not. Gabe briefly wondered at Stallard's arrogant pace, or was this a test? At any rate, while they pressed down the sidewalk, side by side in the dusk, Gabe felt he would have heard the slap of reins on some wet flank, had there been sound effects for the minor cruelties of men. Instead, the street was singularly still. No solitary car or man had come as far with them as this, from Main.

Gabe looked up and measured the sky. A strip of daylight on the horizon narrowed rapidly, squeezed down by a dense thinking cap of wooly winter darkness. Tonight, under the spell of reprieve, the universe was Gabe's alone. He couldn't imagine what Stallard's motive was in asking him to come home for this talk. The Judge's invitation itself had been a furtive act. A summons scribbled on a napkin that, somehow, achieved the weight of a subpoena.

Thus far, on the way to Oxford Street, Stallard had kept his own counsel. Gabe was gratified that neither of them broke the small town's roomy, dinnertime silence. All along the five blocks of Montgomery, Gabe harnessed his muscles to stay neck and neck with the Judge. As he did so, Gabe felt that he was rising forcefully from within himself and opening, his soul spreading above, like a vast umbrella sprinkled with stars, newborn to time.

Matthew Stallard abandoned haste when they turned onto the walkway to his own house. In that more stately fashion he followed the brick path, thickset, between black-green beds of pachysandra and sculpted boxwood hedges. By the time they reached the steps to the Georgian façade, Stallard ascended more than climbed, wearing a mantle of decorum. Gabe drew himself up in a bid to match the Judge in this, as well.

Mrs. Stallard opened the door without a summons and handed Gabe and her husband in, smoothly, to a wide, bright entry. If Gabe was taken aback at his sudden delivery into confined space, he didn't mean to show it. He allowed himself to be greeted pleasantly and drawn inexorably away from the front door and to be ushered, without protest, past unlit rooms.

His escorts, Belinda Stallard and her twin in dignity, the Judge, cushioned Gabe between them. His limp was padded by a colorful Turkish carpet-runner, which narrowed and extended as they traveled the hall's length. A star-shaped, leaded-glass chandelier dangled overhead. Beneath its burst of wattage, the trio's progress was briefly empaneled in a floor-length pier mirror that was elaborately framed in gold. Gabe's eyes caught the rippled wings of light shining from their reflections as they floated by. To him they looked seraphic. This was not Gabe's first experience with Belinda Stallard's hypnotic calm. She was one of the few adults in Milan who had emerged from the amorphous, shadowy haze of "big people" which loomed over his childhood. Gabe glanced toward her while they glided along. The woman's appearance had not changed perceptibly. The Judge's wife was pale and graying now, as she had been then. Nor was there yet an observable alteration in her gracious manner, as democratically applied tonight as in his memory. Time's effect had been emphatic only.

While the couple each held him lightly by an elbow, Gabe seemed to sail along as fluidly as they did. Mrs. Stallard stayed with them all the way to a small study. There, at the doorway, she relinquished Gabe to her husband.

Inside Stallard's den the dreaminess that Gabe had experienced while walking between the pair dissipated with a pouf. This room was a dark, tight shell of a place, abruptly different from the entry hall. The soffits and one wall were painted Chinese red and had been hard-glazed. The other three walls were scored with bookshelves that pressed row after row of thick, leather-bound volumes between enameled standards.

Gabe knew at once, tucked inside this cramped chamber, that he and the Judge totaled something more than could conveniently fit. Matthew Stallard, however, looked perfectly at ease. He took a seat behind his desk, settled back against a display of law books, and faced Gabe openly.

"Be my guest, sir," said Judge Matthew Stallard. Gabe decided not to identify Stallard's tone as mocking. Without answer, he accepted the proffered invitation and sat in an ornate chair that faced the Judge. The sense Gabe had of being back in the Grand Jury room gave him a whiff of nausea. Only this time one all-powerful man was both inquisitor and jury.

Gabe knew of course that he was his own jailer. He was not bound here against his will. He could leave. And he just might. At any second, he might withdraw until he was no bigger than a flicker of moth on the glowing green glass lampshade and disappear. Then would the Judge and all his marks of privilege, the polished brass urns on the cabinet and the leaded crystal ashtray near his hand, and certainly the silver letter opener on the blotter with its heavily engraved, King's pattern handle, refit the space. The very timbre of Matthew Stallard's voice, which had caused in Gabe misgivings his whole life, depended on the presence of such things.

Stallard began emphatically: "I want it understood what has just happened to you, Gabe Phillips. And why. Before you get ideas."

Gabe could hardly believe his ears. God forbid that he should have ideas. In his entire speculation about why Stallard had brought him here, not for one minute had Gabe thought that he might be upbraided. If anything, Gabe suspected the Judge might have in mind to deliver a sort of formal congratulation on the Grand Jury's finding, to declare

146

a truce of sorts. That would be consistent with Matt Stallard's style as Gabe knew it—aloof, but seemingly benign. A manner fine-tuned to preserve the status quo. But what the man had just issued was nothing short of a reproof, no two ways about it.

Gabe prickled with outrage. Before he could speak, Stallard continued. "Those of us in Milan," the Judge said, "those of us with interest in the welfare, no, the well-being, of the people in this town, are glad for today's result." And there the Judge did pause.

Ah. So there was a carrot, even if Gabe had obviously just been defined out of those people who cared about Milan. Gabe considered the nicety of difference between "welfare" and "well-being." "Well-bein'." "Well-fayah." The older man had buttered his remark with a prolonged and deeply Southern enunciation. Stallard wanted what he said to go down easy. At that, Gabe felt his gorge rise. Who was more responsible for the town's prosperity than he was? he'd like to know. Gabe grappled with his emotions. He moved his hands casually, moved them naturally, he hoped, to the ends of his chair's wooden arms and fitted his fingers into the grooves carved there and curled his fingers just as those wooden paws curled and waited for the Judge to continue.

"But you may mistake us, Gabe, if you think our interest is, let's say, individual." While Stallard went on breathing words, Gabe switched off and listened to himself, inside.

Us? Had the man said "mistake us?" Gabe began to marvel. At last, Gabe thought. At the long, god damn last. "*Our* interest?" Yes sir. Gabe was actually in the room of power. He had stumbled in without suspicion, blinded by the dazzling whiteness in the hall and his serene companions. But he was here all right. After the quest of a lifetime,

147

Gabe had certainly come to the hard-shelled heart of things. That impenetrable place he had guessed existed. All these years of trying to storm his way in, until it seemed the very theme of his being. And now, this other man, Judge Matthew Stallard, whom Gabe had never fully evaluated, had blithely opened the door to let him glimpse the promised land.

Gabe knew this because the Judge was using exactly the amiable, excluding tone Gabe hated. Had always hated. What gave some men the right?

Few adults in Milan had spoken to Gabe directly when he was a child. For that matter he remembered wishing someone would grant him at least enough credit to look him in the eye. Belinda Stallard had been an exception. In the thirties, after a heavy winter snowfall, Gabe had cleaned the Stallard's driveway. He had pillowed his bad leg in the deep drifts and worked for hours. When Mrs. Stallard paid him, she stood coatless in the doorway of this very house on Oxford. Regardless of the cold, she had given him a long appraisal while she clinked five nickels, one by one, onto his raw palm. There was no pity in her expression during the whole length of her study. No pity. Just a frank and kindly surmise over the whiteness that repeatedly bloomed and closed in front of her lips as her breath warmed the air between them.

Otherwise, Gabe had received little attention in Milan until the last few years. It was his old man who caused talk. Back then "that trifling Charlie Phillips" was everybody's favorite drunk. Done up for laughs, his daddy's binges must have seemed less sodden.

But hadn't Gabe showed the powers that be? He had got from there to here in this tight, red room, where Judge Matthew Stallard looked at him intently and drew a circle in the air.

Gabe tuned in Stallard's voice: ". . . It's not a fancy world, but workable, Milan, or has been so in the past. People recognize themselves here. Some of us feel that the worth of that is vastly beyond its measure."

Judge Stallard waved the circle away. He looked pointedly at Gabe. "But you. You've never felt constrained to honor boundaries, have you? I've always wondered where you would end up. Since I watched you as a boy. Oh, I watched. That look of surprise gives us little credit." Gabe bit his tongue. He might have interrupted the Judge's sermon to point out that, as of this moment, he and the Judge seemed to have ended in exactly the same place. Stallard, however, did not let up. "With your problems, Gabe," he said, "your father and your lameness and all . . ." At that, Gabe started in spite of himself. He did not know a man who would be so bald-faced as to say that to him outright. Matthew Stallard, who preached on, seemed unfazed. "What I predicted was that you would come up scared," he said. "It seemed the likely thing. Instead, I think you lack awe, Gabe. Utterly. It's curious." Stallard did break there, as if questioning his own curiosity. Yet it was he who continued. This time his tone was somber. "I felt fond of you, though, because of your fearlessness. I respected it. Discreetly, of course." Of course. Gabe held his breath.

Stallard lowered his forearms, which had been in the air the while, hands open. "Fond, Gabe. No denying that. And, until the death of Joyce Oliver, you defied all expectation, in gratifying ways. Oh, you skirted the edges. Don't think I didn't know. But you had yourself a start on a family. It was sad they left. Everybody agreed. And you were always willing to put your head down and work. Until last August, you operated pretty much in bounds."

Judge Stallard stopped at last and gave him an opening. Gabe didn't say a word. In a sorrowful voice, Stallard himself broke the silence: "You know Gabe, you really mustn't think that the rest of us are a mere bunch of sorry fools." When that got no rise the Judge returned to his previous tone with an air of niceties aside: "Very well then. As for *what* happened to you today at our fine courthouse, there is no sense in which you have 'gotten away' with anything. Let's make that plain right here."

This, finally, was more than Gabe could silently bear. "You're saying that you doubt my account." His voice cut the quick edge of his thoughts and stung.

The Judge was no less sharp: "Not at all, Gabe. I don't bother with your account. In the given scheme of things, our Grand Jury's decision was well founded. There are common interests."

That did it. Gabe could have cracked the walls. He was furious. Now there were common interests? Where were those interests when he was a child alone, in charge of a drunk and weepy daddy? How many locals had wanted a share of Charlie Phillips' selfish grief when his wife saddled him with a crippled infant then ran off, before Gabe even had an inkling of her touch?

Gabe had long since stopped wondering how his careless daddy, a hapless man already prone to benders, kept a baby alive. Somehow he had managed.

They had lived in an upstairs room at the hotel. His father was the doorman at the courthouse in the days when such courtesies were formalized. Gabe could almost feel the heavy broadcloth morning coat and trousers that were his daddy's uniform. Picked out brightly in gold-colored wire thread, "United We Stand," the state government's logo and motto, glistened on the greatcoat's breast pocket, near a wide lapel. The hard fact was that on most mornings the Commonwealth was on much steadier legs than Charlie Phillips. In spite of his dignified appearance, the day that the old man, flat on his back in a doorway, tipped his hat primly and howdy-do'ed a spinster, he became a laughingstock. And if Gabe's laugh was bitter, who could tell?

But Gabe had got on inside his daddy's pitiable life, determined to burst out and save them. Drunkenness being a thing of romance only in the lore, however, Charlie Phillips had not lived to see it. Shrunken so skeletally that his greatcoat appeared to have consumed him, Charlie died when Gabe was barely fifteen years old. Gabe threw the doorman's uniform into the Hebron during that spring's muddy flood. Through it all, this same Judge in this red room and the rest of Milan had let Gabe head out under his own lead, dragging the reins. And while Gabe hustled pool, while he did any odd job he could lay his hand to, until he was old enough to pinhook tobacco, the entire town, except for Lucy Clement, had withheld everything but judgment. Until tonight. Tonight, according to the Honorable Judge Matthew Stallard, he was part of something. Wasn't that dandy as hell? Now that his fucking payroll paid rent on the whole place, Gabe had a share in the belonging.

Gabe had to ask: "And those common interests would be what?" How brazen would Stallard's explanation be?

"You're a tobacco man, Gabe. Good as any. Set your mind on that point in the curing where moisture suddenly makes a leaf pliable. When nature strikes its perfect balance between age and atmosphere and the plant can be handled without breaking up. You know what I mean. You know well the name of that stage."

Yes. Gabe knew the name. "Order," he said. "It's called order." When tobacco leaves came in order they were soft as neckties. And the rich smell of Burley was heaviest in the barns at that stage, putting forth a dark, moist aroma, redolent as a mix of earth and chocolate.

"Then you understand." The Judge also breathed deep.

"And 'why'?" Gabe interrupted their imaginary detour through the fields. "You said you wanted me to understand 'what happened and why'?" Gabe wanted to know where the Sheriff and the Coroner and Sonny Nolan fit. If Sonny fit. He wanted to see the town's hierarchy clearly. He wanted a name slotted into every tier below the top before he would admit understanding anything about the way they worked.

The Judge shrugged but there was no indifference in his tone. His answer was clear. "The way of life we want preserved depends on balance. Balance and that order we discussed."

Well, if they were setting themselves up as keepers, Gabe would by god rattle the bars. He would terrify them if he could, but he wouldn't be ignored. Not tonight. Not ever again.

"And, I gather, it's your particular way of life you've elected to preserve," Gabe stated firmly. "If there was a referendum, I don't think I had a vote."

For an instant the Judge looked uncertain. Gabe could feel the intensity of his own expression without touching his face. Did he have to use more words, or could Judge Stallard answer what he saw? "You're cocksure, aren't you?" Gabe added. His defiance felt almost lighthearted. "How comforting to be doubtless, absolutely doubtless that what you want is right."

Right there the Judge's features came out from behind themselves and hardened. "There is a purity, Gabe, in what is simple," he said icily.

Gabe knew the gloves were off. "Don't get nasty-nice with me. You're not talking about 'simple.' You're talking about rules, commandments."

"Simplicity is a nicer word, and I think a true one. But maybe there is a better way to state it. Humor me. Let's say that people must embrace and cling to certain values if they want to keep things spinning. The center holds, Phillips, because everything spins in place, and fast enough."

Gabe had to say it, "All these years and you never noticed. I tried but you didn't get it, did you?" Gabe's voice was down to a whisper. "I'm the usurper, your honor. New rules apply. And I have my own people to tend." He could see, though, exactly what the Judge described: the plate of Milan spinning like a top, a toy. So it was a game. That was the part Gabe had missed. Judge Stallard had brought him here, tonight, into this room at the center of the whirl, so Gabe could know, finally that, in truth, it was a game. And whose hand set it spinning? He had seen. He did know. Gabe guessed at last the trick it took to win. The secret was to make it count. Gabe had their secret now.

But Stallard had been right about one thing. Unlike this afternoon, Gabe presently sat fearless before the Judge. "Are you saying that you rigged the Grand Jury?" Gabe asked.

The Judge's denial was wordless, at first. Watery green light rippled across his forehead when he shook his head. "You see, Gabe, using that word 'rigged.' A man wants subtlety. You need things to hurt. What we did, if you have to know, was create an atmosphere. That's all. A gentler climate of opinion. I suppose that postponing the Grand Jury hearing to October was the most overt thing we did. But we had reasons, medical reports, a crowded docket. All good reasons.

Plausible. And with respect to your Miss Oliver, Milan was woefully short of sympathy for her from the start. If we adjusted the rain somewhat, who's to blame us for the harvest? Do you complain, by any chance, of the result?"

Gabe winced to hear "Miss Oliver" tossed out as weightlessly as any other words. They were so smug, these men. He felt momentarily powerless. He, himself, had made this happen. How dare they take the credit? Gabe salved his sense of having won the day, of having orchestrated his own redemption. For if he had done so, he could win his life back. Gabe could protect himself from himself and keep Clara and Lucy and even Nonie safe. He was in control. And if the desperate debt of Joyce Oliver was payable, here had been its infinite beginning.

Gabe felt compelled to talk back, to give Stallard's harsh question its equally hard answer. "I complain of your assumption that you and a bunch of jumped-up farmers and schoolteachers pulled something off. I want to know if Sonny Nolan was in on it. Just how smalltime was this deal?"

Stallard chuckled. It was a sign to Gabe of the Judge's certainty of privilege. For this was anything but funny. Gabe's dragon anger surged. He wanted to sweep the desk, to push those cursed knickknacks over the edge, to hear them crash, clattering to the floor. He would grind the shattered crystal beneath his shoe soles until the particles were fine as sand. Instead, Gabe deliberately retrieved his pocket flap from inside his jacket pocket and breathed a steady fire that heated up the room.

If the Judge sensed a rise in tension, he chose to ignore it. His response was mild. "I am aware, Gabe, that you and Sonny Nolan are an awkward match. Poor Counselor Nolan is as anxious to please as

154

you are unwilling. Well, many say there is no justice. But no. Sonny was never included in the planning, just the plans."

Gabe pressed. "So, I'm guessing the cabal was you and Sheriff Gilliam and Buell Smith?"

"And the Coroner."

"That's all it takes around here to rule the roost?" Gabe's voice was shrill. "Jesus God!" he said, too loud. The Judge's seeming amiability vanished. He chastised Gabe shortly: "Please. I'm sure Belinda is awake. Here we keep a *peaceful* house."

Gabe doubted that a small explosion of minor profanity could damage a woman on whom even time had no effect. Yet he would spare her in honor of what he felt was owed. He dropped his tone and seethed: "Yes, well, above all else, let us not be rude. We wouldn't want sleep disturbed over the tiny issue of lives being used as pawns."

"Ahhh." The Judge's own voice has risen. "You accuse us! Of what, may I ask, Mr. Phillips? Hubris? Ever hear the cautionary tale of pots and kettles?" Matthew Stallard's eyebrows flared at first before settling, darkly, over his next sentence. "We're down to it, aren't we?"

Gabe let the full silence of his answer sink in. Then asked if there was anything more.

The Judge answered as if from a depth. "You do know, Gabe, that the Grand Jury could reconsider. If there were to be a so-called 'public outcry' it is legally possible for this to come up again. Jeopardy does not attach from a hearing. You must tread carefully, more ways than one. Very, very carefully."

The mean chill in the room and the warning gripped Gabe, his throat tightened: "You mean I'm out on good behavior. Lifetime parole."

155

"In a small town, over a thing like this, yes, that's so."

"And this cage of a place is the perfect world you want preserved?"

"I never said perfect, Gabe. 'Workable' was the word. You're the one who demands perfection." Stallard all but shook his finger.

How dare the man? Gabe knew what he knew. "I think this little 'come to Jesus' talk is over." Let Matt Stallard take that how he would. As soon as he spoke, Gabe was desperate for seclusion, for his own rooms in his own house where he could at least seek the solace of regret. When he stood, his movement was abrupt. "I will see myself out," he declared. "I'm needed at Tyrone." The prospect of the silent ride so close to the river, the anticipated, almost sexual allure of solitude and the long curving drive down from Milan to Tyrone swept Gabe suddenly.

Gabe looked back at Stallard from the library door. The Judge's face had a benign expression, but it bled through the shadows in a sinister way.

"You're a despot," Gabe said.

"I'm just."

Gabe didn't accept the tinge of sadness in Judge Stallard's distant voice.

The long hallway was whiter now, between the red room and the dark. Gabe avoided his image in the mirror. Unaccompanied, his limp felt more pronounced. He didn't wish to see.

Since morning, the door had cracked open on such a vast internal space, Gabe half expected the earth to have fallen away and to step outside into nothingness. At first he felt weightless, out the door, descending. But on the bottom step he tripped over an iron ornament, a bootscraper, and reality broke open. There had been no magic; Gabe was crippled as he had been, ever tethered to himself. But all else had changed. Why had he stayed bent on storming Judge Matthew Stallard's stronghold? Lucy came forcefully to mind. His own lusty wife with her fierce love and anger and strength versus that dignity of the Judge's wife. Gabe had wasted himself on men. Here were these women, all of them, Clara and Lucy and Nonie, even Joyce and Belinda Stallard and others. Here before him, the filaments of their differences and subtleties dangled softly in the dark. Gabe was tantalized; he could almost touch them. If he reached with all his power, he might yet gather their strands and re-braid his life.

The revelation pulled him forward, and Gabe retraced his steps downtown. It was enough to lift him from the Judge's purgatory. Gabe's earlier sense of freedom began to reassert itself. By the time he made the left from Oxford, the last bit of crust from Stallard's Milan had crumbled and been brushed away.

Half a block behind Gabe, measured footfalls fell eerily on Montgomery Avenue against the slant of his sideheavy tread. Gabe wondered briefly if the old man he had seen earlier was still wandering somewhere in the dark. But the sound Gabe truly attended on his way to the car was the quiet suck of his own breath, freely drawn. Reprieve.

CHAPTER 21

The Mixing Zone

IRA HUNG BACK when Gabe entered the house with the Judge, but not too far. The washy blue dusk was camouflage enough. In it, Ira Truitt could have been anything, he thought: an idler, out for a twilight stroll, some casual husband, even, whose wife would hurt her lips against his cold, sandpaper cheek when he returned. Ira briefly touched his face. Whatever else he was, this night of October 17, 1953, Ira was certain that the men up ahead were self-important. Too much so to bother with the likes of him.

And they soon proved it to his satisfaction. The careless pair didn't give a single backward glance before climbing steps and disappearing through a glossy black door set in a surround of cut-glass panes. The illumination spilling out when they entered blinded him. As suddenly closed as opened, the doorway stayed darkly afloat in its own luminous frame, a gleaming, solitary mouth into a cave.

Then Ira made his move. Almost on tiptoe, he crept near the house. At the base of the steps Ira turned left and sidled between a row of boxwoods and a wall of rough brick. He groped his way around the corner and along the elevated foundation, wary at every twig's snap but encouraged by the familiar smell of rotten mulch. Way at the back of the structure, a pudding of light spread onto shrubbery under a window. When he reached the source of the light, the room where Gabe and the older man sat, Ira's eyes were just above the level of the sill. He must look like graffiti he had seen as a child. It had been a simply outlined devil's head drawn so that only the top of the cranium, the brain case, showed above a line meant to be a wall. The legend written underneath had been chilling: The Devil Is Watching You. The hollow-eyed drawing and the words had haunted Ira. Some faithless soul had even carved the horned, domed forehead with its satanic message on the back of a pew at church. Ira had been craven with fear as a youngster that he himself had whittled out the leering face when in the grip of evil, as he was often accused of being. The cartoon had even become audible in the recurrent nightmares of his childhood. What did the sound and symbols mean? He could have never faced his father's derision to ask. Ira shivered away the image and came back where he was.

Inside the room, only the desk lamp was lit, revealing Gabe Phillips, sitting opposite the Judge, on Ira's left.

Ira could barely choke down his excitement. He backed away and flattened himself against a shutter. This was the closest he had been. He screwed his neck around taut as a stopper and fixed on the view. Gabe and his companion looked heavily still, except for their mouths, against a red background. At the Dixie restaurant it had been eyes, swimming in pairs and colorful. Here it was lips. Gabe's seldom moved. Ira strained to hear their words until he saw that the window's panes were covered with a thick slab of outer glass which silenced the men completely. But the dumb show Ira watched told much. His knowledge of the world had always come from what he saw; the spoken world had been brutal to old Ira from the start.

Ira studied Gabe Phillips' lips intently. His mouth was emphatic, crimson, and wet around the few words Gabe did use; his tongue showed. The other man, the mighty judge, talked often, though his lips weren't essential for the act.

Ira had wedged himself between a metal pole that supported a geometric aluminum contraption that was rigged up on the roof and a bushy pyracantha. Its pomes of pumpkin-colored fruit were clustered near his temple. Time melted for Ira while he watched, transfixed.

Finally, in minutes or hours, both men inside the red room stood. Then Gabe left the room, alone. With a jolt, Ira anxiously twisted around to fly his prickly nest and creep back the way he came. He imagined Gabe's journey, inside the house, on a course parallel with his own. In Ira's haste, mean little switches of spiraea, out for blood, entangled his arms, but he pulled away, unflinching, and he equally ignored the pyracantha thorns that razored through his thick twill trousers and sliced his calves like rubber.

Just as Ira reached the corner where masonry gave on to an iron balustrade, Gabe emerged from the black doorway above and to the left of Ira's head. Nightfall had by now swallowed Ira down completely and he knew it. Excited, his hands clenched over his mouth, Ira watched, looking up from no more than a few feet away. Phillips stood silhouetted for a moment in the tunnel of light cast by the open entryway.

Ira gave Gabe a head start and didn't move until he could see him a far piece down the block. But this time Ira wouldn't be so silent when he stepped out to follow. From the outset, he snapped glassy blades of frosted grass beneath his feet. Then, emboldened, Ira dragged his heavy boots across the sidewalk in an exaggerated mimicry of Gabe's stride. A pull of one boot, then a quick step with the other. Ira's bootsoles rasped across the concrete like repeated gasps of dying breath. He halfway hoped that Gabe would hear him covering the ground between them, and that the noise would grate Gabe's nerves as raw as Ira's had been that long night on the river, the night that Phillips yelled his vicious curse, his demand for Ira's damning at the hands of God. No man whose life was as vacant and bitter as Ira's should be cursed and damned from such a height.

Ira was exhilarated to be on the move again after being cramped up against the brick wall. He kept his eyes glued onto the tick-tock stick of Gabe's figure while his peripheral vision scanned every house they passed. Most of the odd frame structures that lined Montgomery Street had elaborate wraparound porches and turrets with cone shaped roofs. Many sported at least one stained-glass window. Late as the hour was, fractured, multicolored shards of electric light danced up and down both sides of the street. In the ghostly glow of moonlight, the layout looked bizarre to Ira.

At the corner of Main, Gabe Phillips paused. Ira stopped also. For the first time since he had started skulking after Phillips, Ira stayed in plain view under the half moon. While Gabe turned slowly and looked back, Ira, in equally slow motion, bent down and picked up a large, smooth rock. It was cold in his palm and as heavy as a minnieball.

Gabe cocked his head curiously but didn't hesitate long. He angled right and headed up toward town. Gabe's car was parked diagonally under a streetlamp near the side entrance to the courthouse. Since it was late, for Milan, Gabe's was the sole vehicle in the area. But the spotless, cream-colored convertible, a mound of enameled meringue on a dish of chrome, would have stood out, like Sophie's prize dessert, from any fifty others on the square.

Ira aimed his eyes at the car's small, bomb-shaped hood ornament, which nosed out visibly from the front grille, wetly new-looking. He had never driven a car. Ira could not imagine what it would be to do so. Perhaps like flying. From a vantage point on the bluff above the road, he had enviously watched Gabe Phillips head for home on several nights over the past weeks. The car ran smooth as a knife, peeling the skin of the knob, winding all the way down, Ira imagined, to Tyrone.

Ira ducked into the indented entry to Lovin's Grocery and listened while Gabe started his car's ignition. The engine turned over with a deep, satisfying rattle that began small then stretched out. Instantly Ira drew his arm back high above his head and held it there, cocked like a skeet pull, until the convertible was within range. When he let fly, the stone cracked sharply against Gabe's passenger side window but didn't shatter the safety glass. The car jolted to a screeching stop at the crosswalk. Gabe emerged halfway, furious. His dark satin eyebrows almost made an *X* on his forehead. He searched the shadows, scowling. Ira knew he wasn't seen. Gabe faced a direction well to Ira's left side and yelled, "You lousy bastard. You *better* hide. You better get as far as you can get."

"Bastard!" Ira trembled when he heard it. The voice and the word. This time Gabe's voice wavered, Ira thought, thinned out by the space it had to fill. It was not the boundless and awful cry of "God Damn

You" he remembered from last August on the narrow river. Ira wanted to weep. How could Phillips know that Ira had to get his attention? Gabe was all he had. Ira's heart kicked, *ka-boom, ka-boom,* against his ribs, sharp as the rock which had smacked so near Gabe's head.

After a quarter hour, Ira stumped awkwardly off in the same direction Gabe had sped. He saw himself reflected in pieces on the moonlit storefronts that he passed, severed by their angles into all his bitter parts.

Once he got going, Ira soon cleared the town. Another forty-five minutes and he had hiked the two miles from the courthouse to the point where a mottled-zinc snake of guardrail began its crawl down to Tyrone settlement. His solitary hike was uninterrupted. It wasn't unknown for a stray vehicle to stop and offer him a late-night ride or for him to hitch. But not tonight. And lucky for the driver, Ira thought. Tonight he coveted his own brooding and would nurse it for hours.

With a guttural grunt, Ira clambered over the railing. He was proud of his shortcut, and had he been a man with any friend he would have boasted. He studied the series of rock ledges that jutted from the hillside at that point. They cropped out at intervals all the way down to the creek-bed that creased the bottom of the ravine, two hundred feet below. It was a steep and dangerous decline. If he plopped flat on his behind, Ira had found a way to use the limestone shelving as a staircase.

Ira eased, heavily, out onto the lip of the nearest stone and then ooched his way, lifting on the heels of his hands from rock to rock, like a big, uncertain baby. Careful of dangerously broken beer bottles and loose shale and sharp-edged pinecones, he felt hypervigilant. Everything was out to wound him if it could.

After his arduous descent to the depths of the hollow Ira caught his breath. The air was a fragrant tea of fresh water and cedar. In the moonlight, Clear Creek trickled quietly. Ira leaned over the creek's bank and brushed a soft patter of debris from his coveralls. Nearby, a wavery line of light bounced from the creekstones then ran along the trunk of a towering old sycamore. With that aid, Ira fished around the tree's base for a small fallen limb. He wanted hickory or oak, but he knew there were few hardwoods down here in the deep cleft between the knobs. When Ira found a walking stick that could take his weight, he stood so suddenly that his head drained of blood and sense and sight. Of everything but pungent creekbed odors and his utter sense of desolation.

Ira made his way along the stream. His boat was exactly where he had left it beached, on the mudflat at the mixing zone of Clear Creek and the Hebron. On arrival, Ira grasped an oarlock with his free hand. His rough stick of a cane clanked against the dory's bottom.

There was a cotton-like burr on the moon. The sky was a filmy backdrop behind its muted light. Ira set off in the boat and skimmed his way down the Hebron toward Gabe's camp. His oars dipped without a ripple. How well could Phillips sleep with this burr on his soul, Ira wondered, and all his sins set out plain against it? Did he dream of judgment?

In the two months since Ira started watching, somehow Gabe's simple fishing camp had given birth to a house. That first night Ira spied, the place had looked unfinished or, as he thought then, abandoned. Timbers had stuck up on the river side at different heights. Bales of wire were tossed wastefully. Several planks scattered on the slope had appeared ripe and ready for the taking.

The Mixing Zone

Tonight, as Ira's flat-bottomed boat closed on the site, ironing the Hebron silky smooth, all was orderly at Gabe's. The once tangled hillside had been mowed and manicured. Attached to the house, partitioned segments of a fine screened porch watched the river like a compound eye. It was insufferable to Ira that Gabe Phillips' house should have displayed such order and serenity when his own was what it was.

Out in the main river channel, Ira pulled up the oars and held them dripping, parallel to the river's surface while he allowed the boat to float itself past Gabe's beach. The house above the Hebron was completely dark. It looked like nothing more than a black hole of definite shape in the foliage on the bluff.

Ira lay back in his boat. If a barge shoved its way blindly downriver, the way one often did this time of night, the throb of its great pumps, pulsing louder and louder through the channel in advance of its appearance, would allow Ira time to reach the bank. Once, having heard the warning and headed to the side, Ira saw a deer poised on the slope above Gabe's float. The animal had stood, one clean hoof raised, ears pricked forward, and waited to see what would round the bend to the beat of that terrifying heart.

Tonight Ira defiantly stayed in the center of the Hebron, drawn downstream by a puckered little strip of current. He leaned back until his heavy head rested on the rear seat slat. He thought that he might even sleep. Weightlessly perhaps in spite of loss. The river's smooth unreeling had consoled him. Sixty years' burdens were dissolving like specters into the gathering fog.

The old, red plastic seat cushion Ira used for a pillow crinkled softly against his ears while he settled. The cushion was ripped in the middle but comfortable enough. Because his round, metal-rimmed eyeglasses had pressed deep into his temples, Ira started to remove them. He pulled at the thin goldplate wires that held them in place then dropped his hands and left the spectacles where they were. Eyes closed, Ira's senses were more keen than ever. The smell of mildew from the torn cushion and the sound of lapping water and the river's utter softness against his trailing fingers folded into a dream of Orena. It was a wispy dream that danced tiny reflected stars onto the coin-shaped lenses over Ira's eyelids as he rocked inside the boat. His face looked almost gentle in repose. A thing so vastly different from what he really was.

CHAPTER 22

Thanksgiving

On a cold, cloudless November afternoon, Clara sat cross-leggedy on the front-porch floor in Hickman. Tempted by the blistered paint near her knee, she picked and flaked until she had excavated more than a teaspoonful of red, brown, and green scales. Her finger-nails were too short to do a thorough job on the floorboards, but since her alternatives were to merely sit and jiggle or fall back into chewing her fingers and tearing the minuscule and sweetly painful tags of flesh from around her cuticle, Clara kept at the porch.

"Come on, come on!" she said under her breath. Clara wanted to rattle the glass door pane but that was the last thing she could get by with today. She had, after all, come outside to stay out of trouble. Lucy seemed as delicate as a basket of eggshells this afternoon. The softest tiptoes started cracks. And inside the house, where Clara now glimpsed the trailing brushstroke of her mother's dress, time had dragged by sooo slowly you could almost see it droop.

Clara shivered while she sat and worked. A couple of weeks ago

*I*T WAS THE GOODNESS OF THE PLACE

Hickman had suddenly turned winter. Hot, gray days changed into dreary, cold ones, practically overnight. That was the way things happened in this town, without subtlety or transition, and Clara felt that she was always playing catch-up.

At this moment Clara was so covered with chill bumps that the tiny hairs on her arms and legs prickled straight out. She refused to wear her winter coat. Its buttons and seams clamped too tight and it looked funny too, all squinched in at the waist. So Clara picked and waited for Lucy, bumpy as a cucumber.

When her mother finally did come out, Clara knew that Lucy would have piled herself deep under a tower of their belongings, from the ham platter to umbrellas. Lucy would also be trailing work papers from both elbows, keys ajangle on her right thumb, and worry plain in her eyes that her own child was within an inch of saying something hateful. "Go on," Mother would then prod, all bulky and encumbered, using her hipbone as a doorstop for the storm-screen. "Say something smart."

Well, Clara could have. She could have done just that. She had a sudden ease with sass that made it seem nearly like a calling. It was a gift that had appeared as if by magic, Clara thought, on her eleventh birthday. It would be easy pickings to mock all Lucy's plant waterings and leaf pinchings and drawers patted closed, her repeated "last" trips through the house making sure the pilot light was on and all the faucets off.

But Clara had come out here rather than say a word about Lucy's dithers. (After the fashion of Nonie, Clara aimed to be wiser than she let on, for once.) Unless she could control her mouth and make it do exactly what she wanted this afternoon, Clara was keeping her trap shut. And if all the tenderness she felt inside flowered in her cheeks and smiling silence, maybe Mother would be comforted and feel less fearful of going with Clara to Tyrone for the holiday.

She could now hear her mother from inside the house. Lucy had mumbled and fumbled closer to the door, anyway. Her proximity put Clara on notice that it was time to concentrate on the car trip. It was important to get the mood exactly right from the outset. None of that sighing her mother hated. Clara would sweeten up her tone as much as possible, not too sugary (Mother would be suspicious), but real nice. Clara hadn't done badly so far, she had to admit: tomorrow would be the first time in five years that Gabe and Lucy Phillips had been together except at doorways. Mother was going to actually step into Daddy's house and sit down and eat Nonie's holiday meal. And wouldn't Clara's feathers fluff in the warmth of her parents' talk? And if they laughed, oh, if they laughed, wouldn't her light soul fly? That sound alone could soothe them all in their sadness over Joyce.

Hmph. Clara saw that she had gotten way wide of the point and reined herself in. For the rest of the afternoon she aimed to be nothing more than a determined bolt of hope headed right for the heart of the weekend. No speculation. All plan but no action. Clara was sorry but she could take no chances. Because with this much moving of her mother and daddy already accomplished, Clara saw the stamp of something real on her imaginings. They could well be arriving at the answer end of prayer. It was a settled fact, in Clara's mind, that miracles might occur.

And at that exact moment one of them actually did. Her mother came out of the front door.

"Really, Clara, for pity's sake! Get up, get your coat on and help me here."

Clara did jump up but it was hard to know exactly where to put her hand in and what to disentangle that wouldn't upset the whole affair of her mother's accumulation. Lucy looked dangerously atilt. After a brief survey, Clara snaked her hand toward the slick brown purse that was precariously wedged between her mother's midriff and an elbow. She slid the bag out and nothing toppled. All right then. That was exactly the kind of sly smoothie Clara wanted to be for the next four days.

While she mulled her next move, Clara traced the handbag's big, fake alligator grains with her fingertips. The glossy pattern was almost as satisfying to the touch as the rosary Clara pined for. What good were Baptists anyway if they didn't get the good stuff? It was beads she wanted, beads aglow from inside that were as slick and bright as jellies. That's what Clara needed. She could really get God's attention if she had a rosary. Especially a red one.

Lucy's exasperated voice jarred her. "Well," her mother said, "here we go, ready or not. I hope you're satisfied." Lucy looked as if her words and her mind were on two very different subjects. Before they left the porch, Lucy wrenched the locked door's handle, then twisted it a final, final time, all the while eyeing Clara sideways. After Lucy had had her say about Clara's satisfaction and more or less poured all she carried onto the back seat, she "simmered" down, as she would call it, and they were in the car and the car was moving, leaving Hickman, weaving the curvy road that wormed its way between raw red mining gullies and abandoned quarries, on the way to Daddy's for Thanksgiving.

Lucy had told Clara about these quarries on that first drive down to Hickman the day they left Milan. The story she told then was that the quarrystone had long since "played out." Even though it was almost half her life ago, that fateful trip and its details were as vivid as a reeling film in Clara's mind. Today, Lucy didn't mention them, but every few miles, while they were still close enough to Hickman to be in coal country, Clara noted the round, quarried sites that pocked the land's surface. Gouged empty of rock, the pits stood filled with water and, between their white rock sockets and the sky, reflected, like huge, unblinking eyes, a brilliant turquoise liquid that was absolutely still. Clara winked, slowly, at each of the deep, deep pools they passed. They were the one feature that she would transport to Milan with her, if she were able. There would be no night fears then. She could dream while they kept a gelid, sleepless watch.

But things being more or less reversed between her and Lucy on this trip, Clara figured she'd better tend to the business at hand. It was high time to get things going on the line to Lucy's heart. Clara piped up with a sure thing: "How are the Peays?" she asked. Elmer and Nunnelly Peay were two of the coal miners in Mother's case load at work. While Lucy considered, her face softened and folded and lit and shaded as roadside thickets and clearings alternately bound and freed the sun. "I don't know," Lucy's tone was weary. "I don't have a single miner without a croupy baby," she said.

Lucy's job at the area Social Security Office, coordinating benefits with qualifying miners, had filled considerably more than forty hours a week from the day they arrived in Hickman. The way her mother told it, the men Lucy was charged with helping had trouble in their lives that was as hard to remove as the shiny lumps of bright black coal that they dug out by the hardest and that had, in turn, chipped away their health. And the harder Lucy worked to try and sustain the ailing miners with whatever government aid was available, the more embedded their health and family troubles seemed. However, it seemed to Clara that Lucy had taken to office work as if she'd been thirsty for it all her life, bone dry up until now. Clara's only chance to bind her mother near, she thought, had been to throw herself in on the helping side and hold on tight. Being only eleven years old certainly didn't mean you were of no account.

Lucy elaborated on her answer to Clara's question about the Peay brothers. At least her mother's voice seemed to rise a little while she talked. "I've written a request for a 'Total and Permanent' on Nunnelly," Lucy said. "Who knows. If Elmer qualifies for the designation, his brother should. They both went down in the mines as teens. Their lungs are equally bad."

Clara knew well what "Total and Permanent" meant. When Lucy could wrangle it, the government would pension off a man if one day he came up from the shafts so cramped he couldn't straighten his spine and go back down, or if he had breathed dust and dust and dust until his lungs were caked with soot and wouldn't take in air, except like creaky bellows. After Lucy's vivid explanation about lungs, Clara had overbreathed for weeks, trying to keep hers pink.

In order to obtain benefits, Lucy had to prove the miner's misery on government forms using check marks and *X*'s. Clara had helped file the completed submissions. To her, they looked more like math than pleadings, and she wondered who on earth in Washington could resurrect a needy being from such a form as that.

Most nights when Clara went to bed, her mother was at the dining room table, head bent, at the center of a ring of cigarette smoke and scattered papers, trying again for some miner whose case had been rejected. What Clara last saw before sleep was often her mother's topknot, bobbing in the smoky light, bright as embers.

It was her mother's frequently stated opinion that her supervisor was "less than no help at all." Lucy described him as "offhand" and had been upset when he referred, in front of Clara, to his job and her mother's as "sucking at the public tit." Clara's eyes had popped wide, white and open, when she heard that one. She knew the man had not cursed exactly, but his words had a kind of smear about them that Daddy's actual cusswords never did.

Clara had seen laid-off miners who didn't get the government stamp for the "Total" part, meaning 100 percent disability, of the designation that Lucy wanted for them. On Saturdays the bureau was open until noon. It was those denied men who waited near the Department's office all the weekend morning. Their ribs and breast-bones had bulged forward from years of wheezing until they milled around the hall in the Federal Building as chicken breasted as a yard full of hens. They all smoked cigarettes while they stood. Since being laid off, their idle hands had changed color from soot gray to tobacco yellow. Each miner lovingly inhaled his Lucky Strike or Camel regular (Clara never saw a single one of the fancy new filtered kind) down to a minuscule stub. Before they ground one out and lit another, they pinched the half-inch butt between a thumb and forefinger and all but shut their eyes (in pain or pleasure, Clara couldn't tell) while they sucked hard to get every last bit of good out of the tobacco, pinkies raised as if hoisting tiny cups of tea. But there was no mistaking their swelled-out chests for pride. That was "Permanent."

Usually Lucy could manage some kind of help. Her name was "out in the community," she said, and she meant to live up to it. Clara thought their address must be "out" too. Sometimes, late of an evening, a miner's wife would rap lightly on the back kitchen window. The women's sallow faces hung sadly in the panes like vining gourds. Last Sunday night the supplicant who tapped on the blistered glass had been shoeless. When Lucy brought her inside, Clara was pained to see that the woman had tied an old, fringed headscarf around each long, blue foot. Even though the scarves were dingy, the effect was clownishly out of keeping with the need. Clara wanted to grab all her own laceups and every one of Lucy's high heels from the closet and would have then filled the lady's arms, piling on coffee cans and lard tins, until the poor soul was anchored in the center of the room and couldn't leave their warm kitchen ever. (Clara would have more than gladly donated her own hideous winter coat but doubted that ridding herself of something detestable actually qualified as goodness.)

But whatever they asked for or received, Clara saw that what the families wanted most of was her mother. Clara understood the truth of that. And they were right to do so. But work on those lives was using Lucy up completely. If Clara couldn't fix things soon between her mother and daddy, she was terrified that she would go hunting for Lucy one day and her mother would be nothing but a smudge of coal dust on a messy desk.

Well, her mother was here now, and she was in this very car and going home, for the first time, to visit Gabe's house on the river. And Clara wanted Lucy to be as glad as she was about it.

"Let's sing," Clara said, suddenly. That was the idea.

"Sing? Sing what?" Lucy asked.

"'Farther Along,'" Clara answered without any hesitation. She knew the words to this particular hymn by heart. The song came close

174

to being a specialty of the congregation at the Trammell Baptist Church, where several of Lucy's "families" worshiped. The white-frame Congregation House, as they called it, was in the center of an area called Little Trammell, after the creek that ran nearby. Lucy went out there fairly often to deliver food or late checks for the miners when she could catch them in one spot. Each time, Clara had listened raptly to all the hymns (secretly she planned to go to an all-night sing just as soon as she was old enough), but "Farther Along" was far and away her favorite. She loved the "country catch," as Lucy called it, where the voice hooked up on a little gasp, at the end of the first phrase.

Clara had seen at once that the way to sing this song was loud and through your nose, and it was pure pleasure to get it going, and the singing made Clara forget most everything else while she was bellowing out. And if she carried the tune, her mother would harmonize, wrapping her clear strong voice as close as a vine around Clara's thinner vocal line until the sound was as proudly teary as a wail.

"Farther along, we'll know more about it," the two of them started almost simultaneously and on the same F above middle C.

"Farther along, we'll understand *whyyyy* . . ."

Clara gave it all she could. Lucy sang with her and didn't split her notes off into harmony until they got to the long "why" of the second line, but when she did go off on her own, she went strong, and by the time they were into the "Cheer up my darlin'," Lucy had taken over the emotion of the piece and was matching her driving to the words. The road had cooperated to the extent that there was a little highway rise that built and then dropped smack on the word "darlin'" and ran along low while Clara and Lucy huskily crooned "Live in the sunshine," before building back up to a big finish with "Farther along in the great by and *byyyyy,*" putting all the catch they each could into "a-long" and lingering with a lot of sad love over the last "by." The whole thing was about as satisfying as could be, and Clara could have just burst when they finished and the final sounds died with the afternoon's slowly dimming light.

All this time, the highway slid away under the car, tipping down behind them or up in front. Clara knew State Road 489 as well as she knew the watery woodgrain of their kitchen table, the narrow parts and where it widened, where it fell off the edges toward Tyrone on one end, mine shafts on the other.

They had been traveling for about an hour. Clara was snug. Mother talked along about Nunnelly, her alto voice shaded with concern. A lace of bare redbud and dogwood trees, backlit by winter sun, dropped curtains just off the highway's shoulders. They had fused, Clara and Lucy and the car. They were all one thing.

Tires on gravel woke Clara. It was pitch dark outside. Mother was behind the wheel softly breathing words. "Well, Clara," she sighed, "you're home." Her hands were in driving position even though the coupe was still.

For an instant Clara thought Lucy would leave her here alone, in the house by the Hebron. Mother was going to drop her off then pull away from Gabe's front door the way she always did. Even in the dark, her mother's eyes were as bright as dashboard lights. When Lucy opened the driver's side door, everything Clara was hoping welled up, but she kept silent. Then Lucy climbed out and then, of a sudden, there was Nonie. And back in the short hallway Clara could see Gabe. All the four of them had to do was squeeze by this uncertainty. Tomorrow would be easier.

What floated them through to the kitchen was Nonie. She offered food; she promised Cambric tea for Clara. "Miz Lucy," this and that, she said, and held Clara at her side, and Clara and Mother and Daddy bobbed through the big center room tethered to the boat of Nonie. Immediately, Clara's head was full of Joyce. Was that where? Was that? Clara felt Gabe's hands like pads on her skinny shoulders as they went. He said "Clara" many times and told her that they had "bought the ham and olives that you like." Then said, "You came." And again, "You're here."

The four of them pressed into the white shine and yellow light of Gabe's small kitchen, and each one found a place to sit or stand. Nonie went back to the porcelain sink and started chopping onions on a board fitted over the basin's ridged, sloping drain. Clara and Lucy sat at the corner table. Gabe stood almost in front of the door, leaning stiffly against the jamb. Gabe and Mother watched each other longer at a time, then back to Clara or Nonie.

"You were safe on the road, then," Gabe said. His words were limited but real. "And no trouble with the car? I wondered about the car, or if you'd had a flat." Daddy looked, to Clara, more worried than he should have been about their direct trip, a journey often ordinary.

Lucy gave a start on a smile, but she avoided Gabe's questioning gaze and scanned Clara's face, instead. "We got away a little late," she said. "I had those things to bring."

Gabe offered to go back with her to the car for the platter and their bag. Clara noted the quiet of her mother's "No" to Gabe and that Lucy added "Please," in the much more final tone of "Thank you."

When her mother returned from the neverland outside the kitchen door, Nonie said that there were jobs enough for hours. Gabe told a

177

little story about the "lawyer Nolan's self-importance" to Lucy. Mother put her knuckles to her lips and almost laughed aloud a time or two.

Nonie was the boss of chores. Clara cracked small, blond hickory nuts out of a granite bowl and sometimes ate the nutmeat. Not one grownup said she couldn't do it. She threw out, unbroken, all the shells where worms had made a minute bore. Why not give a worm the world of his undoing? Let the little fatso live it up awhile, Clara thought, he'd never get back out that pin-sized hole.

Lucy and Nonie seemed well aware of what they each could do. Nonie blended country ham and onions and celery and sausage and the hickory nuts together in a heavy metal grinder that was clamped to the sinkboard. Mother dipped into a bubble-topped tin of oysters and lifted out a handful mounded on her palms, then layered the miniature, pearlized pillows on alternating beds of saltine crumbs. Gabe soaped the turkey in the sink like a heavy, naked baby. All talk was of ingredients; the words were warm and smelled of sage.

The arms and hands of her adults fascinated Clara. The way they moved. Nonie turned the grinder handle slowly, round and round at an even, steady speed. With her other palm, she caught the stuffing, one plump dollop at a time, and molding as she moved, winding the handle as she molded, Nonie tucked the egg-shaped packets snugly into a glass baker that sat a few inches away. Mother's fingers lifted above and lightly in and out of her creamy oyster pudding as delicately as dancers on a cloud, and Daddy's strong arms guided the slippery clean, fourteen-pound bird with such sure grace, it could have weighed an ounce.

Clara wished she possessed long fingers and willowy arms and hoped when she was fully grown she would have the skills she witnessed. Something else was in it, though, she knew. There were secrets beyond size. Clara was already almost as big as Nonie, and Clara was only in the fifth grade. She wasn't the biggest fifth-grade girl, either. But she could hold her own. She scrambled on the monkey bars at school, braids sailing behind, as agile as any monkey. Clara had lately used the interlocking pipes of the jungle gym to swing away from all the taunts. Singsong, a few came through, over the slap of her fists gripping from rod to rod, "Your daddy is a . . ." or "Mother loves the miners, *na, na* . . ." The miners' children went to the county school out the pike and down a dirt road. They didn't have to hear themselves jeered. But maybe having quick hands, hands like her own, hands that were learning to fly fast and faster than even Mother's and Nonie's, meant that Clara could grow up and stand in a yolk of light as yellow as tonight's, doing pretty work that smelled like sugar ribbons or a blend of sage and bay.

Mother patted the oyster pudding done and began cracking eggshells to make meringues. She used the shells' halves as tiny, sharp-edged cups and poured the whites from cup to cup until the yellows were completely separate. She set them, glistening, aside for later use in béchamel. Next, Lucy whipped the eggwhites and smoothly added one teaspoonful of sugar after another. Yellowish foam turned thick, then slick, and finally into blue-white peaks that curled like stationary waves and lapped up high above an elongated aluminum bowl. Satisfied, Lucy disengaged one of the beaters from the head of Gabe's old Mixmaster and handed it over.

"Lick," she said to Clara. "And then it's time for bed."

The house only had two bedrooms. Nonie led Clara to the one

where she always slept, on the other side of the bathroom from Daddy's. From the side of the double bed, Nonie watched and waited while Clara put on a flannel nightgown and climbed under the sheets. Even though she eyed her intently, Clara could tell that Nonie was seeing and thinking clear off in another direction.

"You leave your Momma and Daddy alone and let them talk, you hear?"

"Yes, ma'am," Clara said, politely. Clara was all full of asking, only she didn't dare mention it. Nonie had already announced in the kitchen that she was "leaving out." No point in trying to hold her back then, because when Nonie started leaving she was gone.

But Nonie didn't move. "I see you looking," she said. "You got something important to say to Nonie?"

Clara probably had only one chance. She'd better find out the worst thing. "Will we eat in there?" Daddy's house didn't have a dining room. There was just the kitchen at one end and the two bedrooms and bath opposite. The hollow room with its huge fireplace ran between. No point in even asking about the porch.

"I expect you'll eat where he puts the table. In front of the fireplace, I reckon. You haven't done all this gathering together, have you, Clara, to show out about the room? There's enough trouble, as it is. Don't go borrowing from tomorrow."

"But will it be all right?"

"It'll be what it is, child." Nonie rose and faced her real hard. "You just sit tight when your mother comes to bed. She'll be along shortly. You got to show some gumption, Clara. I know you got some."

In Milan, if she went uptown with Gabe, there were a few old sort of Sunday school ladies who grabbed Clara and scrubbed her cheek with their bristly chins every time they could get her in their clutches. Clara usually turtled when they came at her because this wasn't a family where hugs were passed around like biscuits for just anyone to grab. Nonie, specially, wasn't much for touching at all. But for once Nonie now leaned forward. She picked up Clara's hand and held it against her ropey, darkskinned throat as if Clara were deaf and she wanted her to understand the words by feel.

"You rise and shine early, Clara, 'cause I'm coming first thing. We'll play names and anything you want while that turkey gets to gleaming in the oven. Child, we're going to have us a day! You'll see if Nonie didn't tell you right."

A few minutes after Nonie left, extinguishing herself and Clara and the room with a snap of the light switch, Clara felt the bed shift downward under Lucy's weight. Eyes squinched shut, she prayed that Mother couldn't see her eyelids jiggle and would think she was asleep. Mother was good at knowing, but Clara was getting real good at faking, too.

Evidently her act was believable because Lucy rolled away and stilled, with her back toward her daughter. At once, Clara really set to praying. She puffed every single word to its biggest size. She wanted the whole house filled, wanted it to bulge as full as a silk balloon with her prayers for Gabe and Lucy and Nonie, and if the little river camp lifted high and floated free, so much the better.

Before she fell asleep, an abrupt prod of fear nearly pushed Clara, falling, into another room, a room she almost remembered. It wasn't like this bedroom, or even the hollow room here where Joyce had died. In Clara's anxious mind, the echo of a fearful place was not of a long space at all, nor narrow. This old enclosure went up and up, but it was just as scary. And Lucy shouldn't be there, in that other room. Clara held her breath and groped for her mother's unpinned hair across the pillow. What had Clara done, with all these plans, to gather them together here? What had she really done?

But at six in the morning when Clara heard the stove door creak open and the furnace kicked on, things were exactly as they had seemed last night in the kitchen. She was in Tyrone with Daddy and Mother and Nonie, and she could smell dust blowing up from the register, catching a warm ride, and life was human-sized and real.

Clara's cold-footed trip from the bedroom to the kitchen was fast, fast. She hardly noticed anything between. If you went that quickly and were silent, it was like it wasn't there.

In the coziness of Nonie's presence, Clara softened. "Morning, glory," Nonie said and slipped the world in place.

They had their meal at the table, which Gabe did set up in front of the fireplace, in front of a big open fire. Nonie's dress, gray like her hair, and her white apron stayed spotless while she served them. After he sliced the bird's buttery breast meat, Daddy invited Nonie to "stay a minute," and he raised his glass and Lucy raised hers and Clara lifted her water glass to clink against the other goblets. There was a curve of fireshine off Lucy's hair and also in the wine, where it lapped back and forth in the stemware's crystal bowls. They all waited for what Daddy would say.

"I've bumped along the bottom . . . ," he started. Several pops from the burning logs finished that sentence for him. Gabe cleared his throat and tried again. "This isn't something I'm easy with, but, for the three of you . . ." There, too, he stopped and Clara wondered if everything had stopped and what it would take to start them up or if Nonie would simply turn toward the doorframe behind Daddy and rewind and set them running or if they would stay here poised in firelight, hands raised, listening in lovely silence, for what Daddy didn't say. But when Gabe lowered his arm and offered them, at last, the single word: "Thanksgiving," they sped forward once again. And though Nonie did not smile, her burnished cheeks caught the curve of light from the wine and Mother's hair. Clara, too, thought, with a catch, that the word was fine.

CHAPTER 23

With Other Things than Time

Sᴏɴɴʏ sᴇᴇᴍᴇᴅ ʙᴇɴᴛ on acting conspiratorial: "You know, Sheriff, that trotline that Gabe runs across the river?" As if there were anything hush-hush around these parts concerning trotlines. "He wants his rig set exactly right. He's sure somebody's robbing it." Sonny buzzed on but Ben's attention faded out.

It was the tenth of December. The gray light that drifted through Ben Gilliam's office windows settled on surfaces like ash. The resulting gloom made Ben feel like he was chin deep in the quicksand of winter. Sonny Nolan roosting on his desk like a vulture didn't help.

When Sonny stretched even closer, Ben tried to scowl him away. The lawyer did retreat slightly. That was about the most to be got out of a "look" with Sonny.

"This has been going on for a long time, Sheriff. I mean it. Now Gabe thinks he's being followed. And you know he's not one to take on about matters."

Ben knew that well enough. Phillips didn't "take on" and he

didn't let on. It would have eased Ben's mind if he did. In his estimation, during all the years he had observed Gabe, the man had been vulnerable to interpretation exactly once: the night Joyce Oliver was shot. And then Gabe dropped his guard for no more than an instant. When he moved to smooth Joyce's skirt over her parted, tallow-colored knees, his face had been a pane of glass.

"Wait a minute, wait a minute," Ben was abrupt. "Back up and start over. And for God's sake, talk out loud, Sonny, because I thought you said that Gabe Phillips, the richest man in the county, is upset about a missing string of fish."

"Laugh if you want to, Sheriff," Sonny needled furtively. "There's something in this, though. It's not only the fish."

"I don't doubt you. I'm sure Gabe does feel he's being followed. He's going to catch eyes, Sonny. That's for certain. Gabe Phillips was the one to watch before Joyce was dead. If you think people are looking the other way now, you got another think coming." Sonny's eyes were unreadable. "He'll just have to go on with it, though," Ben enlarged. "There's no hiding place in Milan County and you know it."

"Hold on, hold on. Don't get in a huff, Ben. That's not the kind of thing I mean. Gossip's no hill to a high stepper like Gabe." Nolan leaned back. When he spoke again, he crossed his arms and raised his voice. "But if you want my opinion, only half this story has been told. Sounds to me like some varmint's got his ears laid back with regard to Gabe."

Ha. The real Sonny Nolan, as sharp as a pinprick and just as quick. No votes in the balance here. In Ben's office he could be himself.

Nolan held the floor. "Gabe met with Judge one night up at

Stallard's house. There's an old man from across the river, Gabe says tell you the one used to walk up and hang around the streets, it looked like him following when Gabe went back to the car."

"You don't mean Truitt? From over in Moccasin County? Is this coming down to Ira Truitt?" Typical Nolan idea. "Ira's not a bother. His wife died up here at Memorial is all. You've seen him. He's a barrel-topped man, in coveralls, no shirt. Has that big merle dog. Its coat's almost pure blue." Ben explored aloud more for himself than Sonny. Ira's history was curious. "He hovers around where they took his wife that time. Goes to the hospital, over to Morton's, then gets his fill of the past and heads for the barn." Ben looked up pointedly where the attorney perched. "Gabe's worry box must be empty. Those Truitts have always been peculiar. You tell him he's got worse on his plate than Ira."

Sonny stilled completely, then all but visibly bristled quick as an outraged porcupine. "Let me ask you something, Sheriff," he said, and his tone was as short as his words. "Have you ever, once, thought your take on things was wrong?" Nolan's face was so bare Ben hardly knew him. That wasn't a real question, not the kind of thing you answered, was it?

Nolan continued, driving his point in hard. "Gabe thinks he's seen the fellow hunched over in a flatboat down on the Hebron, near the trot. He put the glasses on him but didn't pick up much besides a familiar looking bulk. But if it is Truitt, the one you're describing, that could have been him."

Ben knew what was coming, and he already hated his part in it. He wanted order as much as any of them. Hadn't he played his role for years in that conspiracy of order headed by Judge Stallard? All for the

186

best, he agreed, for Milan, and other places, like Tyrone, where the county's population had spread. But this next move was sad. He knew well what Sonny wanted. Ben had done the same for others. There was probably more reason this time than most. Nolan wanted Truitt warned off. A simple thing. And you got it done in circles, Sonny had that part right. There was a slow but constant turning of a wheel of votes and favors hereabouts. Ben rubbed his neck. Better to be the miller than the grist. The Truitts of the world made perfect grist and, truly, they ground exceeding fine.

"I've got no jurisdiction across the Hebron, Sonny, and you know it." Worth a try.

Outside, a cloud shifted. A swing of sunlight widened the room. "Come on, Sheriff," Sonny wheedled. "A neighborly call is all we ask. You want jurisdiction for a social life? Gabe thinks mighty highly of you, Ben. He's not begrudging a single vote he got you. But this needs doing. I aim to see that it is."

"And you're just the man to hold the lantern while your Mama chops the wood, aren't you, Sonny?" Ben would have the last word even if Sonny Nolan had his way.

On the road to Truitt's place, Ben practiced his little speech aloud. He wanted a certain niceness of tone. There wasn't much time. Already he could see where Tyrone bridge spanned the Hebron like a highwire, a thin black line across blue sky from cloud to cloud. Up close, the construction wasn't delicate at all. Its girders were lashed to the hills on both sides of the river by huge concrete squareknots that were pierced with bolts the size of a man's leg. A hundred yards below Ben, the water glittered bits of winter light that had broken where it fell. A few tenacious, gold-red water maple leaves spurted occasional dots of color onto the rusty bluffs above his head.

It was enough for him, still, this place: the county that had mixed him from field clay and river water and bony limestone palisades. Briefly Ben quit talking to Ira in his mind and breathed it in again, the life, the land.

Across the river, Ben cocked an eye for the turnoff down to Truitt's acreage. He had spent months, seemingly years, of his boyhood rocking like this in the back seat of his father's old Ford while it rattled from mailbox to mailbox. From those years of early practice, Ben spotted the mailbox, although its post was all but hidden in a chest-high clump of broom sedge. A crude, lowercase *T* was painted large on the box's dented side with brown paint. Except for the period after it, the letter looked like a rough drawn, splintered cross. Ben parked, stepped down from his truck and listened, one foot on the running board.

When he knew he was alone, Ben tried out the phrases he had settled on earlier. "It's come to my attention . . . ," he started, then switched to "We've had a complaint in the office . . ." but the words felt awkward. "You been rooting around on our side of the river, Ira?" was more like it. At least it was direct, and maybe Truitt had some humor about him that would make this easier for them both. Unlikely, Ben thought, recalling Ira's stony face, but it was possible.

Other than Ben's voice, the afternoon was hushed. When he was little, Ben had often sat on a nest of brush in the hollow by the creek that lazed across his parents' farm. He had sat in an identical kind of daytime quiet, waiting there for his life to arrive. Anything might happen, he felt as a boy. Here on Ira's place the feeling was the same. Buckeye trees had grown together overhead. The Sheriff half expected to hear his mother's voice reaching all the way from thirty years ago. "Benneee, Bennneee . . . ," she had called back then. Her tone had always been as clear as springwater, and his name, drawn pure and long, hung on the air until Ben allowed the line of sound to catch him up and reel him close.

Ben bestirred himself and rustled onto Ira's property through waist-deep weeds. The whole place needed to be bushhogged. He fended huckleberry snares along a barely visible path. Off to his left, erosion had caused the hillside to break open, leaving a straggly grass eyebrow arched over exposed dirt. The soil was reddish and angry looking. Ben hated to see land neglected. In his estimation it signified a moral waste, and he judged Ira for it. Ben clambered down a faint trail, past a burned-out house, until the path dropped steeply toward a cluster of saplings.

Ben tried to control his labored breathing. When, after a quarter hour's hard descent and toil through a windbreak, he reached Ira's cabin, he tensed before he knocked. The smells that spiced the air were easily identified: dry timothy and fallen hickory nuts. The pleasant background odors and vegetation of Ben's childhood were here, all ragged and overgrown with other things than time. Then Ben laughed slightly, relieved. Ira Truitt noisily pushed the door back and stared out, blinking. He was as pale and harmless-looking as a grub, uncovered, in the cold, slanty sun.

"Afternoon, Truitt." Ben waited. Ira didn't acknowledge him. "You know who I am?"

The heavy scent of sweaty flesh diffused around Ben. He could have sworn that Truitt had expected him. The old man's expression had an edge of smugness, as if he were victorious in some small, mean way. "I'm no forgetter. I know you, Sheriff."

Behind Ira, Ben could see a sink, in grainy light. Water ran from the tap into the center of a mound of suds. Ben watched the bubbly stomach rise around its deepening navel.

"Better see to your faucet. Could I step in for a minute?"

Ira didn't move back and he didn't turn to check his sink. A dollop of suds started over the enamel.

"You're stretched mighty far across the county line, aren't you Sheriff?" Truitt paused. "Aren't you afraid? . . ." His words rolled to a slow stop.

What was Ira asking him? Ben's muscles contracted. He wasn't asking Ben about fear, was he? Nobody ever asked him about that. Even Mollie. They assumed that he was fearless and he let them. Ben preferred it.

"Many's the one would find it troubling," Truitt leered at Ben and paused, then he concluded: "Coming onto a man's land like this. Specially where a fellow might be licking wounds from last time. Not you though, I reckon."

Truitt's inflection implied a crude attempt at banter. Ben decided to give him the benefit of the doubt, but he was puzzled over Ira's reference. "Last time?" Then Ben remembered. How could he have forgotten? A few years back, a nurse had called from Milan Memorial and complained that a man was seen staring up at the same window for hours. It was Truitt he had chased out of the parking lot. Ben kept it simple that evening when he went over to the hospital. "Better move on before it's too dark," something like that. Given the word, Truitt had shambled away, headed straight west on Tenth Street. The old man didn't vary his gait. He plodded along heavily until his bulk dissolved into the purplish line of dusk that limned the skyline. Ben had neither yelled nor followed after to soften his admonition. The Sheriff had merely taken Truitt's place for a bit. Ben stared gravely at Memorial's uninspiring planes of brick and glass. The idea of Ira's mute mourning had sickened him. He recoiled from imagining the pain such surgery as the loss of a wife would inflict. Ben shuddered again now.

"Come on, Truitt. It's not like that. Let's just have a word or two." Soap dripped off the sink and fell, like curds of rendered fat, onto a worn carpet square.

In no hurry, Ira stepped back. With one undeviating sweep he cut the tapwater and dropped a grimy rag on the floormat. As a politeness, Ben pulled the metal door shut behind himself when he stepped inside.

Ben found himself standing uncomfortably near a small iron stove that was busy overheating the air. Layers of dirty quilts mounded up on the cot between the sink and the bucket-shaped heater. Torn sections of a coverlet were even taped over the window. The place was a suffocating confusion of patchwork and pattern. All the quilts were splotched; batting oozed from their frayed panels. Draped over the sink's corner, a dark coverlet bled inky stains into the spilling water. Ben felt slightly queasy.

Ira stood for a second in front of the Sheriff, then sat heavily on the cot. A little needle thrill of danger pierced Ben when the old man unhurriedly looked up. Ben prickled with the knowledge that he was hemmed in, narrowly, by strangeness. The sensation lessened when Ira spoke: "And you've crossed the Hebron to say . . . what, to Ira Truitt?"

"I came to ask. There's a man lives on the other side. He's got a trotline, crosses and comes up close to where your place hits the river.

He thinks it's being tampered."

"Mr. Phillips you mean. The 'broken-footed man.' Mr. Gabriel Phillips. He's got fishes he won't share? Not neighborly, is he?"

"It's his right, Ira. You know how things are on the river. A man can have a trot and wants it respected. The catch is his."

"You've come fairly far with a trifling complaint, Sheriff." There was no mistaking Truitt's defiance.

"It's not just the trotline, Ira. You seem to know Phillips? Do you?"

"What I need to know, I know. Do you?" Truitt didn't wait for Ben's answer. Ira went on: "You ask about a profligate. A man who wastes what he's given. No husbander."

"Well, Ira, we're not here to judge him. . . ."

Ira was impatient to continue. "Oh we're not? You're quick enough to judge me," Ira shot back. Ben was completely startled by Ira's willingness to grapple verbally.

Ira wasn't through. "Besides, Gabe Phillips has already been judged." The cut in Ira's voice was deep and raw. "I saw your lists in the courthouse." Truitt was down to a rasp. "He's gone free while I'm condemned. But there are other places where names get written. John told it. Men love darkness because their deeds are evil."

Ben had craned forward to hear. This was more than troublesome. The man seemed mad.

Ben took a step away from the heater. The long bill of his cap grazed the overhead bulb and set it swinging. A pendulum of light and shadow swept back and forth between the men.

"Well, let me tell you something, Ira. Across the river, I do have a bit of authority. More than a little. If you know of anybody robbing that trotline, or if you hear of anybody from this side of the bridge going on to Phillips' place, you better warn him off." In the periodic gloom, Ben's voice sounded grim.

Gradually, Ira stood up. Ben reached behind himself for the door hasp. In the confines of the shed they were both too big, too close. Ben was alert and wary.

"You making me a deputy?" Ira insinuated the question with a sneer. "I'll be checking on my pay." Ira reached for the hot lightbulb and held it still. No pain showed in his expression. He squeezed blistering lines of light from between his fingers like juice from a radiant fruit.

Ben groped, suppressing the unthinkable urge to turn tail and run, until he gripped the makeshift doorknob's strap. He pushed back awkwardly and the door gave with the slightest metal protest. Ira stayed inside, a huge, dark presence swaddled in the shabby, half-light of his shack.

Unaccountably shaken, Ben backed down off the step and continued backing slowly toward the path. A smoky prism of sunlight struck a barrier between him and Ira, near the thicket of saplings. With a sharp intake of breath, Ben turned and set off to retrace his way to the mailbox. If Ira came out, he thought, he could duck and creep among the foliage.

Inside the ring of maples, Ben watched his feet to make sure he skirted the rim of the sinkhole. On the far edge he stumbled over what he thought, at first, was a mound of dirt. But dark as it was under the upturned basket of bare interwoven tree branches, he saw that the carcass of a dog had tripped him. Ben knelt, trembling. It was obvious to him that this was a fresh kill. The dog's silvery blue coat was dully tarnished but intact. A tight wire, looped twice around, cut into the animal's downy muzzle. Ben delicately reached to free its jaws. He jerked his hand back as if stung. The lip and nose leathers, once velvety, wriggled with hives of vermin. Ben stood and stared. From above, except for a few bloody skull fragments which had matted on an earflap, the carcass looked peaceable. As if in death the hound might yet be whistled up to run and howl its mournful bay, eternal, through the woods.

Waves of emotion washed over Ben all the way back up the hill. He checked his wrist for the time, but his big steel watch face was as unaccountable as his fear. Only a quarter past five. Hours had passed in minutes. The Sheriff paused after each careful stride in and out of the dappling afternoon cedars and hawthorns and stunted horse-chestnut trees, tuned for the grating noise a corrugated tin door would make, scraping on linoleum, if it were pushed in place.

From however far away, there was no sound of anything but the whispering of grasses gone to seed. Only Ben's heart beat against the day's silent cooling down, the closing in of shadows, while he drew near his truck.

CHAPTER 24

Mercury Glass and June

CLARA WAS PROUD of her daddy's stride. She had been so from
her first recollection of him. It was nothing less than he deserved, she
thought, that Gabe's gait should be as distinctive as he was himself.
"High, wide, and handsome" were the words that came into Clara's
mind walking beside him this morning, called up by the way Gabe
held his head and rocked his shoulders toward his bad leg as it swung
forward.

The air was crisp as a bite of chilled apple. Following Gabe's
striking example, Clara pulled herself up as tall as she could and held
his warm hand hard. Whatever they said down in Hickman, she did too
have a daddy and here was proof: the two of them strutting down
Milan's main street as big as life, on the last day of Clara's after-
Christmas visitation. Tomorrow Gabe would take her back home to
Lucy. School started the day after.

This morning Clara had never seen more men, women, and
children parading the downtown sidewalks and in front of stores. All

of them looked cheerfully chubby, bundled as they were against the cold. Clara was proud to believe that Milan's pervasive air of satisfaction stemmed directly from her daddy's business. "Tobacco money" was a phrase she heard more often every time she visited. No matter who said it, the tone was almost always praiseful.

Clara and Gabe waltzed in among the people on the street. A huge cloud, bulging with snow, had settled over the courthouse. The air bore the barest hint of the talcum of snowflakes on its breath. Beneath the cloud's gray cast, the crowded sprinkle of multicolored wool coats and knitted mufflers and long, striped toboggan caps with their invariable red tassels, some tied with bells that jingled when they shook, were as bright as Christmas ornaments.

McCauley's Ten Cent Store was within sight on the far corner. Clara looked beyond the crowd toward the tinsel swags on McCauley's red and gold marquee. She squinted to travel her eyes through its looking-glass entrance into the world of treasures beyond. Her own little tobacco dividend, tucked heavily inside her pocket, had made her antsy. At breakfast Gabe had given her a new fifty-cent piece, and she aimed to spend it while it shined.

Nearer to the five and dime there were fewer people on the walkway. Clara and Gabe swooped rather grandly, she thought, from among the clusters of families and moved along. Gabe was to leave her at McCauley's then meet her for lunch at Spiro's when she was through. She would order deep dish pie. Clara already savored the idea of fleshy, befloured Sophie. The woman's larder of buttery sweets seemed to be as ample as Sophie was herself.

Clara had barely begun a tasty contemplation of her noon meal when she was startled out of her reverie by a fearsome sight. A huge, bespectacled stranger with a grizzle of tangled hair loomed out of nowhere and blocked their path. Gabe unsuccessfully tried to steer Clara left, around the pillar of the other man, before there was an impasse. But the aged intruder stepped in front. And he did it again. Wherever they veered, in fact, the old man got there first.

In the first scandalous seconds of these awkward do-si-dos, Clara was embarrassed for her father. The air around them felt like it might crack with static. She was desperate for Gabe not to stumble or feel ungainly, not while Milan's eyes were burning on their backs. When Gabe suddenly clamped tightly down on her waist and clapped his other hand protectively onto her opposite shoulder, Clara was pricked by an unexpected blade of fear. She took a hard look at the wild-eyed man who confronted them.

Though the fellow was old, it was clear to Clara that he was anything but pitiful. He had a massive, weathered head and torso. His bristly gray hair was long over his ears and onto his neck and his spectacles glittered so alarmingly that his body had the startling, top-heavy appearance of a wood torch. Clara instinctively recoiled. She shied back from the toe-to-toe standoff and tried to pull Gabe with her. But the apparition had already accomplished his evil trick of turning her daddy into stone.

Before Clara could think of any way out, the old man looked down and gave Clara a full and horrified study. It was Clara who was immobile now. But Gabe had found his feet and when he moved he did it forcibly. In one fell swoop Gabe lifted Clara and forced the grizzled stranger to the edge of the sidewalk. First Gabe scorched the man with the single word, "Fool," before he snatched himself and his daughter furiously away, down Main Street. Clara, dangling beneath

197

her daddy's arm, clung as hard as she could to the cashmere smoothness of Gabe's overcoat sleeve and tried to look behind.

Her daddy muttered something but did not speak again until he grimly deposited Clara at the entrance to McCauley's. Gabe said he would meet her where they had agreed. She entered the store after she made sure Gabe did not head back the way they had come. The prospect of that looney man turning up again made Clara shudder.

Inside the ten-cent store, Clara stood still until the bones in her legs found their marrow. Clara knew McCauley's layout by heart. At one time or another in her short life, she had made leisurely studies of the wares on every aisle from the oversweet perfumes near the front register, which now made her think vividly of Joyce, all the way back to piece goods in the rear, righthand corner of the building.

First, Clara spritzed one of the perfumes on the air then had to step aside to escape its pungent mist. She worried her way past a few bins of marked-down items. For some reason, nothing looked quite as brightly painted or desirable as Clara had pictured it before. After wandering up and down the rows for a while, Clara loosened her coat and stood stock still and thought. Then the very thing caught her eye.

In a bin fenced with rectangular panels of glass, a group of silver-colored vases, each one no more than five inches high, had been neatly arranged. The words "mercury glass" were hand printed on a sign taped to the front of the bin. Clara gingerly picked up a vase and checked its price. Forty-five cents. But well worth it, she thought. Daddy liked a nice decoration. This June when she came for her stay, Clara would fill the container every day with flowers she picked on the hillside below Gabe's house. Even dandelions and clovers would be pretty as their shaggy yellow and lavender buds reflected a fringe of color onto the vase's shiny little hips. She would leave the bouquets on his desk for Gabe to find. So the vase was like a promise to her daddy.

At lunch Gabe didn't ask her what she had in the paper sack, and that suited Clara very well. He hadn't mentioned the scary man from the sidewalk dance either. If her daddy meant to ignore the set to, Clara knew it should make no never mind to her, as they said in Hickman.

The rest of the day and evening passed quietly. But Clara's mind was like a jumping bean with anticipation of the weather and of giving Gabe his present.

Clara awoke the next morning from a nervous sleep to find that yesterday's clouds had, in fact, plumped a twelve-inch thick comforter of downy, snow-white snow down over the entire bed of Milan County in the night.

Gabe declared he would put chains on his tires and get on up to the warehouse but that he wouldn't chance the two-lane down to Hickman today, not with Clara on board. He sent her off to Nonie's cabin to suggest that the two females should spend time there while he was at work.

Clara, decked out in galoshes and Gabe's deep-pocketed hunting coat, set off for the short trek to Nonie's house while Gabe squatted in the driveway and worked to attach collars of rattling chain around his convertible's thick tires; the sidewalls' wide, white bands were as pristine as the snow against his reddening hands. He seemed happy enough at his chore and smiled Clara on her way. Through the weather-bleached air, which had the clarity of lead crystal, Gabe's teeth sparkled as brightly as his surroundings.

Out of Gabe's sight, among the trees, Clara slipped sideways. To steady herself she caught a bur oak in a tight hug. Briefly, she rested her cheek against the tree's icy bark and stayed perfectly still for a moment, lost in thought at the heart of the morning. When she set off again, Clara wondered what people down in Hickman, where the only drift was soot, could possibly know about such a powdery hope chest of a world as this one.

Clara continued slowly and firmly. She dropped her feet as purposefully as anchors, from the knees. Occasionally, she looked back at the deep wells that her boots made in the snow. Nonie's thin feet, the same color as autumn oak leaves and hardly thicker, probably wouldn't even make a mark. Clara bet that Nonie could brush across this snowfall without ever breaking through its crust. There were times when it seemed possible to Clara that Nonie might some day skim the surface of the Hebron, its current lapping up, tickling at her delicate pink soles. She seemed to touch that lightly where she walked.

Clara paused again and raised her elbow to check on Gabe's vase, which she had cushioned in her muffler and brought along to show. She quickly verified that his surprise was intact and nestled in her roomy pocket. From the nearby clearing, Clara could see across into Moccasin County. The steep banks on the other side of the Hebron were thick with saplings. Bare of leaves, the distant tree trunks were as black as ermine tails against the white pelts of the hills.

Before long she reached Nonie's porch, and within seconds Clara was unbundled inside the small oven of a house.

"If you're not all gussied up, I never saw it," Nonie greeted, meaning Daddy's jacket and the boots. She dried and polished Clara's face briskly with immaculate huck towels. As a seeming afterthought, Nonie pulled a nylon stocking over her outstretched fingers and smoothed Clara's hair with it.

Clara impulsively put her hands on Nonie's cheeks to thaw them on the woman's warmth. For the millionth time, Clara peeped inside the woman's tiny, heart-shaped smile, at the jewelry of teeth outlined in gold. "You hold still, you hear me," Nonie cautioned, "If you're going to have the fidgits, I won't be able to do a thing."

Nonie dropped and spread a protective carpet of old newspaper over her bare wood floor. Clara neatly placed her boots, side by side, as she knew was expected.

"Daddy couldn't take me back to Hickman," she explained. "I guess you can tell that since here I am. He's calling Mother himself from the warehouse. I suppose I'll have to go back there tomorrow."

"I should think so," Nonie observed. "School holidays is one thing, young lady. Mamas alone is quite another." Nonie wadded the nylon stocking, the one she had used on Clara's hair, and took dead aim at her bedstead.

In fact, Clara didn't feel quite easy concerning Lucy. Nonie had hit on a sore point. Clara tuned up her ears but Nonie didn't offer more advice. The sun was already hot at its work of undoing winter's spell. In the background, a rain of snowmelt trickled gently from the eaves and plashed onto Nonie's stoop as quietly as tears. For an instant, Clara despaired. She didn't know what on earth to say about Lucy's aloneness. It was proving impossible to be everywhere at once.

At that moment, Clara was kneeling. She helped Nonie dry up the puddles her boots had tracked inside. The room's white pine floor planks had been scrubbed down with water and sand so often that they were as smooth as a satinwood bandage against Clara's thin-skinned knees.

There were more than a few winter nights that Clara could remember having spent in this very room. The metal heater in the corner had a pattern of perforated dots on its casing that Clara knew well. She could have mapped them blindfolded. Firebugs of orange light often escaped those holes and skittered toward her across the slickedy floor in the dark when she slept over. That image brought Clara back to the thing that had been scorching her heart since yesterday morning. Until now, she had been able to tamp its fires with a fair degree of success, because there was no place fit to tell it except right here in this spare, clean room. And nobody safe to tell, save Nonie Pulce, about the thing that happened up in town.

Nonie eyed the floorboards and used one of her two ladderback chairs as a handrail to pull herself upright, indicating the floor was wiped and dried to her satisfaction. Before she was fully on her feet and could turn hands to another project, Clara blurted: "Up in town yesterday. We met a person."

"What do you mean, you met 'a person'?"

"Daddy and I did." Clara paused. "A man. On the sidewalk. We were going to the Ten Cent Store."

"Well. It's pretty likely that you would see a man in Milan, isn't it? Why are you telling Nonie?"

"This man wouldn't let us by. He kept stepping in front."

"And Mr. Gabe, he says what during all this?"

"Nothing. I think he was embarrassed though, you know, because he's . . ."

"Crippled." Nonie's voice was low and matter of fact. Clara knew that was the truth of it, but was it the only one?

Clara kept it to herself that Gabe had never raised his eyes to face ·

the man at whom he had spit the single word: "Fool."

"Well. Do you think Daddy knows him?"

Nonie had turned aside and started reaching down dishes from the rack above her two-burner plate. "Was it a big old man with a heavy back?" she asked, her own back twisted up into her job.

Clara chilled to think that Nonie had seen him too. And seen him where? "Is he from Tyrone?"

"No ma'am. And that's enough. Here we are squandering most of a fine morning on yesterday. You set places. I'll be fixing lunch."

Nonie stepped outside and retrieved a rind of fatback and a loaf of yeast bread from the zinc ice box on the stoop.

Clara was afraid she was fairly shouting into the frozen air, into the snow's glare that blanked out Nonie's figure beyond the open door. "Daddy seemed to hate him right off the bat," she cried.

"Honey, I'm going to say this plain," Nonie announced upon reentry. "There's not many your Daddy does like. He's got plenty of acquaintances but a single friend that I know of. Now there's an end on yesterday, I hope." Batted by Nonie's elbow, the door thumped shut. The rattle of frying pans being separated and the clatter of busyness took up the space of talk. Nonie handed down a packet of brown sugar from the wooden box she had nailed on the wall for use as a cabinet.

Clara opened out the narrow drop-leaf table and placed two thick, spider-veined crockery plates just so. She then trotted over and stood near Nonie for a good vantage on the slicing operation. Before she had a chance for one big-eyed blink, three strips of fat had fanned smoothly away from the knifeblade under Nonie's expert hand. Each piece of bacon was a good quarter inch thick and had a seam of pale pink porkmeat across the bottom.

Nonie patched the burner's bright red eye with her iron skillet's broad bottom and cooked the meat through. She was expert at avoiding the stinging spray of fat that sizzled out. The strips of fatback curled and fluted while they spit, taking on the appearance of toasted ruffles when they were done. Nonie set the rashers to drain on a square of paper, then she deftly fried up four nice planks of whitebread in the fry pan's residue of hot grease. What was left of the bacon's precious fat, she strained through a perforated lid into a tin can and set off to the side. At the last, Nonie patty-caked a thick layer of brown sugar onto two pieces of the fried bread and topped them with portions of the crunchy bacon and a final, topmost layer of toast.

They ate the delicious concoction companionably and washed their sandwiches down with mugs of steaming, woodsy sassafras tea. Clara wiped the table while Nonie piled their plates and utensils into the dishpan. Clara could bide her time before showing off Gabe's present, allowing her lunch and Nonie to settle.

"Do you ever think what would happen if we moved back, Nonie? I could come stay with you most every day." Clara was more or less thinking out loud and Nonie seemed to know it.

Once or twice, though, Nonie seemed on the verge of starting up with her. Instead, the slight woman took her dishpan into the small, cinderblock bathroom that Gabe had added onto the back of her previously one-roomed house. In this addition there was a commode and a poorly formed but definite concrete tub. The darkish room was, Clara thought, too rough-surfaced and clammy for Nonie, but if she had complaints, Clara had never heard them. Nonie had laid a narrow, pink chenille rug on the stone floor between the bathtub and the wall and let it be.

Pretty soon Clara heard the sudsy dishwater emptied into the toilet. Next, she listened while it flushed down with a gurgle. Afterward, Nonie settled lightly beside her on the bed. She pulled Clara close with the iron band of her featherweight arm.

"You seem to be doing a lot of plotting, child. If you're worrying plans around more than usual, ponder this: your mama's getting strong down there in Hickman, honey. She's thickening up, finding her own substance. And you got to let her do it. Nobody hurts you when you find your own substance."

She asked: "You hear Nonie? You hear me, girl?"

Clara heard her. But, no need to tell. If they were living here, in Tyrone, Clara herself could keep them all safe, not only Lucy. Her entire life Clara'd been studying on a plan to do so. Going back and forth the way she did now, it had become almost too hard to hold anybody close.

"Who's Daddy's one friend?" she asked, trying to buy time.

As she intended, Clara caught Nonie off guard. The woman inquired wordlessly what Clara meant by raising and hovering the tiny wingspan of her eyebrows above her wide-set questioning eyes.

"You said he only had a single friend that you knew of."

"Now that I've said it, I wouldn't call them friends, exactly." Nonie indicated a direction with her head. "There's a preacher lives down the road here in Tyrone; he tends a flock of Free-Will people up in Milan. He and your daddy tease and argue some when they meet up. About beliefs and such. But I can tell you this: each one's listening well as laughing, all the same."

"Are you much afraid, Nonie?" Clara couldn't help but ask it. The time seemed right.

"You put an end to worry quick enough, once you believe yourself."

There was nothing Clara had to say to that. She eased herself off the bed where they sat and retrieved Gabe's jacket from its hanger and from the pocket, his vase.

"This is mercury glass, the lady said so," Clara told, equally proud of the gift and its name. "Mercury glass," she repeated. She then tipped the vase onto its side and held it out for Nonie to examine close-up while it cooled Clara's sweaty palm. In the room's unnaturally bright light, reflected from the whiteness outdoors, the miniature container looked iced. The one unthawable object in a melting world.

Nonie regarded Clara steadily. She reached across and rolled the container gently with the tip of her index finger. There was a brief winkle of opalescence. "That's fine," Nonie said. "Gabe Phillips is going to like that fine."

The rest of the afternoon, Clara and Nonie took turns reading aloud from an old book of stories Nonie kept by the bed. Gabe had warned Clara to be home before five. By the time Clara left, the temperature had dropped outside. The surface snow had refrozen under a syrupy glaze that crackled when it broke where she stepped.

All the way back to her daddy's place, pine limbs, weighted with clumps of snow, tumbled puffy dust brooms around her, near the base of trees. Cold air on Clara's face kept her alert inside the spell cast by every magical sight and sound. Throughout her trek she held a warm idea focused on the path, of Nonie propped in bed, her finely molded head angled toward a fat book that was all plumped out from use.

In spite of the stiffening cold, Clara managed to pull Gabe's gift from its twisted-up muffler, as she had earlier. This time Clara kept going, but she held the vase pendant between her gloved fingers, while fitting her bootsoles gingerly into the slick blue caves of her own morning footprints.

Next summer, Clara thought, when the sun kissed up close again. When she and Mother and Nonie and Daddy were all gathered here in Tyrone above the banks of the warming Hebron, Gabe's mercury glass vase would summon this good day with the clarity of an icicle. If only June would hurry.

CHAPTER 25

An Odd Kind of Space

THE NIGHT OF the snowfall Clara fell into a weighty sleep from the day's mental and physical exhaustions. There were double doors in her bedroom at Gabe's house that gave onto the porch. Her mind sailed dreamily through the glass panes across from the foot of her bed and slipped, as easily as air, though fine mesh screening. Freed, it sailed itself upward and glided, like a swallow, far above the black ribbon of the Hebron, which shimmered between the white-furred hills.

It touched down faint as a wisp in another room, where she was younger.

The room in Clara's memory was filled with blocks of slanting light. It was an odd kind of space. Walls angled in at the top and compressed its volume high above where she stood, eye-level with the arm of her father's chair. Clara was only six, yet she knew that what she felt was planted deep and would never leave her.

A quality of heaviness weighted the room, a weight under which Clara was absolutely still. She didn't breathe the dusty, oven-dry air, she didn't rub her palm across the armchair's clipped, brown-fuzz covering. Her sight was microscopic. On the rug, less than a giant step away from her sandals, a dark, reddish stain disfigured two flowers in the carpet's overall design. The rug was otherwise drab, worn through along the rigid routes her parents walked, Daddy to the chair, Mother to the sofa.

There, between their paths, the stain was plainly visible. It marked an area where Clara played, where she had pressed sheets of waxed paper against the rug's raised floral pattern and rubbed, with crayons fatter than her fingers, until, magically, glassy green and blue bouquets appeared. Clara made them for her mother. Their blooms were cabbage-sized and simple, in colors nothing like the stain.

And looking at the stain, and knowing that the fear she felt was permanent, Clara's gaze penetrated dye and fiber. She saw her world and her family's woven red. Young as she was, she understood the vision as a prophesy.

But if she could hide the stain, Clara thought, if she could push the chair to cover it, she would have control; she could stop its spread. Clara stepped into the bay window behind the chair and squatted down for leverage. Silent, she reached up and gripped the backrest and steadied her arms. Knees bent, she shoved her elbows with every bit of might her fifty pounds could muster against first one side of the chair back, then the other.

Upholstery tacks along the side seams nicked Clara's skin. They pricked bloodspots on her forearms. But Clara had strayed from what was usual and she couldn't pause.

She didn't slip or falter. For once, Clara's shoe soles held against the rug so she made the chair move slightly.

There was nothing beyond that room.

CHAPTER 26

The Best Time in a Timeless Place

AT ALMOST DEAD center in the immense space of his warehouse, Gabe stood alone on the selling floor. It was the middle of the third week of February, 1954. His arms hung loose. He craned his neck and studied the exposed underside of his building's peaked roof for a goodly while.

It was Gabe's nightly habit during the sales months, November, December, January, and February, to walk from his office for a slow three-sixty, checking the visible details of his realm. Among other things, the solitude here had become an addictive form of comfort that he craved. His need for it had grown to an all but insatiable thirst.

It had been at least a quarter hour since the last workman punched his time and left. Gabe peered through half-light at the inch-square dial of his wristwatch. The three tiny phosphorescent hour, minute, and second hands had nearly merged on midnight. In this windowless space there were no other clues to time.

Without moving from his usual spot, Gabe lowered his eyes by degrees. Nothing showed that cried out for his attention. At seven o'clock in the morning the last tobacco auction of the season was scheduled to begin. And it would do so promptly. Gabe would see to that.

This time Gabe was more than ready. It didn't suit him at all that scheduled auctions had pushed this deeply into the sales calendar. February was always iffy. The crop's quality and price were each affected if they were left go this late. The leaf was the ruling thing, Gabe reflected, the almighty. There was hardly a time to let down in its devotions, from the minute the minuscule seed, no bigger than a spider mite, was incubated out. It wasn't tyranny, though. The crop was a loving charge in Gabe's eyes. And growing more so all the while. At the end of tomorrow's auction, the caller's gavel would ring down, by God, on the most profitable harvest Gabe had yet seen.

Gabe hectored the growers constantly about tending their acreage, housing the crop, avoiding house burn, detail after detail. Preaching to the choir. Gabe knew that well enough. But here in Milan County at least, they had better all be clear on what was at stake. If the farmers and tenants and sharecroppers would only hear Gabe on these matters, if they would just listen, they could all sweep right up with him into the coming abundance of cash.

First he had had to convince them that Burley wasn't local anymore. Overseas, American giveaways of cigarettes during the war had created a tidal wave of European demand. In Gabe's vision the tobacco industry was afloat on a worldwide flood of consumers. Manufacturers in the U.S. were scrambling over each other, racing for the high ground of supply, ably steered by their savvy, sharp-eyed buyers.

The industry's envisioned energy fairly coursed through Gabe.

Like the mite of its seed, he felt his tobacco ventures ready to explode into something impossibly broadleafed, full and greening in the sun.

These days, early in the season, factory reps poured into Milan County to be here at the warehouse. Gabe had often seen the men ride in, sitting up high on their smooth grain pinseal leather billfolds, in flashy cars. But no car was fancier now than his own.

Some of the biggest cigarette manufacturers were based in Louisville, a city so highfalutin it was almost in another world from small towns out in the state, like Milan, but they, too, sent their representatives to Gabe.

Other buyers came all the way from North and South Carolina and Virginia. And they came right here, to G. Phillips Central Burley Warehouse, No. 1. Because Gabe was sitting in the catbird seat. It was this tobacco, smack dab in the center of the state, that was in highest demand, industry wide. Little Milan County's own species of broadleaf Burley had a sugar content that guaranteed it would ripen the color of maple candy then cure up the sweetest. And finally, they came here because Gabe, when he was a boy, had seen it, had recognized the crop and business for what it was and could be. Because he had had enough of not having enough.

Each season, when the big-city buyers arrived, Gabe brought them into his warehouse. He ushered them proudly into this place he had created that was as well-ordered as a hallowed hall. And they bought big.

Thank whatever gods there might be, a few reps were still in the market this late, trying to bulk last-minute quotas.

Gabe's gaze slid down an electric cord and settled on a row of metal-hooded light fixtures that dangled from the struts overhead.

Every damn light had better be working, Gabe thought. If you couldn't see product, you couldn't by God sell it. It seemed, however, that Gilmer, the maintenance man, had done his job for once. Shades and bulbs alike were clean as mirrors and each one was illuminated. Every single lamp sported the only kind of bulb Gabe tolerated: the big, old-timey, pear-shaped globes of clear glass that had visible tungsten elements for works. From twenty feet above him, they cast a spare light that Gabe thought fitting. On balance, Gabe admitted, Gilmer Crow did as he was told and that right pleasantly.

So Gabe continued his onceover. He stood in the shadows of his huge, windowless building (six and a half acres under roof), resting his weight on his good leg, and took things in. The feelings that welled up within Gabe as he did so were damn near worshipful. He was that close, as close as he had ever come, Gabe thought, to a sense of sanctuary.

So many nights since last August, Gabe had simply known that he was doomed. Tonight, practicing the tobacco rites he had done for years, put Gabe in mind of any harvest's promise, far from Joyce and the sowing of regret. Yet at this late hour, Gabe was more fully aware of his remorse than ever. And still it seemed, impossibly, that a grave kind of happiness was just within his grasp.

Grudgingly, Gabe stopped woolgathering and came back to the business of the night. All the circular flats of woven reed, the so-called tobacco baskets, were in place. Each basket in the house was piled waist high with up to seven hundred pounds of hands of tobacco arranged in perfect, crinkly circles on the flats. Hands of tobacco were tied during the stripping process. To make one, a man took up a bunch of fresh leaves of a like stalk locus, gripped their stems tightly and bound the stems together with yet another leaf, in the manner of a nosegay. To be effective, the tying motion had to be both quick and forceful. It ended with an upward jerk that secured the leaves and was anything but delicate. Done properly, it was an artful labor. After the leaves bulked down, the hands went flat as fans, with similarly convenient handles. The fans of leaves were placed and stacked so that they radiated outward from the center.

All day long Gabe had had his crew shuffling and reshuffling the finished baskets. As was his wont, he demanded that the rows be orderly. In addition, they were necessarily far enough apart for a queue of sellers and buyers to move among the bulky stacks and not straggle.

Gabe had always held his arrangements to a strictly observed plan. He kept the widest aisle formed and centered underneath the row of hanging lamps. Done that way, the overhead fixtures cast onto the warehouse floor a path of milky-colored, steppingstone circles that led directly to Gabe's office. In such light, the baskets of tobacco on either side of him appeared fanciful, as circular and ruffled in the gloom as antebellum petticoats.

The press of paperwork was on Gabe, but he was reluctant to pull his gaze. This was the best time in a timeless place. All was as it should be, as far as he could tell. Finally, he headed down the lighted aisle toward the indentation in the far wall that was the door to his inner sanctum, his office where the big steel safe and the tools of accounting, ledgers, adding machines, and best of all, deposit sacks, awaited.

But again Gabe halted. This time for the purpose of one last straightening of a single basket's tag. The little flutter of paper that was wired onto each stack of hands designated that basket's particular grade.

The Best Time in a Timeless Place

The tag Gabe adjusted stamped the bin of hands as being composed entirely of redleaf. Redleaf, or tips, was the highest government grade of Burley. It was cut and culled solely from the very top leaf sites on the stalk. No flyings, tans, or lugs need apply. Gabe plucked a solitary hand from the basket and snuffled into a dark-smelling blend of sugar and nicotine that was as deliciously pungent as a cloud of incense. He then ground a portion of leaf between his thumb and forefinger. After catching the grains on his palm, he spread them with the pad of his left thumb. Their color was consistently blond. They would roll smooth and burn smoother. Gabe could almost taste the smoke. His mouth went slick with saliva at the thought.

Within Gabe's line of vision a dark trough ran the entire length of the side wall of the warehouse. For the merest instant, Gabe thought he saw a washy swirl in that direction, as if something, or someone, were about to congeal out of nothing more than a scoopful of pure night air. The idea shivered down inside him. He cocked his head and peered as hard as he could into the ink-black well of shadow. Gabe had himself designed the trough that drew his attention. The depression was in reality a concrete slot running along the far wall, the length of two football fields, entrance to exit, and formed a pass through for delivery trucks. When in the lane, a truck's flat bed was exactly level with his warehouse floor. Gabe's innovation had streamlined the previously labor-intensive work of offloading.

Again, Gabe ran the area with his eyes then shrugged. Auction jitters. He continued down the row, brushing crumbled redleaf from his hands. Constantly touching successive baskets, Gabe felt for texture, eyed color, and peered disgustedly at mordant, frog-eyed spots. He sidled along evenly, the way he could sometimes when there

215

was no one to see. A peerless warehouseman, in his element, and he knew it.

From pinhooking to this, Gabe thought. Jesus, what a tortured road. He didn't want to feel oversmart. Never would he get above himself that way again. God almighty, though, Gabe was glad he was on this side of things. Like in the song, a wretch like him was saved.

When the government had first regulated tobacco in 1936—had it only been eighteen years ago?—Gabe had instantly grasped what allotments meant. The regulation had solely limited supply; prices were free to soar on demand. Gabe's one abundant asset to that point in his life, sweat equity, was suddenly good as gold. In that same flash of recognition, Gabe had also seen the vein of shrewdness within himself. At the time he couldn't have even put a word to such a thing. If Charlie Phillips' one claim of drunken pride was true, that they came of educated people, Gabe had not been the proof. Merely doing enough schoolwork to get promoted with his classmates, he had earned his diploma in the fields. It was Lucy who had refined him.

Like it was yesterday, Gabe remembered being sixteen years old, chopping tobacco. He hacked out weeds and broke suckers to make the Burley plants go bushy. The blister-hateful hatchet that he swung was no bigger than a tomahawk. Like so much about the raising of a crop of Burley, the hatchet dimly connected the boy Gabe had been to the state's untamed, Indian past. A history Gabe felt but didn't know.

In the cold warehouse, Gabe relived his boyhood for a second more, its agonies of energy and appetite, soaked in perspiration. By God, he'd been determined. With one hand he had weeded himself up and out of the fields. With the other he had caught hold of Lucy and held on for dear life. At the thought of her, Gabe winced ruefully. But looking back now from his office door, the soft-lit picture was soothing: the basket-skirts poised to waltz away, the truck-well's shadow river running near, in silence.

How could it be that he had built all this by dint of an idea and by squeezing pennies out of nothing but his own hide? That Gabe had been plunked down where his desires and talents met within him was amazing to him tonight. And him a cripple. But he'd been hellbent to beat the odds. The day he was able to bargain for a rattletrap of a truck was the day he had called himself a pinhooker aloud. Gabe felt honored by the name, and he had vowed to honor it, in turn.

And the whole time he worked tobacco, Gabe had reworked himself, hard. He had studied ways to look the part and talk the part, big-timing it, if necessary. From this doorway, looking back, Gabe's efforts appeared desperate to himself, like the youngsters he'd seen chewing their lips, stringing their daddy's broken flyings on baling wire to sell for pocket change, with no idea of what was stacked against them.

But if styling himself had been hard, the rest of it, the feeling for tobacco, had come easy. Gabe had been an excellent judge of the raw leaf from the get-go. Here, Gabe whistled low. He had been knowing. There was no denying it. What had made him go so wrong about himself?

A pinhooker made money by being shrewd or sometimes just owning transport. Soon as he got his truck, Gabe had gone field to field with a vengeance and bought up what he could, promising a certain price. Some farmers had no means of delivering their crop up to the market. In those days the nearest warehouse had been well over a hundred miles away. And the roads from here to there were bad. So

Gabe had bought what he could and sold it where he could with nothing more than himself squeezed in between, because he gave a fair price, which he didn't always get at market, in return. The main thing was, if Gabe put his word or his hand to a thing he by God made it good. The farmers had kenned at once that they could trust him. Gabe sighed at this realization that he should have always been in love with the elements of his own life.

The cold brass doorknob in his grip brought Gabe from his reverie. Just there, when the black-green enameled door swung back, he heard the tiniest sprinkle of sound behind, no, above him. It was like a rain of pea-gravel on tin.

"Who is it?" he called. Gabe's voice flew high then perched on hidden rafters. There was no answer to his call. Furious in an instant, he yelled out again, enraged: "It better not be you!" Silence took roost and settled its feathers in the dark.

For good measure, Gabe slammed the door shut and was merciless with the clipboard that he smacked onto his desktop. The small office was comfortingly warm. He sat heavily and pulled his lamp close. Who was he to feel haunted? Let the others have their fears; Gabe would have no truck with running scared.

He brushed out his mind and pulled a ledger near. The government grade sheets had to be gone into. Gabe had no intention of heading into the morning without a thorough understanding of what the tobacco that would be sold was worth, according to the graders. He extracted numbers from his ledger, compared them to the established grades, and multiplied those by volume. Once he had the baskets priced out, Gabe situated his Burroughs adding machine and set to work in earnest. Shortly, a tongue of paper tape stretched unbroken down the front of his desk. The tape furled onto the floor, where it coiled deeper and deeper for hours. Gabe viscerally enjoyed his skill on the slippery, black enamel keys. The whirr and clack of the machine's wood-handled metal arm accompanied the rushing swiftness of Gabe's working mind. All the while he calculated, he felt like he was running, a thing he had never done, of course.

At 6:00 A.M. he was still immersed in figures. It was Gilmer Crow's job to raise the huge wooden warehouse doors, first thing of a morning. At the sound of the activated pulley, Gabe left off where he was, stood stiffly, and clumped out to the loading dock for some air. It was dark out yet. The huge wooden panel that Gilmer had first hoisted gave access to the drivethrough. Gabe cheered at the sight of foggy rain splattering down outside onto the patchy grass near the entrance. If today's experience was typical, bad weather brought good prices. His set of buyers would huddle under roof, companionably loath to leave.

Satisfied, Gabe headed back toward an immense aluminum coffee urn, Gilmer's pride, which steamed softly by the office door on its dented trolley. That was the only source of warmth, besides the human kind, out in the open warehouse. A few sleepy men trailed in and climbed the steps up from the trough. Gabe nodded to the man who ran the forklift for him, an expert at his job, who made his mechanical lifts and turns look like figure eights on ice. Some of the farmers whose tobacco would be sold were already here. A little shy of Gabe, lest they get another lecture about early marketing for breakfast, they shuffled close to the trolley then moved quietly away and aligned themselves comfortably on either side of the nearest row of baskets.

Nobody was talkative. The people who assembled knew this routine by heart. At five minutes before seven o'clock, Gabe wordlessly took his place at the head of a line that the ragged collection of farmers had formed, somewhat unevenly. Gabe surveyed the row behind himself and felt a click. Preparations, at least, had come right. He was satisfied to this point.

As warehouseman, Gabe provided the auctioneer. This caller, Gabe's favorite, a man in demand throughout the tobacco belt, had been available today because there was little competition for his services this time of year. He was a courtly looking gentleman in a trademark tweed cap who wore a kind expression. Exactly with the tick of seven o'clock, the man stepped into his accustomed place of preeminence. Gabe sensed a collective intake of breath at the importance of beginning.

The auctioneer stood opposite Gabe, scanning down the line of sellers. After that, and before he uttered a word, he eyed the set of buyers who were arranged behind himself. Each man stood a bit taller under his inspection. At the pointed end of tension, the caller nodded and began a drawling, smooth-toned chant. He walked forward slowly as he sang the special chant no outsider could have understood.

Both queues, sellers and buyers, followed closely behind the auctioneer, kept apart by the first row of baskets, which they now bought and sold. Most of the men, Gabe included, kept a palm on the uppermost hands of leaves in the gauntlet between them. Many tweezed lit cigarettes between the fingers of their other hand. The lines moved separately but, inhaling and exhaling and coupled by the hitch of baskets, each man smoothed and cupped and patted leaves the way Gabe had the night before, always moving, always leaving their lovers' lingering touch on the best grade of goods. Above the trains of men, two trails of breath and smoke condensed.

The Best Time in a Timeless Place

The established order was that Gabe preceded farmers and farmers preceded taggers. On his side, the auctioneer led the company buyers down the row. These last were well-dressed men whose expensive cars, which in the past Gabe had envied, were parked, frosted and rain-etched, in the lot across the street. But in spite of what distinction they laid claim to elsewhere, in this world they didn't hold themselves apart. Here, they gathered in among the rest, reached down into the leaves to check for quality beneath the graded level, nodding bids, sometimes speaking outright if they weren't heard.

Smooth as these proceedings looked, and the sound was even smoother, no single sale component lost its necessary edge. In a heightened state, Gabe listened, and his eyes were everywhere at once. He noted the blind accuracy of the designated marker, the man whose job it was to pitch sold tags onto the goods behind them as they walked. And, as with every auction, from opening day to this one, the buyers' finger signs and the sellers' narrowed eyes, and above all, the resonant, native Indian cadence of the headman's spiel, that regularly rose, "come on," or "go on," then dropped, in sync with the imaginable beat of an ancient tom-tom, connected the endeavor even more forcefully, in Gabe's mind, to its ancient roots.

Only once did the line stall out. A farmer named Ainsworth balked when it came time to accept the bid on his basket. He had removed his hat and clutched it now, two-handed, by the ragged brim. The halo of unaged white skin that topped his weathered face made him look pitiably vulnerable, like a half-dyed egg. "I done worked it like a borreyed mule," he said, adding a postscript into the bib of his overalls: "I'll smoke it myself. Or burn it, if that's all you're giving me."

Mostly lugs and flyings, Ainsworth's bundle of tobacco had been rough handled. There was no doubt from its condition that the entire lot had been left curing too long. The stack didn't deserve the bid it got. Gabe could readily see that the leaves were discolored and damp. Ainsworth hadn't even aired it right. The man probably didn't have a pot to pee in, Gabe thought, much less a vent barn or a coke stove.

The auctioneer called the product again, a tinge of sweetness in his repetition, but the price didn't rise. The buyers seemed like kind men, but this was business, and they were accountable to others than themselves.

Gabe watched Ainsworth step outside the line. The slightish farmer backed himself into the dark scrim of air just behind the rows, continuing to wring his hat as he went. "I'll not go begging," he mumbled. Then he disappeared on cue.

"You should of knowed," his wife would say, custodian of their sadness. "I told you. Hadn't I told you before you even went?"

Immediately the line closed up and Ainsworth's spot filled in, like liquid, with another man. Not a soul would make it worse by staring after. The queues flowed smoothly forward. It was little enough to do.

After the last consigned basket sold, the players moved over to Gabe's own stock. The warehouseman always held his tobacco, the stock he accumulated by buying baskets that he didn't think brought their price and some that growers plain wanted to cash out early, until last. Here was where Gabe shined. "Buying low and selling high," he joked aloud, with a lilt. From past experience, his little audience was in on it with him; the way Gabe hammed and almost buddied up, they felt better for it every time. Today he even parodied the caller's singsong. Have them leave the warehouse feeling good, he thought. Gabe always thought it, whatever serious business had transpired. As he had anticipated, this was a record last-day sale. Gabe calculated his margin by the second. He could afford to take a dive. "Oh, no, you've killed me," he lamented, laughingly dramatic, near a certain basket, then nodded his acceptance of a lowball bid.

Gabe's section sold up in minutes. By eight o'clock, the auction was over as Christmas. More than four hundred baskets had changed hands in less than an hour.

When the bidding and the buying ceased, the two lines of men merged and padded off toward Gabe's office like a human centipede, each man as anxious as another to pay, or be paid, and be gone. Crowded near his desk, buyers and sellers and Gabe's crew stirred around in a snowy paper swirl of checks and drafts and money orders. All cleared through Gabe. His percentage from both sides and his own from the middle swelled his accumulating mound of profit. Before the morning ended, Gabe damped the noise in his ears and stepped mentally away to observe his own creation—this clearinghouse where men and tobacco and money flowed in and mingled and flowed out again, purified and changed, rinsing the once marginalized lives of these men's women and children with comfort and warmth.

Gradually the flurry settled. Sound siphoned away with the departures, and Gabe was practically alone again in his warehouse. Gilmer had taken his coffeepot into the bathroom for a scrub. The urn clanked against the sink where Gabe could hear it ringing dully through the plank wall that separated the main floor from his office.

Gabe went back out and checked the unpeopled space. Each tobacco crinoline now wore its claimer's brand on a tag. He read off a few of the elegant old colonial names: Pall Mall, Tarryton, Lorrilard,

Kent. Others had been stamped with a manufacturer's imprint: American Tobacco Co., R.J. Reynolds, and more.

Tomorrow, the Burley would be forked and shipped and re-dried, by its new owners, then stored, aromatically, in gigantic hogsheads for at least three years. The warehouse already appeared emptier in Gabe's eyes, even though the tobacco was still in place on the spacious floor. The space looked higher roofed, dwarfing everything it held. Gabe's heart swelled. He could be as big here as he wanted to be. And come next November the whole, heady process would begin again. Right this instant, Gabe would bet, there were tobacco farmers who were preparing their fields for the March burnoff, aiming to kill the weed seed before it grabbed its hold.

How Gabe wished that time would fly. His longing had little to do with money. It was the founding in hope the growing cycle gave him, that he, too, might reemerge, this time a tenderer plant. Clara trusted in him now. And he could woo Lucy the way he had done once. He would sell her on his own belief that the rage had been cured out of him. That was surely true, same as these raw, green leaves turned honey-smooth and pliable when housed. And Lucy Phillips would never be rough handled again. Not by Gabe. Not by him.

Gabe had thought he was alone. There was no warning before Ainsworth's hand brushed his shoulder. "I come to say," the farmer who had refused to sell announced, simply, "I didn't mean nothing by it, Gabe." Gabe's nod was as weighty as the words.

CHAPTER 27

Inside a Tender Envelope of Skin

LUCY THOUGHT SHE heard water running. She had been gripped in sleep, but the sound—she thought it was water—had finally roused her. Gradually more conscious, Lucy tried to find a comfortable depression in the lumpy bed, twisting from her back to her stomach and over again until she had wound herself deeper and deeper into the mattress. Exasperated, she tugged at a stack of quilts and burrowed under. But still Lucy had a sense of something playing on her nerves, like tapwater flowing in an old sink. There was pressure on the air around her. Was it water?

Outside, in Hickman, the early March night was a sponge of rain and cold. Lucy had wakened from her recurrent dream of traveling with the miners in their tunnels. Nightly, if she was lucky enough to get to the place of deep sleep, Lucy condensed an underground maze out of her unconscious. She wormed her way through its shining crawlways, a nether land entirely formed of tubes of black volcanic glass instead of coal. While Lucy dreamed, she even felt the tunnel's

225

floor beneath her palms. It was curved and cold and littered with balls of obsidianite. But Lucy had surfaced now and she was alert. Had it come from the kitchen? No, from the front room, surely. Clara or she had left a faucet open. Merely that. But there were no water pipes to the front of the house.

Lucy wanted her dream back. Once there, her symbolized cave country route was usually as endless as she willed it. Lucy summoned her visionary creation. Karst passages burst open into huge, domed limestone bubbles and shadowlight flickered on natural caprock arches. Released from reality, Lucy had always lingered in her reverie, squinting upward at glyphs of painted animals, furred and long-taloned, which were caught forever gathering air between their front and hind legs for a powerful, motionless spring into eternity. But Lucy had, tonight, to get up and trace the sound. The impulse was too forceful.

Lucy rose and slipped quietly into the celluloid negative of her unlit bedroom. At midnight it was a stage set, almost as unreal as dreamland. She made her way through succeeding zones of black and white to the front hall. By the time she steadied herself by touching, briefly, the corner of the drop-leaf walnut telephone stand in the entry, Lucy felt composed of filament entirely. When she left Milan and divorced Gabe, Lucy had thought to reconstitute herself, to stand full bodied on the ground in the sunlight. But these wrenching recent months since Joyce's death had made the glare of Gabe's affection stark. I've become a night dweller, Lucy thought. A hidden woman. All because of Gabe; loving Gabe has made me this.

From the density of midnight, some dark light escaped and spilled through the big windows in Lucy's front room and the entry hall's small lunette. The light, permeated with silence, edged in from triple-hung, floor-length glass panels in the living room and dining room. It slid through the leaded pane over the bookcase and spilled down the wall opposite the phone stand. Outside, in Lucy's front yard, she could see the damp trunks of two walnut trees which looked dipped in silver, liquid silver that ran down and puddled. It's so quiet, she thought. That was what the noise was. It was silence seeping in. Lucy covered her ears with her hands to make the silence stop.

Lucy had smothered the phone's receiver with a pillow before she went to bed. She dropped her hands and nudged the pillow ticking softly aside. She glanced at the perimeter of stealthy light that closed around her. Gradually, clouds opened and she saw, revealed in the leaded-glass lunette, the bare center of the full moon's face—a luminous, circular opening at the top of night's tent. Her sweetheart, Lucy thought, the Man in the Moon. Gabe had loved to hear that song. And "Behind some dark cloud, Where no one was allowed," she had made love to the Man in the Moon by singing.

When the phone trilled, Lucy answered. As she expected, Gabe's fateful whisper tickled down the line. "Did I wake her?" he asked, meaning, of course, their daughter, Clara. There was no first hello. He sounded near. Lucy felt his breath inside her ear, the way she had when their double bed was as wide as a room and she and Gabe were warmly woven together in the center. Tonight he was at least one hundred miles away. Thus Lucy connected herself to what was real. She would remain aware, she promised, the whole time she kept the line open, of Clara's sleeping, of the dreamy suspension of her daughter's stream of thought, behind the wall behind her.

Lucy realized that Gabe was waiting for her response. Had he

227

waked her? "I was nearby," she said. He didn't need to know about the pillow.

"Thinking of calling?"

"Thinking of not calling, to be exact." In spite of her submission to his inevitable call, Lucy would not be submissive. Had she wished to, she knew it was not in her. She did not have that to give.

"Will you stay on the line?" Gabe asked. When Lucy didn't hang up, he continued. He spooned out words which she took in careful little sips. Gabe had phoned, he told Lucy, to compare notes with her on Clara. "She says she can't fit in with other kids . . . ," he said, concerned, he claimed, about their daughter's oddball manner when the child discussed her classmates at the grade school. But however slanted his approach, Lucy felt that Gabe was closing in. Gabe, and Clara too. The two of them were closing like the moonlight on the transparent center where Lucy sat and hoped she could remain invisible.

This was Gabe's strength, of course, bargaining hard and easy in the same smooth breath.

Lucy knew what they wanted from her. It was plain in every way but words. Clara and Gabe both wanted time, her time. Only her vacation to start with. Two weeks. Was that so much? But Lucy thought she must be vigilant. Thieves of time were sly; the treasure was that precious. Thanksgiving had been one thing. This was quite another.

For a minute or so Lucy floated away from the muddy dark of March into an idea of the summer Hebron's fizzy green heat and the gooey gloss of its banks. Gabe was waiting, though, and Clara was waiting while Lucy meandered through the future. She could feel her child and husband pendant. The cloudy moon stayed pasted up in place.

But Lucy was also enamored with her present. She thought she wanted it "for keeps," as they had said as children. "Tickalock" had worked the magic then. Lucy thought of her job, the miners, the families. Even worn-out Hickman. They had knitted up to give such unexpected warmth. At least to Lucy. But all her fight seemed drained away.

Lucy tuned Gabe back in. The oddity was that if she felt herself slowing, winding down, becoming more and more still, Gabe seemed renewed. He sounded like he had as a boy when she first met him. Lucy smiled for the benefit of shadows. Did they still tell it up in Milan how she took a shine to Gabe the minute she laid eyes on him? Lucy expected not. Grim tales were the more exciting. Poor Joyce. Poor child. She had grabbed for something that wasn't hers to take. And it had killed her. With Lucy's free arm, she tried to rub away a sudden chill.

Over the phone line, Gabe tried another tack. "I've sent your check," he said. For child support, he meant. It was a thing he really didn't need to add, did he?—Gabe had been faithful there, at least.

Lucy responded, "As much as anywhere." She had suddenly returned to his earlier question about Clara, whether Clara fitted in at school.

If Gabe was confused by Lucy's non sequitur, he didn't sound it. He said, "Well, she seems fine up here," after no more than a second's pause, finishing: "Loose on the river, that child's as natural as a ripple . . ."

Ahhh. Lucy let him talk. Their daughter as a widening ripple, flowing away between the banks of Gabe and Lucy. Gabe had always been like that, able to say more than he uttered. It had been part of what she loved. And tonight he was no different. Lucy felt, as well as heard, what Gabe really meant: "Come back, come home," brushed feather soft beneath his every word.

When his phoning first commenced, the call after the January blizzard that stranded Clara at Gabe's place, Lucy had lifted the receiver, blithely unaware. On recognizing Gabe's voice she heard him out, lightly, staying on the line only long enough for his explanation about Clara's late arrival. Then she had re-cradled the handset and padded silently away. The rest of that January day she had moved gingerly, to keep the tumbrel in her head from rolling free. Lucy had fooled herself, the whole while that she continued dressing, into thinking that nothing of her balance here in Hickman was leastways disturbed.

"I saw Sonny Nolan yesterday," Gabe presently offered, in an attempt to whet her thirst for conversation. The smarty-seeming lawyer had been a great joke between the two of them when Nolan was a newcomer to Milan from West Virginia. He had moved to town around the same time Gabe hired Joyce. She and Gabe had made great sport of Sonny in the months before Lucy's fears about Gabe and Joyce Oliver loomed more heavily over her life than the palisades above Tyrone. The day Sonny had a huge ESQUIRE lettered after his name in thick, gold paint she and Gabe laughed until even tiny, three-year-old Clara had caught the infection of their glee at supper.

"He hasn't changed a bit . . . ," Gabe said now about Nolan. "Success has swelled him up like a puff adder. He'll run for office if he doesn't explode." Gabe liked to speak that way, the way he did around the field men. He would use the line again, she knew. And when he did, the quote would be repeated, drawing bigger laughs each time it passed along.

Lucy wasn't sure during this next time if Gabe spoke or whether she interrupted him. Did he try to ask if there were anything left of love or was it gone? And did Lucy then opine, "Sad to say, that's not the question now"? Or were they both still mesmerized by memories? When at last Gabe did say aloud, "Why don't you spend your vacation on the Hebron, with Clara and Nonie and me, here in Tyrone," had Lucy answered, "I don't know, Gabe. Once I was sure of where my life would take me but now the course is vague,"or had she remained mum?

But suddenly his words were unforgettable enough. "If you're afraid . . ." Gabe offered, his voice grave.

One thing Lucy knew. He mustn't say that yet.

"We'll see," she concluded in a hushed tone. Each word separate from the other. Again. "We'll try and see," she said. Lucy gently placed the fetal curl of the receiver in its solid cradle.

There was a floor register in the corner by the bookcase. Lucy stood over it after she hung up and let the air billow her gown. Against her bare feet, the ornate metal grill was almost too hot.

Clara had been so afraid of this house when they moved in. "All the doors," the child had said, over and over. Lucy had been exasperated. Evidently Clara thought the windows worked like doorways and the more you had of either, the less safe the place would be. No matter how many times Lucy explained it to her, Clara whined. She had been implacable for months, and she professed to have no memory of how forbidding the house had been that Lucy and Gabe rented in Milan. Those dark, high-ceilinged rooms, piled crookedly on top of each other because of a sagging foundation, had more than their own share of narrow, looming windows. Of course, Lucy ruefully admitted, the dangers had got in.

Lucy hunched her shoulders up as if to pull the Hickman house in around herself. Its wooden frame exterior had shrunk with age, and the place was slightly rickety. It was true that a stout walk across the floor might set her china rattling. But on sunny days, when every one of its window panes was squeaky from a recent vinegar rinse, the cottage looked as shiny as a vitrine. And whatever the beliefs of her eleven-year-old daughter, because Clara's complaints about the house and its location had hardly abated in the five years since they had lived here, Hickman did, in fact, have a sun. A giant, lemon-yellow sun that burned every bit as shiny bright, above the coal dust, as the one at Milan.

From its deep basement corner, the coal furnace suddenly thumped loudly for attention, then clicked off. Lucy felt her soft nightgown settling, settling against her skin, like plumes. The sensation reminded her again of Gabe, the soothing way he had touched her with his big, even-weighted hands. These nights he was whispering "Come home, come back," across the miles. But he had said "Come here," the night he hit her. Lucy, remembering, ran her finger down the line of her jaw around to her chin. No trace in the bone.

She had stepped close when Gabe demanded. Lucy had been as mad as mad could be. She had wanted to brute her husband into the corner, topheavy with anger as a buffalo. She had pushed her fury at him with her chest. What on earth had Gabe been thinking? Tied up at the warehouse night after night, he had told her. When Lucy knew what his late nights and distraction meant. She knew! In spite of all not knowing.

That particular night Lucy had felt furiously invincible. What kind of funny business was it that kept Gabe from ever having time? Not any time for her or Clara. In all the mental pictures Lucy had of Clara from that time, the girl pressed her macaroni elbows close and trained big eyes, worried, on the world. Wasn't Gabe the one who had declared that his wife and daughter were his life? What kind of wastrel was he that he would put them all at risk? Did he aim to turn into his daddy? Yet Gabe had snapped "Come here," that night to Lucy before she had fearlessly stomped closer. They had both been huge, in rage. Lucy yelled. She had called Gabe "Mister" in a braying voice she would not have claimed. "You just better tell me, Mister, whatthehell? . . ." Lucy almost heard the echo, the shouts had been that loud. "You nasty bastard," her voice had shrilled at Gabe on authority of its own. And she had continued throwing razored words she knew were drenched in venom, aiming for the vein.

"Come here," growled the face of Gabe she had not known, the awful mouth around the set of awful teeth. Lucy had pitched nearer, fearless. Gabe's sudden left arm swung toward her like a bat and when his hand connected, her own white teeth, with their fine enamels padded by the cushion of her cheek, sliced deeply into the plush vermillion border of her lips. Everything went quiet when she fell.

Lucy had suppressed her memory of Gabe's blow since the day she moved from Milan. But nothing of its impact was lost. After falling she had remained inert for a second or two before she opened her mouth slowly, as if waking into silence with a yawn, and bled her brilliant chrysanthemum of blood onto the carpet. The rug's raised fibers, which created its dull pattern, had rapidly absorbed the stain while Lucy studied the phenomenon as if unaffected.

As he had done earlier tonight, Gabe had breached the silence then. "Jesus. Jesus," he had cried. "How could you make me do that." Gabe had nearly screamed before he clomped crookedly away and out the door.

After all these years he wanted to draw her near again. Lucy looked through the living room archway toward Clara's bedroom for fear a sound might have waked her girl. But the door was firmly shut.

Lucy had fainted in front of six-year-old Clara when she came in from the dentist's office that next day after the fight. Standing over the heat duct now, her gown re-inflated, Lucy felt the exact sensation as when she had passed out. Instead of falling, the floor had caught wind and flown up around her, full-bellied like a sail. Lucy sank inside its cloth. She remembered smothering pleasantly, until the world came back from black.

Little Clara had been kneeling over her in the bedroom when Lucy opened her eyes. The child's skin was whiter than a nurse's white-starched uniform. She had brought Lucy a wet washrag when her mother asked.

Their dentist, Dr. Claypool, had washed his hands repeatedly while he worked, regretfully, it seemed to Lucy. The man had looked down at her, lashes long above his mask, from the intimate position of a lover. The bright light he aimed bore down on Lucy like a locomotive. But they shared no secrets.

Those last few days Lucy spent with Gabe in Milan had been oddly tender, she thought now. Lucy had virtually tiptoed through the house, picking what she would take with her from Milan to Hickman when she left, besides Clara. Each morning she chose a room and stayed put for hours at a stretch, considering small items. It was artifacts she craved. A teacup or an ashtray. And nothing could be damaged. That was her one rule.

Gabe had stayed away from home except at night while Lucy made her preparations that December. He, too, had had his pressing work. It had been the start of his second auction season as owner of the tobacco warehouse. His dream. Before daylight every morning he was gone. When Gabe returned, late afternoons, Lucy saw his eyes strike spots where something had gone missing.

Lucy had slept in their same bed with him nightly that long, last week. They had been careful not to touch. "If I could take back one thing," Gabe said once, near dawn, enunciating clearly. But he never named it.

Back within the here and now of Hickman, Lucy moved from the corner furnace vent to the living room sofa. She settled herself lightly on one bolstered arm. She was so thoroughly of the same temperature as the air in the room that she felt bodyless, her gown a mere slant of moonlight against the ivy-patterned slipcover.

Oh, she and Gabe had had such passion. Bouts of wet-skinned lust that drove them each so hard they were amazed when something petal delicate like Clara had sprung from their intensity. So was it loneliness that had her asking herself if she might return? Or was it the aching absence of that satisfaction?

Perched on the sofa, Lucy held in tight. How had she left him? How could she presently bear to leave herself?

Cloud cover hid the moon. Lucy's cottage turned as black as it was quiet, inside and out. Cautiously, she picked her way back to the bedroom. In the dining room Lucy trailed her hand slowly around the oval table. The mahogany wood felt cool and silky, like an extension of her own tender envelope of skin.

CHAPTER 28

Time as a Souvenir

I N HICKMAN, CLARA skipped down the hill. It was April and she was homeward bound on an errand of flowers, flowers to bring back to school. On her right, the trees in the park were just leafing out. Celery green and soft looking, dotted pink or white, the dogwoods there were more bouquet than tree-like. Their petals stirred and Clara bounced in a breeze that was as chill and fresh as sweet tea.

For the first time since last fall, screened doors and windows on the houses opposite stood open. Their black frames danced up and down while Clara bobbed past; then they settled behind her. This unbottling of spring was oh, so delicious, Clara thought. Even Hickman seemed tolerable this morning. She would take her own sweet time about the flowers.

Songs and voices from radios across the street ran out from every open house. Clara noted the sounds but kept right on bounding lightly down the sidewalk, springing gleefully through the mingled words and music. She felt as wriggly as a pup.

At the corner of the block, when she was one house away from home, an old two-seater coupe slowed in the street. "Help me, little girl," the driver called. Clara could barely hear the man through the other sounds that had her attention. "Come on over here," he crooned, singing a scary song, "I need some help from a little girl like you." His thin, young face was solemn.

But it was class day, after all, and Clara had flowers to bring from home, and she wouldn't let that stranger frighten her by any means. Quick as a flash, she wheeled immediately left and started a diagonal path to her own front door. The slippery soles of Clara's new sandals fairly skated across shoots of rye and dandelion. The young grasses were as slick and green as jade. "Mrs. Honaker," she yelled in a singsong, "I'm on my way." The car picked up speed and went through the four-way stop every bit as fast as Clara's racing heart.

Then Clara was in the house, and then she was elated by the starlike glints of light reflected from the sideboard silver, and in the kitchen, off the stove. If there were a Mrs. Honaker, a name Clara fancied, her Mrs. Honaker would be built in incremental mounds of white, much like a snowman, and would have greeted Clara with a dough-soft hug.

Out in the backyard, Clara saw that flowers were winning over weeds. That's how potent spring was, she thought. She wanted to go on tiptoes only, to balance her basket and her scissors on upraised fingers in the air. But Clara was greedy, too, and she could hardly wait to plunge and cut the different colors.

Clara knew a few plant names already. Tucked up next to the alley there was an azalea that had gone stalky. It hung heavily lopsided from the top. The bracts showered sparks of hot persimmon-colored petals from several drooping clusters. Start with that, Clara thought. Get a little sizzle in the basket first. Then Clara dropped onto her knees in gushy soil and began separating blue ajuga spikes from their copper-colored leaves. She snipped six or eight carefully at the base, the others more hurriedly.

All the while, Clara kept finding lilies of the valley everywhere. Their tiny, pearl-sized bells popped up in tangles of ivy. And they dangled over a rock border that was almost completely overgrown with mint. Clara pinched and cut everything she thought most likely to delight until she and the basket were stuffed full of blooms and scent and she was about to burst from so much liberty.

This was her good world, Clara thought, and getting better: By midsummer she would be with Mother and Daddy in Tyrone. On that note, Clara topped her collection with one last spire of snapdragon. Its small, lemony pouches waggled in the air when she held it aloft. Now she was perfectly pleased. She could go back to school, hightailing it all the way.

The hill was too formidable for even Clara to skip up. But she made it a light-footed trip and carefully pressed the basket between her elbow and waist so that none of her armload of stems spilled out. Clara thought that her mother wouldn't mind this garden robbery. Wouldn't Lucy be ever so glad that Clara was finally showing signs of taking some advice? "Be part of things," Mother was constantly urging about Clara's friendless state. Well, wasn't this a case of being part, this bringing of bouquets? Why, Clara felt like part of spring itself, nearing the peak of her ascent. And she was breathlessly pink-cheeked, abloom to all who saw her.

It Was the Goodness of the Place

***

Back in Milan, at almost that exact moment, Spiro propped a bentwood chair under one of the double door's chrome bars; then he pushed it back until the Dixie's entryway was wedged open. People in his restaurant looked up and waited, blinking patiently, as he did so, while April streamed in and at first diluted, then replaced the stale, steam-table air they had been breathing and rebreathing since autumn. The patrons seemed faintly surprised by the scent. Those who were seated with their backs to the door twisted themselves around for a better view and pulled their sweaters close.

The pin oak trees which lined both sides of Main Street were visible from most of their booths and tables. Tiny, chartreuse leaves spotted the trees' conical crowns. After a swift appraisal, the men and women returned to their newspapers or neighborly talk, satisfied. The world of open windows, open doors, was back. Shortly, the noon whistle would blow. Unmuffled by winter, the sound was less mournful. Theirs was such a sweet town, they thought, with its stately courthouse, right in place at the center, and spring more punctual here than in other places.

At Spiro's hindmost table, Judge Stallard and Ben Gilliam waited for the Coroner to arrive and complete their trio before they would order lunch. Ben teased the Judge about the air conditioning unit and television set the older man had recently bought. They were the first (and Ben earnestly hoped the last) of such things in Milan. "You'll be missing out," he told Stallard. "You'all are going to be closed in with nothing but cold air and pictures of foreigners. You won't know you're here and you won't know it's summer." Stallard smiled and Ben returned it. A slight current stirred the napkins stacked at center

240

table. The Sheriff felt as airy and good-natured as that breeze. He felt newly produced, more on the Judge's level. This green season had pushed him right up through the darkest winter Ben remembered. Maybe only in his mind had it been so bleak, fixated as he was on Joyce Oliver's death and the implications for Gabe Phillips and Milan. Not to mention the business of Ira Truitt's acting up, stalking Phillips, or whatever it was he was doing. Well, it was time to let go, Ben thought. Like those pin oaks, he knew he had held his winter leaves too long.

In only a few weeks this town would wilt in summer's heat, and when it did, all the sounds that escaped through screened openings, the voices that rose from fields and lawns and from Milan's tiny city park, even the oiled buzz of engines in the street and on the farms, would melt and run together. That hot blend of noise was Ben's favorite; it linked his present with the sameness of his past, and he heard in such music the echo of his children's future. Yes sir, this was a fine day, he thought, a ceremonial day. Ben washed its freshness down with the glass of springwater he took now from Spiro's hand. This April morning Ben understood, he thought, for the first time what it was to remember, that it was to become a part of memory, not the other way around, and that time was a souvenir of the mind.

While the noon whistle blew in Milan, Gabe and Gilmer, from the warehouse, stood down in Tyrone with Nonie and considered an open can of paint. "That color don't look like it could occur," Gilmer said.

Gabe had to agree. The liquid was a limpid green in a new bucket. Seen from straight above, the can had no depth and the paint looked for all the world like a silver-rimmed enamel disc, which had been discarded as thoughtlessly in his side yard as a huge, green tiddly-wink. Alternately Gabe studied the paint and squinted in the appropriate direction. He was trying to spot the tin roof on Nonie's small house. Within his field of vision, the paint's unnatural color emphasized the subtlety of every other tint.

The trees and undergrowth between Gabe's house and Nonie's were now, in April, variously and profusely pastel. Gabe finally spied the roof's metal sheeting through the foliage. It was dull brown like the flank of a deer. Along his sightline, among shiny water maple leaves that looked as wet as newborns, redbud and whitebud trees were scattershot. Their explosion of flowers hovered delicately in the air over the spindly tethers of their trunks. Woody vines as big around as half-dollars, which Gabe had tried to hack away last summer, were visible today only as spidery connections, seemingly no thicker than pencil lead.

"I don't know, Nonie," Gabe said, "whether I want that paint applied or not. I thought it would do, but, now it looks a little . . . unsubdued." Nonie was presently taking in the sky, not the can of enamel. She had seen enough in an instant to know what she wanted. Perched right out on the edge of a big, shiny marble, she felt, like her mother used to say she was. Oh, Lord, this was some day, Nonie thought, all fresh-washed and billowy. A keeper day, surely. Those two men hadn't even glanced for one particle of a second at that blue up there or at the Hebron below so full of sky that every now and then a puff of cloud drifted downstream.

"Well, it's your roof and your paint, Mr. Gabe," Nonie answered when it suited her, taking her time about eyeing her employer instead of the clean sheet of heaven or mirror river. "It's your house, too, which I know," she said. "But it's *my* opinion that any other color would about spoil the whole project. I say the top of Nonie's roost is going to hold cool air when everything else is hot and dry in August. It'll be so green, spring won't want to leave me, ever. That's what I say, Mr. Gabe. You do what you want."

Gilmer's mouth was a such a perfect *O* of surprise that Gabe laughed aloud. Gilmer had never in his entire life given Gabe a response more personal than a list of his favorite vegetables. That *O* on Gilmer's freckled, wrinkled face was exactly right, Gabe thought, laughably right, for too-bright paint. Because of so much rightness, Gabe was in the mood to grant all wishes. "Well, okay, Nonie," he announced. "If you think you can put a lid on this weather, you are sure as hell welcome to try."

Nonie and Gabe and Gilmer stood and considered. They gazed down at the bold, primary green in its winkling can. Almost simultaneously the three of them raised their heads and mentally applied it.

"And if it *don't* suit, that ain't awful," Gilmer cracked, willing to say almost anything to join in. There was a faint breeze. The sun heated the skin on the backs of their necks, softened their postures. After a while, Gabe started toward the toolshed in long, relaxed strides. Who cared if he was crippled? Nonie wiped dew beads from a lawn chair's fan of wooden slats with her forefinger, then wiped the finger's damp tip all the way around her lips. Old Gilmer, in no hurry at all, squatted and stirred the viscous paint with a twig.

That morning, in the wheel of fields between Tyrone and Milan, farmers disced manure from their cow barns into soft dirt. They sighted back over their shoulders at the slightly wavering lines that trailed behind their tractors. In light as bright as sunflowers, newly turned clods showed black. With an even rhythm, the men worked the earth until it was alternately ridged and furrowed, a dank, dark mane of soil separated by the wide teeth of a comb. That mane of combed turf flowed and blended from farm to farm to farm all the way around Milan, as loose and wavy as the gentle breeze that now stirred trees along the fencelines.

Come May, growers would set tobacco plants that were this minute being coddled in warm beds under acre-long strips of gauze. When it came time, each leafy starter plant would be as small as a head of Bibb and just as fragile. The farmers would take up those clumps of new Burley with their thick, calloused fingers and handle them as tenderly as baby chicks. Raising tobacco was fine work, they thought. Even in the face of chance, in spite of worries about weather luck, or bug luck, this was a job they understood. The cycle made sense. When it went right, the men could stretch up from cramped, bent-back jobs, sweaty, and stand with their wives and children, sighting down row after row of green-leaved stalks that were pink-topped with flowers. In those moments, the crop caught their hearts. It meant almost too much, they thought. But today the farmers jounced easily along in the breeze, simply content, working their portion of April beyond the ordinary limits.

Two blocks from the courthouse on the square, near the grade school, Milan's cemetery took up several acres. In the cemetery, too, a man rode a tractor. It was time for the first spring mowing. The smell of spring onions, just cut, traced the air. The driver stopped his equipment for a minute and turned his face, eyes closed, full into a slight breeze. Then he started again, artfully weaving around those headstones and statues that were situated on large plots. Later he would take the push mower and cut the section where small brass plaques were no farther apart than the width of a casket.

There were willow trees leaning this way and that throughout the grounds. The crowns were just greening, and the long whips of their branches draped forward over many graves like hair mournfully tossed from the nape of an arched trunk. The maintenance man had several scratches on his forearms from using the tractor instead of a hand scythe to get under where they hung.

He was towing a small tool cart. On the bed of his cart sat a new granite marker, minimum size. The marker had been engraved block style with only a name and dates. There was no message. When he figured the years, the man whistled low. Twenty-six. This was a town where people died old, generally, and he always figured the years just to comfort himself. But this Joyce Oliver only got twenty-six. Hardly a handful. He'd seen her up in town looking more than a little bit lively, and he meant to set her stone nice. The girl had kept herself that way, wearing red bracelets and barrettes that matched. And he liked her tight dresses, too. From the back, when Joyce Oliver walked, her bottom jiggled, creamy as a custard. She wouldn't have picked this here gray monument. He knew that. But he could brighten her site, transplant a little something from an area around one of the mausoleums. A white mountain laurel maybe. Or even clematis. She would like that one. The flower was showy. There were some clematis vines on a wrought iron rail near the Mapother vault. When he pruned them in the fall, a handful of blossoms had showered onto his palm like a catch of purple stars. Bright white flesh highlighted their centers. Late this afternoon, after the granite house was in shadow, he would get a cutting, all right, and wrap it in peat. Who would know?

His tractor putted along slowly, almost at the idle. And why not pace himself? For his part, people could rush around all they wanted. He was sure in no hurry to get, well, where he was. Even if, on a day like today, the Milan cemetery had to be about the prettiest place anywhere.

Over the engine sounds, he could hear the whispery, rhythmic whoosh of the blades. Breathe it all in while you can, he thought. Ride and breathe. The work was as pleasant as sunning on a rock.

Late that afternoon, Ira Truitt used a beech trunk like a tent pole and settled back against it. He scanned the underside of the foliage. What sunlight there was had a silvered look.

His new shotgun was balanced across his lap. "Smooth bore," the clerk had said. "Side by side" was another phrase the man had used. Ira, remembering the sales pitch, sat in his thicket and released the gun's top catch, where the barrels attached, and broke it open. He squeezed his left eye shut and peered down into one dark chamber. The tube was so clean inside that a few dust specs looked outsized and magically attached, as if they might break free any instant and bounce along, pinging endlessly off the walls of their miniature vault.

Satisfied, Ira clicked the stock back into place and stood. He walked to the rim of the sinkhole with the gun butt in his armpit, barrels threaded lightly over his thick forearm the way he had been shown. "See how it feels," the man had advised him. "Grow accustomed." Well, Ira thought, it felt like part of him, no less than the missing part.

246

The shotgun had been costly. A full eighty-nine dollars for a "rabbit gun." That was a lot of bunny killing. The salesman had also made him practice raising the wrist that supported the Winchester. The idea being to lift the business end with that single gesture. He was told that the proper hold made it easy as pie to fire after you spotted prey. Just raise the arm ("making the move real silky"), grip with the left, and slide to the trigger. Raise, grip, slide. One, two, three. There was nothing to it. Simple as gliding on the river, Ira thought. No sense of constriction.

The air stirred around Ira's head; then a breeze picked up. The cool scent of April swept the thicket. He knew well that he needed a sweater. A few reedy saplings were blowing against each other. They were too supple to make much sound. But Ira watched them, tap, tap, tap. He stood utterly still and watched. Tap, tap, tap. About five yards away, to the left of the sink, there was a jack-in-the-pulpit. He slowly lifted his shotgun and sighted. The erect flower was an exotic, botanical chalice of palest lilac, dashed with green. He centered a metal bead under the plant's lipped bowl. Pow, Ira whispered.

CHAPTER 29

Sweet Time

THE LONG ROOM in Daddy's house, shaded by the screened porch, was as cool as Clara's favorite mudbank, a little slap of land where she often played between river shallows and overhanging trees. Clara would remember the light in the room. No matter how bright the wash of sunshine outside, this room had a pleasant, watery depth all its own.

Clara was sitting in a wicker rocker by one of the double doors, and Daddy lounged contentedly on the leather chair near his desk. His feet dented a plump hassock. Clara had spent her morning on the river rowing a teeny dory. Back and forth she had plied in the juicy air while Daddy talked warehouse business on the phone. This dozy, afternoon tiredness in the half-lighted room with Gabe was her reward. And it was ample.

It was the third weekend in May. Clara was on her last, unremarkable visit to Tyrone before school let out in two weeks.

But she would remember the light and how she and her daddy talked.

Those things were every bit as important as what they said. After lunch Clara had washed up, unpeeled damp, mud-spattered jeans from her skinny legs, and stepped like a fawn into her new three-tiered, circular cotton skirt. She couldn't wait to show off for Gabe. There were so many yards of material gathered into the skirt's layers that ruffles swaddled her knees and calves whenever she moved, increasing the pleasant sensation that especially today, here in this room and on the river, there was no break between one sort of goodness and another.

For fun, Gabe had let her choose one of his hats to wear this afternoon. Clara went with him to the door of his closet and surveyed the setup. His suits were hung in perfect order, ranging from her favorite light blue three-piece at one end, over to the striped charcoal wool on the far right side. "By color and weight," Gabe answered, even though Clara's wondering had been silent. Several hats were perched upon the shelf above his suits, and a row of shoes marched along below. He called the dress-up pair "French Shriners," which Clara thought was a better name for laceups than any she had heard. She and Gabe had stood there amiably, his warm arm comfortably heavy on her shoulders, while Clara pointed out a fedora in the center of the shelf. "Snap-brim," Daddy had said gaily, his voice a rubberband.

Clara now retucked her braids inside the hat and rubbed its rolled edge with the palm of her hand. The honey-colored felt was as solidly soft as a bird's smooth breast.

"There was a snake on the river this morning," she said. Clara's voice came out a mite smaller than she planned but she went on with it. "It just kind of skeetered along. I was trying to row the same way." Gabe had told Clara that she should learn to make her boat go smooth.

She hoped he would say that she had, that he had looked down from his high porch and that the dory hadn't left a single mark on the Hebron.

Instead Gabe cautioned her. "You have to watch out," he said. "Water snakes are tricky devils. They've been known to wriggle up an oar every now and then. Some'll get right in the boat with you if you let them. But as long as you keep an eye out." In spite of the warning content, Gabe's impish tone and his eyes, shiny bright, were as much as telling her that no danger was real.

Clara felt secure, then, bragging to Daddy that even when she saw the snake she hadn't been a bit afraid. And she truly, almost, meant it. Like people were always saying about one thing or another, Clara figured that the river was plenty big enough for both. Especially if the snakes weren't real, she thought.

At that, Gabe told Clara she sounded exactly like her mother. "Lucy was a rascal at your age," he finished up, swallowing a chuckle at the end.

Clara stilled. This room didn't frighten her either these days. Not the way it had last Thanksgiving. And this afternoon the memorable and welcoming light behind her daddy's brown eyes made her feel perfectly at home.

"Did you say rascal?" she asked him. Clara would give a pretty just to hear Gabe declare "rascal" again. He had hushed the word and given it the lisp of secrecy. She was glad, though, when her question didn't divert him, because Gabe continued about Lucy: "There was a ropeswing not far from here when we were kids. A boy tied it up onto a huge old butternut that must have been a hundred feet tall . . ."

Clara had spied such a tree. It soared out of the cedars and undergrowth that topped a palisade upriver on the Tyrone side. Daddy went on with his story while Clara pictured her tree through seasons. Its sky high trunk was twisted like a rope of taffy.

"Butternut's a hickory," Gabe told her. "This particular tree topped the steepest bank for miles, and had a big rack of branches that stuck out that far over the Hebron." Daddy encompassed the air in his long, strong, arms.

Gabe gestured and paused and spoke and paused. Taking his own sweet time, Clara thought. So this was what that meant. Sweet time. While she listened, Clara gently adjusted a tier of her new skirt. A triangle of gathered fabric fanned slowly, enjoyably, down along her shin. Sweet time.

"I guess I was in the eleventh grade," Gabe continued his story, "which puts your mother in the ninth. She and I would meet at Tyrone landing sometimes." Daddy stopped. He flipped his lighter cap, then sparked the tiny wheel with his thumb in one fluid roll of the hand. Clara was enchanted. She watched and waited for Gabe to tell her more, so much more, as his cigarette smoke twisted upward on the air like a ghost of the long-ago tree.

"That day, a bunch from school showed up too," Gabe said, now that his lungs were satisfied. "Some boy in the group, a towheaded kid named Arland, I'll never forget, had got hold of a spool of one-inch braided hemp. Quite a find during the Depression. Arland wasn't big as a minute. But I saw what he meant to do, even though I was standing off to one side. Your mother was in with the others. See, I usually stayed apart. Anyway, Arland jumped on that hickory bark like a monkey and started shinnying up, dangling a tail of rope. God, he climbed high."

Clara could see the boy plain as day. During his ascent, tiny Arland's white silk hair twinkled like a sunspot, in and out of clouds of leaves. Across the room, Gabe's gaze was also focused on the ephemeral.

He went on with his description. "The way he was going, it wouldn't have surprised me if he'd pulled the rope up after himself and disappeared," he said. Clara relished the shock of the possibility Daddy had put forth.

"If he'd fallen I think the impact would have squashed him like a bug. But he didn't. Not in this telling, anyway." Gabe laughed low and continued. "When he got where he meant to go, Arland crawled out about as far as he could on a riverside limb and knotted his rope."

Every now and then a heavy outboard engine zoomed down the river. Clara breathed the faintest whiff of gasoline, which was fanned up, she knew, from the bottle-green Hebron by a spreading, white-feathered wake.

This scented air and the light and Arland aloft in her mind, she thought. All this.

"The best thing was that when he had the hemp knotted and tightened, he rode it straight down like a shot. If he burned his palms, he didn't tell us. Made the thing look slick as a ribbon." Gabe spoke easily, the line of his voice slack. An aimless, two-winged fly spiraled lazily in the filmy space between him and Clara. "I don't know who fixed the grip on the rope's end, but he had the swing ready for business in a jiffy."

"The point is, you should have seen your mother." At this, Gabe shook his head. The gesture was plainly visible even in the changing light.

"A few of the boys gave some half-hearted tries at swinging over the edge but they fell short. None of the other girls, nor half the boys were even willing to attempt it. Except your mother, as you might've guessed. Lucy Clement, she couldn't wait. Absolutely could not wait to jump. She grabbed that rope and drew back up the hill, far as the strand would reach." Gabe stopped there, the way Lucy must have when she did it. Then he started fresh and full of breath: "She came running fast. You could hear her coming, thumping like a pony. I'd have stopped her if I thought I could have. At the exact right spot, where the bluff turned to air, Lucy picked up her feet and sailed waaay out over the water. Clean as a whistle."

Clara would remember that this odd light in the room was a flawless light.

And she could hear Lucy running with the swing as plain as if she, herself, had suddenly jumped to her feet and raced toward Gabe.

Gabe didn't leave Clara to ponder long. "Lucy had her timing right," he observed, "I'll say that. She swung at least as high as the branch and waited til the tip top of her arc to let go." Daddy smiled before the next part. Oh, this was fun. "When she did let loose, she hung in the air. Stayed up there while we all held our breath. Then she tucked her elbows, hugged her knees, and went spinning right into the river like a pinwheel."

In Clara's giddy imagination, Lucy's red hair wound around and around the pinwheel's center, as she spun down and down from the loopy ropeswing. Her father had made it luminously clear. Here in the light of this room, Clara pictured the bright star of her mother spiraling into the Hebron with a pointed splash.

Lucy's vivid presence from that long-ago day lingered there

between Clara and Gabe, just beneath the surface of the afternoon. But in one month, Clara thought, her mother actually would be here. In this very room, perhaps. And she would be in Tyrone for two whole weeks. Because she had promised. Lucy had finally, finally agreed to spend her vacation at Gabe's house.

Suddenly, Clara had the perfect vision. They would all go upriver and find the tree. They would. They would take chicken and sandwiches and tea. The butternut hickory with its twisted taffy trunk still soared above the thicket, Clara was sure. The loop of its magical rope, which had once swayed easy in every season's breeze, was no doubt ingrown into the branch at the depth of heartwood.

Gabe's chair was several feet away from Clara's. After a long, silent study, she was afraid he didn't plan on speaking again. But he did. "Well," he concluded, "she was a pistol."

Gabe then faced Clara. His eyes were steady. He was happy with his tale, she thought. Was she supposed to talk now? "I think she isn't different," was all that she could add.

Was that okay to say? Clara wanted so to please Gabe, to repay him for spinning out the fine thread of his and Lucy's story until Clara was included.

Gabe accepted Clara's observation about Lucy. He went on in a more curious tone. "Your mother and I, we're just hard to figure, Clara. You must wonder. We were bound too close, maybe, and for too long a time. I always felt my life through Lucy, though. We were so young when we started with each other. Maybe that was it. But I think we have a chance."

It was the first time ever, *ever,* that Gabe had talked to Clara this way. Here in this room with the syrupy light. This was the way he talked to people at the warehouse, or uptown. To Nonie, most of all. Her excitement over his manner brushed Clara's skin.

"And if it's up to me," Gabe said, "your mother and I have more than a chance. That's something I want you to know, Clara. I'll make it a pledge."

Clara wished to put her hand on her heart and swear allegiance together right that second.

The room expanded like a bubble in her mind. Clara was right where she was and far away at the same time. She could see herself focused on the bubble's convex sheen, turning her shoulders this way and that. Did Gabe think that she was pretty, in her circle skirt and his jaunty, snap-brim hat?

Gabe had more to say. "It's funny about people, Clara. When you grow up maybe you'll figure it out for us. Whether people change events, or events change them."

Clara didn't know how on earth Gabe meant for her to take that, but she loved the way he weighed his words, their heft and balance, though she bumped to earth about as fast as Arland had when he said: "You know, Clara, you shouldn't expect too much this summer."

If Daddy's warning wasn't Nonie talking, Clara never heard it. Nonie would be here shortly. She was probably already taking her last few minutes "easy breathing" out on the bluff before slipping back over to fix supper. Clara had noticed more than once that expectations seemed to be about the only things in the whole world Nonie did fear. The woman made a regular habit out of lecturing on the topic. And whenever Nonie preached, she gripped Clara's hand or shoulder, as if she could wring out every single drop of expectation by squeezing on that bony point.

Well. Daddy didn't seem to be looking for an answer, so Clara stayed mum about her ideas with respect to next month's reunion. She could keep a secret. Good as gold. And it was her own business what she had or didn't have for summer. Hope or expectation, who could say? Surely not her parents, from what Clara had observed.

To her delight, Daddy started with another tale. He was telling her about his and Lucy's high school dance. Clara worried for a second. It was impossible for Gabe to have really danced with Mother, or any other girl, and Clara couldn't stand to think the memory would make him sad. But when Gabe joked that he'd been "the best damn intermissioner in the lot," she liked his face. Right that minute he looked happy as a clam. She would have loved to say so.

Clara leaned back in her rocker and tilted her face up to the warm, delicious rain of Gabe's words. Every single drop felt good. It seemed like the beginning of loving Gabe and Lucy in a different way, as people separate from herself. Clara held the children her parents had been tenderly in her mind. But while Gabe relived the past, Clara registered the diffusive quality of shadow in the long, cool room and the gradual extinction of the light.

CHAPTER 30

Absolute Summer

Nonie watched through a pane of glass that was as clean as air. It wasn't quite noon but Mr. Gabe had already shut his kitchen windows against June heat. His house, under the overhang, was as dark and cool as wet moss, and Nonie knew he meant to keep it that way. Come nightfall, he would open up, Nonie thought. That was his habit of doing. All three sets of double doors would stand wide this evening, allowing the house a big gulp of the chill that started rising off the river by suppertime.

Nonie could see Gabe outside on his knees next to the walkway. He was digging at lime-colored grass with a pointed spade. She shook her head. Too ready, she thought, that's what he was trying to be. The man ought to just hold his horses and look around a little bit. Keep still, for a change. Clara and her mother weren't coming to do inspections. And after all Gilmer's mowing yesterday, if as much as a sprig of jimson was popping up out of place, Nonie would be surprised. But she reckoned it wouldn't be the first time.

It Was the Goodness of the Place

***

Gabe wore a sun-whitened, cotton dress shirt. It wasn't five hours since Nonie had pulled it off the clothesline over to her place early this morning. She had ironed the dew out of it first thing. When Mr. Gabe buttoned it up, the cloth had probably still been warm from the pressing, the way he liked it, even in summer. While Nonie looked out at him, the shirt's cloth reflected midday brightly in her eyes, until it obliterated shade and detail and caused her to squint.

Since Nonie was glassed in, she could only imagine the soft chink of Mr. Gabe's spade into soil. The corner of the house where she stood was always quieter than the river side. But today the kitchen seemed as unnaturally hushed as an empty church. She pulled her work bowl closer to her flat bosom and kept her vigil. A tiny noise disturbed the silence only slightly. It was Nonie's knobbed knucklebones rattling against the rim of her favorite crock. She respectfully accommodated the tremor, same as she did the grave age that caused it, and kept right on working, watching. Once in a while Nonie cupped the bowl's edge, just to cool her palms. The crock's blue, saltware glaze was slick as ice and right effective.

Nonie meant to cook at least a double batch of strawberry jam and had several quarts of fruit to prepare. Berry capping was, for her, in the way of being soothing. An absentminded job, Nonie felt. And a good day for it. She discarded another sprigged hull onto newspaper, where a shaggy mound of caps had already accumulated. Without missing a beat, Nonie snagged the next fat strawberry in a smooth left-handed loop and mercilessly plucked its top.

Nonie's performance was as seamless as it was nimble fingered.

And the motion satisfied, she thought, standing, moving her keen arms and hands from memory, with her eyes on the figure outdoors. Occasionally, Nonie even hummed a bit, swaying unconsciously. But it was Mr. Gabe's hands, not her own, that held Nonie's attention. For he looked to be doing magic where he sat, poking a hole in the turf, then reaching through and coming up with things. He made it seem that the carpet of yard was one-ply thick and that wonders were tucked, like Cracker Jack prizes, in a batting of clouds below.

Just now, Gabe had added a bow-knot root to the small pile of gypsum-crusted rocks near his thigh. He scooted over and adjusted his crouch until he sat smack down on a patch of rye. His unmatched legs stretched out of Nonie's sightline. Inside the window sash, the rest of his figure was framed for her against blocks of pure color: waxy green sod and freshly sealed macadam, which was as black as a telephone. Mr. Gabe had had the pavers run his driveway down the hill while they were at it, so he could launch or pull a powerboat more easily. Under morning's ripple of wavering heat, the stream of asphalt poured from a zero point and gradually flared behind Gabe until, at the widest, it plunged over the edge of the lot, a dark, liquid-looking waterfall of shining tar that cascaded all the way to the Hebron.

Nonie looked out on a square of absolute summer, caught and held. That was the truth. Her eyes locked themselves into an unwaveringly pleasant stare, the way it sometimes happened, until finally, Gabe's shirtback, ever brighter, dazzled a hole in the center of her vision. At the last, there was nothing for it but for Nonie to pull her gaze within the kitchen's shady shallows.

***

Because the windows were shut and the oven was on, the kitchen had become close, to the point of stuffiness. Mr. Gabe had gone out through the laundry room and left the outside door ajar. But Nonie didn't think the air had stirred from here to there since then. She would have traded more than a few degrees of heat, about now, for roomier breathing and called it a bargain. Nevertheless, Nonie ignored her dry mouth and let her thoughts float like tufts of cottonwood seed, landing where they would.

Her mama's Red Red Jam. That's what Nonie Pulce was making. And proud of it. Nonie meant to have a row of Mason jars filled with the goopy sweet strawberry spread and gleaming ruby on the windowsill in time for Clara and Lucy's arrival. Unless something happened, Nonie would be well ahead of herself by nightfall.

When the stove timer dinged, Nonie left off capping, pulled a metal roaster from the oven and set it across two cold burners. For the thousandth time, she wished her mother's battered, oblong sugar-warming pan hadn't got away, like so much else. Nonie would be using it this minute. She knew that.

Back at her window table, Nonie lifted the berry bowl and deftly gathered newsprint, one handed, around the mess of hulls. She held the parcel away from herself and carried it like a stork's bundle over to the sink. A tiny stream of juice dot, dot, dotted through the soggy paper. Minuscule splats marked her path on the polished linoleum floor.

Nonie quickly re-covered the work surface with clean sections of Sunday's *Milan Daily News*. She overlapped the pages and ironed them flat with the side of her hand. It was her mother's moves that she was making. Like always, when she cooked, before Nonie ever donned her apron this morning, she had stepped inside her mother's body and slipped her own thin arms into those ample, long-ago arms, like a pair of invisible sleeves.

Nonie was specially willing to confer her mother's grace and blessing today, on the advent of reunion. For there was an unlikely point where Nonie felt that she and her mother and this odd white man connected. Mr. Gabe drove hard, she thought, but he drove himself harder. There probably wasn't a thing he asked that he wouldn't do or hadn't done twice over. And whatever the secrets of his heart—Nonie wasn't in the business of excusing or accusing right now—he did seem to have built his world by hand. The same way that Mama, always worrying her own hold on life, had taught Nonie, herself, to do.

Nonie knew she was on dangerous ground in her thoughts. If she started following that line, she would soon come to the sharp edge of considering exactly what Mr. Gabe's efforts had brought him to keep while Nonie, like her mother before her and on on on back, through all the sweat- and blood-connected women before that, had washed and ironed and cooked and sewed and cleaned and swept and dusted her way up from nothing every day. Every single day. Minute by minute. "Spit your bitter to the side," Mama had said in each night's secret counsel. Nonie always had done the bidding of her mama, but bitter left a potent taste.

Right now there were sweeter things to think on, thank the Lord, because Nonie knew perfection when she saw it. Like this red, gold-dotted strawberry, that sat on her palm, big as a top, and sliced like butter when she cut it. The cottony down in Nonie's mind floated to rest for a moment on herself, as having settled into something like a family. With that, she tossed the berry into the pot and went on spearing the tip of the knife into the plumpest fruits that came to hand, releasing their moisture in a steady, satisfying trickle of dark-tinged whey.

After fixing a first layer of cut berries two knuckles high in the aluminum deepwell, Nonie added scoops of warmed cane sugar from the roaster. She then alternated layers of sugar and strawberries until the pan was near full. For the topper, she drizzled an inch of the sweet granules through her fist like sand and patted it flat. "Flat as a flitter," she said aloud for no particular reason. Juice on her hands stained the white surface and left the reddish print of her delicate palm perfectly in place, lifeline crease intact. Old woman that she was, Nonie gave herself a Mama hug around the waist and settled back against the stove to wait for the first syrupy bubbles to blister their way to the top.

Out the window, Mr. Gabe was all but completely out of sight. Last time she looked, he was ooching over to edge the strip of bluegrass by the garage. His big shears caught the sun, and Gabe Phillips flashed down the row in his shirt that was still as clean as a barber's coat, leaving a fringe of soft, green clippings on the drive. Nonie knew he would sweep them up within minutes.

She idled happily, leaning there, lips pursed over a swelling smile, blowing ideas along toward next week. The meals were ready in her mind. Yesterday, Nonie had prepared a cured ham. She singed its rind free of bristles then scrubbed it clean as a whistle before boiling the thing all afternoon. When the time came, Nonie sawed off the hock, painted on a thick paste of hand-ground mustard and cloves, and put the whole package to bed in a slow oven for overnight cooking and sweetening. Right now the product was cooling on a shelf in the laundry. It was done up in brown paper bag like a present. A few spots of greasy transparency hinted, delectably, at what was inside. Clara would be quick to spy it.

The long, narrow concrete room where the ham rested held the temperature down like a springhouse. Nonie loved the hollow chill of the laundry, all stone and enamel; it put her back in time and contained the past as if it had been pleasant. But Nonie usually dipped the bucket at the well where she stood. So it was coming days she wanted to think on now. The things she and Clara would get up to. They would take hands on the twisty path between this house and her place, lace themselves together with their fingers, and leave Gabe and Lucy to whatever acts of bruised mercy either could commit.

The faint sound of liquid just starting to percolate turned Nonie back to the stove. She held a wooden spoon by its bowl end and pierced her sugar handprint with the footlong handle. Next, she streaked the handle slowly, slowly through hot pulp. A crimson swirl, bejeweled with glistening blisters, formed on the surface as the mixture juiced up where she stirred. The room was hotter but moist and sweet to breathe. After adjusting the flame lower, Nonie again took her mother's pose. She checked the yard.

Mr. Gabe was back up in a kneeling position. He had placed one hand on the garage wall for support. He raised his head and Nonie looked with him where the driveway flowed in from the road. There, next to the boxwood Gabe Phillips had been nursing through a winter tip burn. There. The man in coveralls was walking in.

In spite of bubbling liquid, Nonie's kitchen was immediately more silent than it had been before. And since they were soundless to her ears, the man's steps, as he came walking in, looked light, and measured even. In fact, almost balletic.

The gray-haired man walked in, but later it would seem he floated.

Nonie started toward the window table, closer to the light, because one of that man's arms looked silver as he moved.

Nonie knew that the man must be an apparition, but he kept walking in. Nothing stopped him. And while he walked his heavy silver arm caught sun and glanced a streak of lightening toward the ground. The wild man's head pulled back too far, too proud, above his chest, and Nonie thought, how could he march so steadily, so lightly? And was he coming closer or stepping forward from one spot each time?

And Mr. Gabe? From where he knelt, his hand was slipping smoothly up the wall, and he was rising, that was him, as if he'd never halted in his life and grace were all his own.

When Gabe was nearly upright, he showed full-faced at Nonie. He all but smiled at his surprise, and when he swivelled back, his black hair, shiny damp, matched the asphalt's unmatched radiance tone for tone.

It took place so slowly and it was over in an instant while Nonie slapped her hands against the glass. Nonie's blows, which almost broke her narrow fingers, had no more effect than if dead Mother did the striking.

Because the man in coveralls kept walking in. He didn't stop. He never did, but raised his metal arm in subtle rhythm with his legs and in three paces joined his other arm to that one.

And then he fired the gun. Then it was that Mr. Gabe, still not full height in his ascent, he lifted from the grass and flew. Not crippled now, oh no, not lame a bit, Gabe Phillips he sailed effortlessly back and landed with his heart exploded red red red on the front of his sunwhite shirt. And in speckles on the lawn.

As for Nonie, she could fly too and she flew now, out through the concrete springhouse room, right through her past and future to this very moment, just this one, and lit, as brown and tender as a cooing dove, by the side of Mr. Gabe.

But he was gone. The instant Nonie touched him, she knew that he was gone, who had been so brittle bright and handsome, and Nonie wished she'd had a feathered wing to brush his eyelids closed.

The man who had come walking in, it was Mr. Ira Truitt she was sure, because Nonie had heard the cruel name and caught a dreadful glimpse or two in secret, that old man, he wasn't moving either, where he stood.

Nonie kept her touch, her precious goodbye touch, on Gabe Phillips' shoulder and then she whispered loud and sad enough to hush the buzz of summer, "You put that gun away, now, mister, do you hear?"

Ira, spent, complied in his confusion, letting the stunted, sawed off barrels slant once more, like veins of mercury, down his forearm. Nonie assumed at last the fully fearless majesty which had been her power all along. "Oh, look at what you've done," she cried. "Just look at what you've done." And, "Are you happy now?"

CHAPTER 31

In the Whirlwind

THE VOICE CAME at Ira from out of the whirlwind in his head. A deafening roar had started when he walked up close on the man and pulled both triggers. Louder and louder now, a huge locomotive of sound bore down on Ira, its whistle an elongated human wail more monstrous than the shriek of damnation that had found him on the river all those months ago, the night of lights, when he stole the fish.

Ira heard the Spirit in the voice this time, when the gun's butt slammed back like a piston against his shoulder in recoil from the velocity of double ought shot, fired off simultaneously from the sawed twin barrels of a twelve gauge. He felt crushed by his own unrighteousness in a vortex that swirled and twirled and caught Ira up and spun him where he stood. The dooming voice of judgment was pitched sky high, like a woman keening, a fugue of anguish created by the friction of an earth that spun too close, too tight against a hard blue sky.

The powder compartments, the high brass bases of the shotgun shells, were still lodged in their pipe-like cylinders while Ira tried to keep to his feet after firing. His weapon had no choke. The blast had been unmuffled so the shot spread fast. Inside the chambers, dull red cardboard casings that had housed the pellets were shredded in long threads as thick as ruptured veins. An hour ago the shells had looked as innocent as penny wrappers slipped into the place of ammunition.

From the heat of detonation, the gunmetal was almost blister hot against Ira's hide, but Ira was benumbed. His ears had usurped and compounded the force of other senses. Dumbly he gawped down at his shoulder where a blood-tinged seepage had begun, caused by the kick of the gunstock. Soon the dingy color of his flesh would be a grisly, glistening black, streaked like tarnish down his arm.

"Are you happy now?" the whirlwind howled at Ira, interwoven with the piercing melody of sirens coming at him from outside the cosmic turbulence. The heavy, heady smell of smoke and creosote coated all membranous linings. Ira knew this was the stench of hell when it was heaven he had tried to scale.

"Looklooklook" the voice commanded but Ira didn't dare. He pulled the gun to his breast, cradled it with crossed arms and turned away to hide, to flee from sound and judgments. Ira's fear was vast. An empty universe engulfed him.

"Cheat," he would have screamed, but his tongue was glued in place from wild wanting wanting. God's woman's voice and pointing arms stretched out long enough to forecast his destruction.

In the world that had been cold to his embrace, Ira hugged himself and tried to pull away from his Apocalypse. He lunged heavily down the wide black path that spread until it gaped open at the bottom of the hill to let the Hebron wet its huge dark throat. At river's edge, Ira kept his struggling pace and walked straight in. He had meant to do God's bidding but the Devil duped him into evil.

"Unfair," he would have howled into the void if the anthem of endless noise would have admitted any other note.

There was one hope of holiness. A sacrament. Baptism by immersion was the means to save his soul. Ira would yet be made Free of Sin, he would be cleansed and Sanctified. Fighting the suck of mud and current, Ira clutched his shotgun like the mainstay of a cross, the full length of his torso, and walked chest deep and deeper.

In the end it was No. 6 steel hooks dangling from the trotline's gangions that settled things between Gabe and Ira.

The trot had stayed tethered but untended since the August night. Spring's powerful currents had stretched the medium weight cotton line until it finally sank limply to the river bottom. For months it wiggled idly back and forth on the mud, forgotten. Well tied, the beckets, loops of knotted twine that secured the shorter gangions and their gear, had held.

It had been Gabe Phillips' pride and soothing occupation to whet the hooks on a small grindstone. The repetitious *grrr* and the sight of spreading beads of oil as he grated steel tips, held flat against the stone, had eased him. The shanks on No. 6's were more than an inch long from eye to curvature. Gabe honed them razor sharp each year before he set the line.

Ira was whisker deep in the Hebron now. The water had to cover him completely to soak the horrors out and release him from the "bondage of sin." Those old words twisted up into the whirlwind that had rushed with him to the Hebron and hung like hornets aroar above his head. The water trickled into Ira's ears when he lifted his chin to draw the breath meant to guarantee salvation.

He would break back to the surface "raised to a new life of grace." From the silt of his life he dredged up hard the recital of the form of words. He wanted to shout them into the dark, musty-tasting water that seeped between his lips. The gift of water, through which the ancients fled their bondage. Blessed waters. When Ira hauled himself above them, he would come up "marked and sealed as Christ's own forever" as the ritual incantation promised.

Ira's coveralls and cheap brogans filled and swelled. Engorged with river water, they were as heavy as the sins he dragged beneath the Hebron's surface. But Ira trudged on until he was locked in the silence and icebox chill of blackly opaque liquid invading ears and eyes and nostrils and wantonly permeating cloth and leather to wet every crease and crevice of his body.

When he was a beleaguered boy, Ira had fancied he could walk across the Hebron on the riverbed if he tried. Some drifter had bragged to Ira that he himself had done so, after Ira saw the man wade in, disappear, then climb out on the far bank. That was the only good childhood dream Ira had had. A small one.

The pain in Ira's chest was near unbearable, the weight of a whole river pressing in, the air in his overinflated lungs trying to burst out. Today he would rise, reborn, and the whirlwind would proclaim him.

Ira's coarse leather shoe snagged on Gabe's hooks. Numbed by cold, Ira hardly noticed the prick when corroded steel pierced hide and caught the side of his foot. He jerked hard and felt it sharp enough but his need to breathe was animal and urgent. It was a gang hook that had snared Ira, three No. 6's tied together at the shank. Their connecting line was caught under a sunken limb swept down in April from a flash flood above the fork. The more Ira pulled the more the hooks struck deep as fangs, a rusty watersnake, biting to the bone.

There was no way to free himself. As there had been no way ever in his life to cry out in grief. The mighty concussion of sound that hovered over and ruffled the Hebron, subsided with Ira's waning struggle. For a time, the tiny anvils in his ears beat out the rhythm of a slowing pulse while Ira wondered dimly, of what use had he been?

CHAPTER 32

The Goodness of the Place

ONE BY ONE, when they saw the cortege in the distance, the farmers with land close to the highway dropped the reins of a plow and left a fat-sided mule standing in the furrow. Or they turned their tractor throttles to idle and clambered stiffly down from black metal seats. Each of the men then made his way with as much dignity as he could around his tobacco plants, big as a plate now, across freshly broken crusts of soil between green rows, and out to the edge of Route Four.

Their women came too, some carrying babies, and stood by mailboxes up closer to the houses. But they came, as far as they could bear to, stringing themselves at intervals along the loose rick-rack of frontage. By some silent prearrangement, even the children left off their chores and got out to the gravel shoulder before the funeral procession rolled by, so slowly that tires barely raised dust.

There was a slight gray cast to the June sky. The silent surf of farmers and their families that lapped up to the two-lane from a sea of land, stood under the grayness and watched, knowing that it was all

271

right to stare straight into the big, dark cars from Morton's Funeral Home. All right because their hearts were in their faces.

Gabe Phillips wouldn't have had them leave the crop and go into Milan for the funeral this morning. There wasn't a one among them who didn't understand that. Not when it was time to plow the rows and chop weeds. Those were jobs that had to be done when called for. And today it looked like rain; see that sky? Worked earth encouraged moisture, they believed.

And they hadn't been familiar with Phillips in that way. Not in the line that called for signing registers. When you thought of it, none of them had known him well at all. Oh, they had heard stories. Who hadn't? There had been talk going around about him and Joyce Oliver for years. But they weren't much of a mind to credit what they heard against a man like Gabe. They'd seen the likes of Joyce before, and like as not, they would again. Wasn't there always some little bit of a girl from out of town? This one had tried to upset everything five years ago for no more reason than that it suited her, just when the Burley warehouse was beginning to boom, when lives were looking up because of Phillips.

No. They didn't know Gabe Phillips well, they thought. But they had taken pride in certain things about him. After all, he did what helped. And he was a man, like them, who had had a wife and troubles and a child. And his handshake was a clasp that had been as sure as signing on a deal. They remembered, too, the tick-tock rhythm of his tread which was as familiar as a second hand. It had timed all their transactions. They would come to miss it, they just knew. In fact, they missed it now.

So the farmers and their families hadn't gone to Morton's for the visitation. They had stayed and worked, as always, this relentless second week of June. Because Gabe was stern, when it came to working; a hard man with himself and others. He put the truth of first things first, they believed, and respected them for having learned to do it, too.

But they could do this for the man. They could walk up here and wait, in a thick froth of thistle and wild carrot that foamed lavender and greenish-white around their knees; they could let their feelings show for once, as he went by this last time ever.

And look, there was his little daughter in the Family car. How sad. They shook their heads. The girl's braids and face were every bit as skin tight and severe as you might have thought they would be. She was reading faces through the glass, though, they could tell. And all along the somber line that stretched, both sides of the road, as far as you could see, the farmers and their generations were saying to Clara what they could by trudging across their fields in wilting heat and standing, eyes lowering like the sky with unnamed loss: we owed your daddy this.

Wasn't it a week ago that Phillips' brand-new convertible had sped by? And him at the wheel, laughing to himself as big as life? Now this horrible trip home at a pace they knew the man would just have hated. They half expected him to come honking and wheeling his flashy Buick around the whole procession this very instant. He would zoom past on the righthand shoulder, spinning gravel at the windshields of these idlers in the road. Bystanders would have talked about his driving, later, keeping it good humored, adding just a pinch of rue for the sake of warning children.

But it didn't happen. Mournfully, the men, women, and children stood and watched in silence while the stateliest cars in the county crept by them. The midnight-colored hearse that bore Gabe's casket led the way. His raised bier of hand-rubbed mahogany gleamed almost purple through etched glass panels. They read the metal letters spelling MORTON'S that hung on the side windows of the undertaker's fleet. It was Morton called it that, "a fleet." He caused sniggers when he said it, too. For a while, it had looked like jokes about the long cars might spoil all the solemnity that went with burying. But most had come to see the three sleek, blue, silver-handled Cadillacs as adding something right to grief.

Certainly today they did. This noon, it was those well-tuned engines that pulled the train of mourners along behind them in a grimly necessary way, gliding all in tow without a hitch toward one destination. If the head cars looked sinister, so be it. What else could have borne to do such dreadful work.

Oh. And there. They would swear that that was Nonie Pulce. Slight, the way she was, they could barely see her in the dim interior of the Family car. But it was surely Nonie, sitting right up next to Clara Phillips on a wide gray seat that they just knew was velvet, the limousine itself being fitted almost like a coffin. But if they looked at Nonie, she didn't look them back. The woman held herself erect as any lady and stared ahead directly, not giving any one of them a single glance. And for that they hardly blamed her.

For a second they all wondered where the little brown moth of a colored would light next. She'd been down at Tyrone so long, she had about slipped out of mind in Milan, and was probably too old for heavy work. If it came to that.

Well, she'd find something. It wasn't up to them, thank the Lord, although they would have helped some if they could have. Maybe

Judge Stallard and his wife would bring Nonie into their fine brick house on Oxford Street. Mrs. Belinda had been sickly lately. Yes, that was their idea of a place for Nonie. And it was a good one. She'd go on back to town.

Not a single man or woman or child turned away from the road until the last bumper of the last car vanished and the flat stretch of Four was desolately empty all the way from Milan to the defile where Tyrone Pike broke off and scattered its hairpin curves down toward the river. They stared after for a while, feeling as they gazed that they were left with nothing, where something quick had been.

When, at last, the farmers did turn away and each woman and child turned too, they ebbed back slowly to their fields and barns and kitchens, and wordlessly they took up chores again and checked the sky and smacked the rippling flanks of mules, gee up, but all was plodding for a while.

The people they had watched, the ones passing in the cars, were dry-eyed for the most part. And wordless too, at first. Ben Gilliam was driving his boxy, four-door Dodge, right behind Morton's third limousine, where the Judge and Belinda Stallard rode in their newly emphasized preeminence. The minister could be seen facing backward from the jumpseat. Inside the cab of the Dodge, Ben turned and studied his wife, Mollie. Her soft face had pinched itself together into points.

"I'll bet this humidity is higher than the heat," Mollie said. Then, "My lord. Did you ever see the like, Ben?" He knew she meant the dismal-looking people lining the road and not the remarkably close weather. "There must be a thousand at least," she said. "Between all of us and all of them, it must come to at least that. Why do you suppose? Why would they care that much?"

"I don't know. You don't know what gets into people," Ben answered, simply. And he didn't know. But whatever Mollie had asked him, he didn't think he would have had the answer for it today. Because whatever had gotten into them had also gotten into him. "I mean they prospered when he did," Ben said. "But I don't think it's money." He struggled for a way to say it, or to know. "He was a net, catching up their lives." The Sheriff touched things as he spoke. He stroked the gearshift knob then softly brushed his chest. "I don't know why that seemed to be, but it was so."

"They couldn't have had anything in common except tobacco," Mollie observed, referring to the farmers along the roadside.

"Well, who does up here?" Ben's tone surprised even him. He took his voice down a peg. "It's true though. Gabe was a man of a different stripe, all right. A vastly different stripe."

The Sheriff, looking out now from his new Dodge, recognized most of the faces he could see beyond the open car window. Their sagging, sunlined cheeks had never looked so heavy. He nodded at a few of the men and women. Even their pie-faced children wore forlorn expressions in this milky light. Purchase on their feelings had been dear.

"Look at the toll it took," Mollie said. "Just look at them." She winced. It hurt too much to make this trip. Ben didn't doubt that Mollie's strength was normally proof against the cordon of human pain outside the car. Mollie Gilliam was a woman who could take what came, he knew, provided she had thought it would. But this death had broken Milan's surface tension, somehow. Nothing held the same.

"I reckon it'll be some while before we all go back to normal," she

276

interjected. Her voice welled with the same emotion as her eyes.

Ben continued to steer one-handed. Finally he rested his right palm on Mollie's thigh. Even in this heat, the thin chambray of her dress was cool, sandwiched between the fleshy warmth of Ben's hand and his wife's skin. He shook his head at his own loss of understanding. He wished to console Mollie, that was part of how he saw his job as husband, but he couldn't think quite how to start or end. Maybe Mollie was the one who knew.

"What's normal, now?" he asked.

Mollie raised her hands, cupped open. No answers there. But it was a well-known gesture and for Ben it went some way toward saying "normal" in itself. His wife lowered her wrists and lightly topped his hand with hers when they started winding down the road to Tyrone. The last of the farmers and their families shrunk to specks in the rearview mirror, then vanished on the car's first downward turn.

Again, Mollie broke his contemplation. "I reckon you noticed Lucy wasn't at the service?"

Ben, of course, had looked for Lucy Phillips at the funeral home. She wouldn't have been hard to spot, under that copper glow of hair. Morton had confided Lucy's reasons for not coming and asked Ben to keep it secret. The back of Ben's neck was damp with perspiration. It was a fool who told a man a thing he didn't want a wife to know. Ben's belief was that within the confines of a bedroom, everything got told.

"Lucy didn't think it would look right after all this time. Finally showing up only to make a big display of grief at the funeral. For public consumption, she meant," Ben quoted the undertaker. "Nobody in the world would doubt she was sincere," he added, "unlike Sonny's

277

carryings on at the visitation. But you know Lucy well as I do. And she didn't want to take away from Gabe or Clara today. Nonie either, for that matter. 'It's their time together,' she told Morton." Their last time, Ben reflected. "Morton said Lucy slipped up for her own private viewing. She's down at the house, setting up the food that's been brought. We'll see her there."

"I tell you, Ben, I liked that woman," Mollie said, "but it used to fly all over me the way Lucy always did look at things peculiar. Just full of opinions. And she always was. You know it, too. You wouldn't think she'd be so bullheaded today, for Clara's sake if not her own. But this sounds just like her. Her and that spiny back."

Mollie went on. Ben thought his wife couldn't seem to get shut of opinions herself, about Lucy. "I guess she'll keep to Hickman now," Mollie said. "That'll be the end of Phillipses up here, I reckon. I don't think there's a one of the family left in this whole county. You'd predict that the sheer force of Gabe and Lucy would have spun their line out forever." She then added quietly, clearly not wanting a response, "I always thought Clara would move back, though. But I expect not, now. She'll put this place down to tragic. And she'll leave us there."

They both rode silent on that woeful prediction, all the while swooping the sharp turns lower and slower until the head cars reached the bottom point and nosed into the little burial yard at Tyrone. Ben's oven-shaped car absorbed the afternoon's rising temperature.

No larger than a third of an acre, the rundown cemetery where they parked wasn't even fenced off from the road. The one-room church that had sanctified the land originally had long since been padlocked and abandoned. However, Clara had been adamant, they said, that her father be buried in this earth close to the Hebron. That made sense, Ben thought. Joyce had a prior claim up in Milan, after all. And there was something sweet enough here about the fringe of Indian beans that dangled from a few flowering catalpas. When Ben got out of the car, Mollie indicated that she would wait where she was. He opened both doors wide so she wouldn't swelter and left her with her eyes laddering up over the sparse grass and few crookedy, tablet-shaped headstones, past the blunted steeple of the meeting house. Finally, fanning herself with a program from the service, she rested her solemn gaze on the sky.

Stirred by a breeze, the flat catalpa pods rustled overhead like the sound of vespers. Gabe's grave had been opened under the one good hardwood tree in the yard, a spreading red haw. Its thorny branches stretched over the undertaker's canopy one-sided, as if windblown. There would be days, Ben thought, when the shiny, lobed leaves would provide the only shade around. Some solace there. Not much, but it was something.

Most people stayed in their cars as Mollie had, or leaned, sweating, against the polished doors while Clara and the minister walked to the canopy. Ben didn't get close enough to hear what was said, but he could see the tightness of Clara's fist when she scooped dust and held it, before she sprinkled powdery grains evenly on her daddy's lowered casket. Nor, while Ben studied her, did she ever move her eyes from the gravesite or close them during the final prayer. Ben felt the heat, compressed as it was between the clouds and earth, growing more extreme. The preacher, evidently mindful of his warming flock, asked the ones who were standing nearby to sing the first verse of "Abide with

Me." After one raggedy chorus of the hymn, which rose on "fast falls the even tide" before the lament died away, the burial was over.

On her way back to the limousine where Nonie kept her vigil, Ben got a good look at Clara. The child's face was stamped with Gabe for all the world. She wouldn't be forgetting how her daddy looked, as long as there were mirrors.

Then the line of cars, except for the hearse, formed up again and made its tired way to Gabe's house. They had heard about the goings-on there, but few from Milan had pictured the home Phillips had coaxed into existence from a simple river camp. They gasped to see it now, this pristine place of violence and death. Why, the black-green boxwood hedge, immaculately trim, wrapped it like an armband.

People filed slowly through Gabe's front door, more shyly curious than grieved, but they were acting out of what they knew was fit and, in their minds, would always be so. This was the way they did things here, this ritual of food and visitation. It was as good an intimation of an afterlife as they were apt to get while breathing.

Clara went in first and stood near Gabe's desk in the long center room. This was the first time she had been in the room since Gabe was here with her. She looked down and saw that his script covered the desk blotter. Often, she had seen him writing there, mindlessly, when he was talking business at the house or on the phone. In perfect penmanship the words *Tall, tall, Texan* laced repeatedly up one side of the construction paper. Clara could feel her daddy's pleasure in making that tracery of loops and loops and strong crossed tees. *Tall tall Texan.* She would not forget.

The small mercury glass vase she had bought Gabe at the ten-cent store last winter was near his handwriting. The vase was as cold to her touch as the day had been. Clara had promised then, too, to remember, and she did. She recalled it perfectly. And she and Lucy were here now, in summer, as she had vowed they would be. Clara leaned closer for a more wistful picture of reunion. In spite of today's heat she could almost see her breath and hear ice crackle. But it was too late to change the past.

Grownups came near and looked down at her sadly, or patted, patted, her head or shoulder. More and more men and women filed into the room and pressed their pity close. Silvered glass and *Tall, tall, Texan* and all the sweaty, thick-made hands made Clara feel slightly nauseous. One woman told her that her daddy was a man who always "kept himself so nice and had such pure, brown eyes." Clara fled as quickly as she could out onto the screened porch.

Lucy and Nonie were already out there. They were standing with their backs to Clara, their heads turned in the same direction, downriver. Clara tiptoed over and slipped soundlessly into the complicated silence between the two women. She fit there perfectly.

The gray-green hills, the same color as the Hebron this afternoon, melted into the water and floated on the surface, carried in splendid solemnity by the current. The High Sheriff had said the man who did it had lived over there, across the river. To Clara, the melting was appropriate: The boundaries had disappeared. All was of a piece now, and the slipping out of mind, for some, had started.

Ira Truitt had died in the very stretch of water that she studied, according to what Sheriff Gilliam said. The man was old, he told her. Not right in his head. Clara didn't like to think of that or make Truitt more real to herself in any way. She had asked where he was buried. At Nonie's answer, that his ashes had been sent miles away, Clara felt no satisfaction. She imagined the site as cold, untended and stony. The fact of his cremation made Clara cringe.

While Clara and her mother and Nonie watched, and without the slightest change in clouds or sunshine, the elements converged and a soft rain started to fall. Clara could hear the droplets patter on the dry hillside and see their evidence on bobbing blades of fescue and the dimpled surface of the Hebron. A whisper of cool air stirred her mother's hair.

Lucy's reverie was of Gabe the day they married. They had gone together to the courthouse and stood up before the Justice of the Peace. Two women in the office witnessed. She didn't remember who took their picture, but somebody had a box Brownie. Lucy had found the photo in Gabe's desk drawer. It was a day much like this one, sultry, with promise of relief.

In the black-and-white picture, Gabe held a cane in his left hand and looked rakish as a dandy, like he might tap a little step. It was the first good suit he owned. Her dress had a ruched collar almost as big as a cape. For some reason Lucy had lifted it to cover her mouth when they snapped the shot. The coquettish pose made her eyes look full of mischief. She stood in front on the left, with her back against Gabe's chest. Their "finery" was dark. The print didn't distinguish the side of her dress from the front of Gabe's outfit so they melded seamlessly at the center.

Nonie broke the silence with a sigh. Lucy reached over Clara and rested her hand on Nonie's shoulder. In her own mind Nonie was coming to terms with meaning. She had earned her keep. She had never allowed her swollen heart to empty of its feelings. That was life enough. Endurance had held her up in sadness. Now it had bought her freedom. Nonie was delivered to the beauty of the land, unfettered.

The two women straightened their arms and raised them, slightly, from their sides so the hint of breeze could circulate and cool them down. The bath of air was soothing.

Clara studied the women's arms, relaxed but lifted to a small degree. Every detail within her sightline was essential. Outside, the river danced its dabs of light and raindrops. From within Gabe's house, the blended smells of tobacco smoke and the odor of yeast from buttered, folded rolls and the perfume of baked meats in vinegary sauces flowed over Clara. Low tones of murmured consolation also streamed out from the main room and engulfed her.

Yes. It was the goodness of the place that Clara would remember. It would become the bible of her life. Gabe had made it possible for Nonie to stay on as long as she drew breath, and Clara would come back here to see her often. Here, Gabe Phillips and love would keep, in spite of all. Her daddy and tobacco fields and the earth and bluffs of Milan and Tyrone and the soothing waters of the Hebron. These things were in her mind. They had been glorious to know.

AUTHOR'S NOTE

While growing up, the textures and tones of my southern Kentucky childhood seemed anything but ordinary. I look back with such affection, tantamount to reverence, that I couldn't help but try to make them spring to life again. My impassioned wish was to catch something of the juice of lives and settings. *It Was the Goodness of the Place* is the love letter to a particular past that I want with all my heart to send. Though acknowledging a full measure of regret for the elements of tragedy that swirled around us there, this book is offered in celebration of a way of life which has ended.

ACKNOWLEDGMENTS

My great, forever un-payable debt is to Dick Sullivan and Sena Jeter Naslund who, to employ a favorite racing term, got me between them and bumped me into the gate.

After that, so many cheered me on. Karen Mann read, edited, designed, shipped, reread and called out from the sidelines in her delightfully unflagging and sustaining voice. Fred Burger and JoAnn Barwick, like dei ex machina, provided exactly the boost needed when my spirits sagged and Barbara Mooney, unaware, changed the shaped of this book with her poetic inner sight.

Bert Hornback, a man who knows everything I know about having one's heart pressed between the pages of a southern Kentucky childhood, but knows infinitely more about all matters grammatical, read and edited to invaluable effect. Joanne Heumann had a vision of the setting which I kept before my eyes for inspiration.

Ben Crain, Cliff Todd, and my brother-in-law Leslie Blackburn educated me about tobacco by sharing their knowledge and experience with such straightforward honor and spare elegance of language I was mesmerized. Rudy Vogt passed along a geological guide to Kentucky which became my Rosetta stone for deciphering the state's topography.

Cappy Warner generously researched the liturgy so necessary to galvanize certain scenes. Amy Sullivan dashed in like Wonder Woman and saved the epigraph day.

Susan Johnson, Daly Walker, Bill Pearce, Maureen Morehead, Marly Rusoff, Alice Bingham Gorman, John Moremen, Sam Zalutsky, Kathleen Driskell, Katy Yocom, Brenda Light, Ellie Moore, Liz Tate, Ulla Maria Dodd, Marika Esham, Lucy Gibson Smith, Mary Frances Willock, Ruth and Bob Lehman, Julie and Nick Stone, Camille and Albert Wilson, Sandra and Carroll Teague, Harry Warren and Channing Warren and Deborah and David Stewart read, encouraged and, along with Barbara and Norton Cohen, Anne Williams, Patrick Welsh, Penny and Bernie Weisskopf, C'Allen and Stan Chauvin, Anita Henkel, Nathan Sullivan, Brendan Cahill, Peggy and Weldon Hewitt, George Mangold, Pudd'n Vogt, Doreen Ovca, Jane Walker, Georgiana Noble and DeMaris Edlin, kept the candle burning in the window while I disappeared.

Sisters and sons, Margaret Blackburn (who even lent her clothes), Mary Warren, Clay and Dixon Kavanaugh, daughter-in-law Stephanie Kavanaugh, who out-Ruth's Ruth, and aunt, Diana Rogers, were unwavering in their support of this project in ways that made me feel cherished.

The Fleur-de-Lis Press is named to celebrate the life
of Flora Lee Sims Jeter
(1901-1990)